# THE LAST BLOSSOM ON THE PLUM TREE

## ALSO BY BROOKE ASTOR

Patchwork Child
The Bluebird Is at Home
Footprints

# BROOKE ASTOR

# THE LAST
# BLOSSOM
# ON THE
# PLUM TREE

## A
## PERIOD
## PIECE

RANDOM HOUSE
NEW YORK

Library of Congress Cataloging-in-Publication Data
Astor, Brooke.
The last blossom on the plum tree.
I. Title.
PS3551.S68L3   1986      813'.54      84–42511
ISBN 0–394–53716–5

MANUFACTURED IN THE UNITED STATES OF AMERICA
24689753
FIRST EDITION

*Design by Barbara M. Bachman*

To C. H. M.

OLD CHINESE PROVERB:

He who sees the last blossom
on the plum tree
must pick it.

# THE LAST
# BLOSSOM
# ON THE
# PLUM TREE

### CHAPTER ONE

# THE HOUSE ON 52ND STREET

ON A COOL MAY MORNING IN THE YEAR 1928, IRMA SHREWS-
bury sat in her huge Crane Simplex on Pier 84 waiting for the
*Aquitania* to dock, not at all sure why she had taken the
trouble to greet Emily, whom she had never liked. Why, she
reflected glumly, had she answered Emily's letter by asking
her to come stay at Bella Vista?

"What have I got myself into?" she asked half aloud, which
caused the chauffeur, Whitmore, to turn from the front seat
and ask if there was anything he could do. Irma ignored him
as she clenched her jaw and decided that her husband James
might have fallen for Emily's childish ways—after all, she was
his half sister and they had been through a lot together as
children—but now that James was dead, why should she have
to put up with Emily Codway and those Boston snobs whose
family she had married into? Irma turned to the man who was
drowsing beside her in the car.

"Was Ben Codway rich when he died?" she demanded.

Wendell Ponderosa of Battle, Ponderosa, and Huddlefield
awoke with a jump.

"Why, yes," he said, aware even in his sleep that rich clients do not like to hear about people richer than themselves, "but not as rich as you and James." Irma and James started from scratch, and Irma would have been furious to hear that Ben Codway had been richer than her own late husband had been.

"He was quite successful," Wendell added cautiously, now fully awake. "But of course Ben began with his inheritance. You and James made it all yourselves, and you made a lot more."

Irma sniffed. "Well, I wonder if Emily has squandered it all. Ben has been dead almost three years and I read in the paper that she has been running around all over the place, Biarritz, Monte Carlo, who knows where else?" Irma, whose name never appeared in the society columns, believed that people so mentioned must be mountebanks and ladies of fragile reputation. She paused, then continued. "She was on safari in Kenya when she heard of James's death and wrote that she wanted to come over to see his grave and to see me, but that was almost three months ago." Her aggrieved tone suggested that she had covered this ground with her lawyer many times before. "Is she hard up now? Is it possible that James could have left a special letter for her? Is she coming over for a reason other than just to see James's grave?" Her voice quavered a bit as she said this, for she had never known exactly where Emily stood in James's affections. "Was there a letter?" she repeated.

Mr. Ponderosa shook his head. "Don't worry, Irma," he said. "There was nothing but the will, which, as you know, left you everything except the little house on Fifty-second Street, and that went to your son Joe." Wendell Ponderosa also spoke as if he had been over this ground before.

There it was again, another nagging thought—that house on Fifty-second Street. She had always imagined that she knew everything about James. She had worked so closely with him all their married life, helping him make his millions. But she had never known about that little house on Fifty-second Street except that James had it on a long lease, and he let their ne'er-do-well son Joe live in it for free. Had James been deceiving her all those years? If he had, she thought to herself, she'd make him pay for it one way or another, even though he was six feet under ground. The house also made her think of her son who lived there. The boy was another of her problems. They had never wanted a child. When he was seven they had sent him off to boarding school, and from then on, it had been school in winter, summer at camp in Maine, and finally Princeton. After graduation, Joe declared that he did not want to go into business but wanted to be a writer. His father was disgusted and gave him a small allowance, saying, "Remember, because you have a checkbook, it doesn't mean that you have money in the bank."

"There she comes," said Mr. Ponderosa, referring to the *Aquitania*, thus breaking into those thoughts that had drawn Irma's face into a scowl. "The tugs are just bringing her into the dock. I think we should get out, Irma." He opened the car door and stepped onto the pier, putting his hand back to help Irma, who joined him reluctantly.

They looked an odd pair. Mr. Wendell Ponderosa, in his late prime, had a round ruddy face with bright eyes peering out from under thick eyebrows and topped by a mane of snow white hair. He was tall, broad shouldered, a little portly, well dressed in a double-breasted dark overcoat and a bowler hat, which he now held in his hand.

She, small, spry, in her early seventies with dark gray hair, had a thin oval face, large round eyes with drooping eyelids, and a petulant mouth. She was still dressed in mourning, a black silk coat, a small round hat from which hung a long black veil, and black kid gloves. In her pierced ears were small but perfect pearls, and around her neck a small pearl necklace. She would never be noticed in a crowd, and cared little for how she looked. James, however, had insisted on the symbols of wealth. So she owned three sable coats and a silver fox jacket, and although they never entertained, he had liked her to wear jewelry as she sat opposite him each evening in their huge dining room at Bella Vista. However, the jewelry meant nothing to either of them. James had bought it to impress the servants, who would carry the word through their empire of employees that the boss was generous to his wife, a fact which caused much grumbling among these minions, for J.S. never gave a raise without a struggle, nor a cent to charity.

Thanks to Mr. Ponderosa's influence, they had the Courtesy of the Port and theirs was the only car allowed on the pier. So they had a good look at the racy ship as she was eased gracefully to her berth. "I can't imagine why Emily wants to see me," said Irma for the tenth time. "I really have no desire to see her and I think I was stupid to have asked her to come over. She has never been a part of my life, and now that I've taken over James's business entirely, it is most inconvenient." She narrowed her eyes and thrust out her jaw. "Incidentally, in looking over some of James's papers, I was surprised to find how careless Battle, Ponderosa, and Huddlefield have been, particularly in their dealings with the Magnum Bank. Have you any idea how much I've lost on my bonds?"

Mr. Ponderosa was annoyed but replied placidly. He knew that the portfolio was in excellent condition. "The market has been down a bit," he said, "but you personally are all right. The general feeling is bullish for the entire market in 1928."

"Bullish or bearish doesn't mean a thing to me," Irma snapped. "I simply hate inefficiency, especially when it comes to business. It surprised me, Wendell, that you never told me about these losses."

Mr. Ponderosa drew a deep breath to control his temper. "My dear Irma," he said in measured tones, "the loss is so little compared to your principal that—"

Irma interrupted him, raising her voice, and Mr. Ponderosa looked around uneasily. "I think I may sue the bank. Who knows what they'll get wrong next?"

Mr. Ponderosa, with a sigh, was about to reply that suing wouldn't get her anywhere, when fortunately, the ship having been tied up, the gangplank was wheeled into place. "We must go over there," said Mr. Ponderosa. "The passengers are starting to disembark." A man from the Cunard Line descended the gangplank rapidly and came toward them. He had spotted their Crane Simplex and assumed correctly that they had come to collect the attractive Mrs. Codway, who tipped more heavily than any other passenger on the ship and was just the sort of passenger to be met in a grand way.

Irma raised her lorgnette to her eyes to observe a slender lady in a bright green coat trimmed around the hem with black monkey fur and a head-hugging green cloche. She was escorted down the gangplank by two ship's officers, followed by a dowdy but agreeable-looking woman clutching a large black jewel case and with a sable jacket over her arm. Behind her was a pretty young woman who seemed to be part of the group, and trailing her was a tall man, a foreigner with a small black moustache. Irma noticed that he never took his eyes off the woman in the green coat who, Irma now concluded, must be Emily. Was he, too, perhaps coming to collect money? she wondered. Emily and her friends were laughing and talking to one another.

Irma disliked them all at first sight, whereas Mr. Ponderosa, an old hand at such situations, seemed intrigued and, to judge

by his suddenly animated expression, scented something afoot.
Obviously, that good-looking man was having an affair with
Emily. He could see at once that she was not a bereaved widow
nor would one have guessed that she had come to mourn a
brother's grave. She had the ease and grace of a woman who
was sure of herself without being arrogant, and she looked
anything but impoverished; but Irma, on the contrary, unable
to admit that she might be wrong, wondered whether she
were putting on a show. These strange people might be gam-
blers that she had picked up in Monte Carlo. Irma, though
sharp in business, was as unworldly as a bushman. She moved
aggressively to the foot of the gangplank, arriving there just
as Emily set her elegant Franch-shod foot on the pier. The two
women looked at each other in silence.

Emily took the initiative. "Irma," she said, kissing her on
both cheeks. "How very dear of you to come to meet me."

Irma disentangled herself, adjusting her hat and veil. "Good
heavens, Emily," she exclaimed. "You almost knocked my hat
off."

"I am so sorry. Forgive me," said Emily. "It was just my
delight because I never expected for a moment that you would
come yourself. It is so very early in the morning. Thank you,
Irma."

"I always have my breakfast at seven," replied Irma, who
felt that Emily's enthusiasm was uncalled-for. "James liked
to get an early start, and now I have so much desk work
myself that I never sleep more than six hours."

"Ah, yes," murmured Emily, having decided not to be
emotional with Irma again. "How you must miss him. My
brother was such a shrewd businessman." Irma narrowed her
eyes—was Emily being spiteful?

Emily, however, had turned to Mr. Ponderosa. "Wendell,
how very nice to see you. I haven't seen you since you stayed
with us at Cypress Point."

"It is a great pleasure for me," said Wendell Ponderosa. "I find you looking more lovely than ever."

Emily laughed. "It's too early in the morning for such compliments, but thank you just the same."

The young officer from the line who was hovering nearby interrupted to ask if he could help with the luggage.

And well might he ask, thought Irma as they moved down the pier, where under the supervision of the lady with the black jewel case, porter after porter was arranging huge Vuitton trunks and bags under the letter C and an obsequious customs official was chalking each piece as it arrived. Emily went straight up to the official and laughed, putting a hand on his arm, then turned to Irma. "When may I ask this nice young man to come and see me?" she whispered.

Irma drew back stiffly. "Certainly not at Bella Vista," she said.

Emily laughed. "Don't be silly, Irma. Of course I am not asking him there. But a man as nice as this deserves a big tip. He's just told me that he has a wife and two children and an old, sick mother and an invalid sister, so I would like to give him something substantial. It would not look right to give it to him here. Where is James's office? I can send it there, but whom should he ask for?"

Reluctantly, Irma told her. She disapproved of tipping. It was un-American and, as James had told her, encouraged dependence. Emily had obviously been corrupted by those weeks (if not months) in Monte Carlo. She was overdressed too. The green coat with all that fur seemed inappropriate for traveling. Besides, she had seen one just like it at Hattie Carnegie's several weeks ago and had overheard a saleswoman quoting the price, which was far more than Irma would ever dream of spending.

Emily finished talking to the young customs officer and said, "Goodness. I forgot to introduce you to my traveling companions. This is my friend Lady Chatwood coming toward us, and that is Prince Pontevecchio behind her."

Irma glanced at the newcomers. She took a quick look at the prince, but it was the young woman she had seen coming down the gangplank who interested her. Was this woman being forced on her too? Also that foreign prince (if he really was a prince) was probably coming to America to find an heiress—which in Irma's opinion was the only reason that men with titles came to America at all. A closer look at Lady Chatwood, who was now standing in front of her, did not make her more appealing to Irma. Lady Chatwood was thin as a pencil and wore a long white polo coat and white stockings with black clocks. A dozen gold bracelets jangled on her wrist. Her golden hair was in flat, shining waves close to her head, and huge pearl earrings almost covered her small pink ears.

"How do you do?" she murmured as she held out a slim, bejeweled hand. "My first visit to America. 'S wonderful."

Irma stood her ground and said only a brief, "How do you do?"

Emily, seeing the look on Irma's face, interrupted to say that Lady Chatwood—Molly—was going to stay with some friends who had sent a car for her and that Prince Pontevecchio was staying at the Ritz. Irma's relief was unmistakable.

"Oh, there's Reggie now," cried Lady Chatwood, who ran off to throw herself into the arms of a tall, good-looking but red-faced man wearing a yellow-and-blue-striped Brook Club band around his straw hat, tilted to the side of his head.

"Well, well, if it isn't Molly," he said. "Never thought you'd make it, old girl."

"Reggie, you darling," screeched Molly. "I would follow you to the end of the world. You can't get away from *me!*"

"Nor me," said Emily, laughing. "How are you, Reggie? It's been a long time."

Reggie then hugged Emily and gave her a kiss. "You look divine, younger than ever," he said. "Ben would be proud of you."

"Now, don't monopolize dear old Reggie," said Molly, hanging on to his arm. "I'm all set, Reggie darling."

"Great," said Reggie. "But where is your luggage? They wouldn't let my car in, so my chauffeur is sitting in it. It is a red Hispano-Suiza. Why don't you go and wait for me there? I will see to the luggage. You can rest for a while; you will need it because we are going to a great party at the Crystal Room at the Ritz tonight. Emily, I didn't know that you were coming, but will you join us? I want to show Molly the town. We are really going to have fun." Molly gave him a kiss.

Irma, standing to one side, was shocked by this performance. This half sister of her late husband was ignoring her. Did she also intend to turn a time of mourning into a party?

"I can't come tonight because I expect to be with my sister-in-law, if that's all right, Irma?" said Emily, turning to her.

Irma sourly said, "Yes. I thought you had come only to see me. I didn't know you had all these friends."

Emily laughed. "Don't worry, Irma, you will see enough of me. You will be quite sick of me."

Many a true word is spoken in jest, thought Irma. Wendell Ponderosa, noting her expression, felt that the visit might be short but certainly not sweet.

"Well, anyway, do call up," said Molly, giving Reggie another hug. "We must all have a get-together, however and wherever, soon, sooner, soonest." After whispering something in Reggie's ear that made them both laugh, Molly said goodbye to Emily and Irma, and walked off arm in arm with Reggie, saying she did not want to lose a minute with him by sitting alone in his car.

Irma caught the glint of a gold bracelet around Molly's

ankle as she walked off. She wanted to ask Emily a question, but she had to postpone it when Prince Pontevecchio stepped forward. He had kept his distance while Lady Chatwood said good-bye; now he obviously wanted to speak to Emily. He took her hand, raising it to his lips, and said, "I hate to say good-bye to you after the wonderful six days that we had together on the *Aquitania*. It put new life into me. I am going to Detroit on business, but I shall be back in a few days. Perhaps we can meet then. I will be at the Ambassador, not the Ritz, unfortunately, as they were full up. I shall always remember our trip. For me it was the happiest time in years." He looked into her eyes.

"Yes. We did have a good time, didn't we," said Emily, playing down his enthusiasm under Irma's baleful look. "Thank you for that. You made the trip a delight for me." The prince bowed, kissed Emily's hand again and, glancing at Irma, bowed again politely. Emily's old governess, he thought as he walked down the pier to find his luggage under the letter *P*. But why the pearls? he wondered and then decided that they must have been a gift from Emily. He smiled.

Irma, noticing all this, felt confirmed in her opinion of Emily. She was obviously a flirtatious, stupid woman, too easily impressed by a broken-down Italian prince, years younger than herself, and a ridiculous hand kiss. James would not have allowed him in the house.

At last, the luggage was safely put away and what didn't fit into the trunk of the Crane Simplex was stowed on the roof under a canvas cover. Mr. Ponderosa said his farewells, and went off in search of a taxi. As the two women got into the car, Emily introduced the woman with the jewel case as her German maid Elsa. Irma nodded and quickly shut the dividing glass that closed off the chauffeur, and then she asked her a question about Emily's friend with the gold bracelet around her ankle. "Is she a chorus girl, that friend of yours?"

Emily laughed. "Far from it. She is the daughter of the Earl of Bottomley and the wife of Lord Chatwood. But you are right; in one way she *has* got theatrical ambitions, although a bit above the chorus line. She has come over not only to see Reggie, but to join a great Austrian impresario who is here forming a company for a play he's reviving. He might give her the part of the Virgin Mary."

Irma was not religious, but she was shocked. "The Virgin Mary!" she exclaimed.

Emily laughed. "Why not? She has a beautiful Madonna-like face, and the part doesn't give her much to say."

"And that man, Reggie, who is he?" Irma asked unpleasantly.

"Reggie Beekman, a man much younger than Ben, but a friend of his. They belonged to the same shooting and fishing syndicates. Actually, Ben was devoted to him, and we saw him here and abroad. He is a dear, but stuffy sometimes."

Irma sniffed. Emily said such absurd things.

Driving out to Rye, the two sisters-in-law had time to size each other up. Emily, still alluring at forty-nine (the official age she had chosen since the death of her husband), looked at Irma and thought a woman will not die from lack of love, but she will certainly wilt. Irma's skin was fine but wrinkled, her neck wattled, her combative eyes half hidden by her drooping eyelids, her full and surprisingly sensual lips petulant. Emily sighed. She had never felt sorry for Irma before, but now she did. James obviously had been so interested in money and power that the love and tenderness that he had shown to Emily in her childhood must have vanished years ago. James and Irma making love, if they ever did, was beyond Emily's imagination. Emily, a connoisseur of emotions, saw all of this in Irma's face. Irma not only looked unloved, she looked mean, as if she unconsciously wanted revenge for what she had missed. And the look she had given Carlo Pontevecchio! Was it because he was a foreigner or did she feel jealous because Carlo had not spoken to her? How can I possibly stand a visit with Irma? she said to herself. I had thought only of James; I had quite forgotten about her. I must certainly go to the Ritz as soon as possible.

These thoughts depressed Emily, who took out her gold cigarette case embellished with a large diamond monogram and lit a gold-tipped cigarette. Heavens, she thought as she fitted it into her cigarette holder and then blew a smoke ring, it's going to take all the fortitude and tact I have . . . and even that may not be enough.

Irma waved her hands in the air to blow away the smoke and, looking more closely, was astounded by Emily's appearance. Irma had never liked Emily from the beginning, but now, seeing her so sure of herself, so obviously pleased with life, receiving ridiculous hand kisses and lighting a cigarette, made her seem like an actress.

As she continued looking, she noticed that Emily's skin was absolutely smooth, her cheeks either naturally pink or lightly rouged. Her eyes were one of her best features—green and sparkling—her nose retroussé; her dark hair came out in curls from beneath her hat. It was her skin, however, that Irma's eyes went back to. How could there be no wrinkles? Emily was only twelve years younger than Irma. Why hadn't her skin become wrinkled?

Emily, catching her searching and obviously antagonistic look, smiled. "Face-lift," she said laconically. "They do it in Paris."

"What!" exclaimed Irma. "What do you mean? I never heard of such a thing."

"I had my face and neck lifted two years ago," said Emily. "I was getting a bit saggy. I had it done in Paris soon after Ben died. They don't do it over here yet. They did a pretty good job, I think, don't you?"

"How do they do it?" asked Irma, ignoring Emily's question.

"They simply pull your skin up over your face and neck and sew it up on the top of your head."

"I wouldn't think of doing it." Irma winced, her eyes still fixed on Emily's face. "Why do you want to look younger than you are?"

"I want to look younger because I hate looking at an old face in the morning in the mirror," said Emily agreeably. "And besides, I believe that a woman should look as young as she can, as long as she can. Don't you agree?"

Irma shrugged nervously. "When you get to be a certain age, what does it matter?" she said. "I believe in looking neat and tidy; but doing all sort of things to yourself, I think, is ridiculous." As she said this, she took her handkerchief out and waved it ostentatiously in front of her face to drive the smoke away. Emily put her cigarette out.

As Emily looked again at Irma's frankly unadorned face, she wondered if it might be better to be a "never-been" than a has-been. At least Irma would never have to hear people say, "You should have seen her twenty years ago," words that haunted Emily. Irma obviously was never depressed when she looked in the mirror.

Emily's heart sank. To be alone with Irma in the country even for a short time would be a trial, and it was plain that Irma did not want to be with her either. It was all a mistake. Emily tried to concentrate her thoughts on James. After all, he was the reason she was here. He had been very good to her and to her mother, whom she knew he disliked. He had come often to her house in the suburbs when she was a little girl, and had bought her stuffed animals and other toys; once he brought her a tiny ring and a small necklace of turquoises which she still had, buried in the pages of her prayer book. It was James who had sent her to a first-class boarding school, but when he married Irma, the checks grew bigger and the visits became fewer. Eventually, they ceased entirely. He had not even come to see her graduate, but he did take the train up to Boston to give her away at her wedding (Irma had pleaded a cold), but went back right after the ceremony. It was only Ben who had, through business, remained in real contact with him. On safari in Kenya, hearing of James's death, all of his kindness had flowed into her mind, and she felt a longing to see where he had been last, to pay her respects at his grave. She owed all her happiness to him, for she had met Ben while visiting his niece who was her schoolmate. If Irma was a little difficult, Emily had met many difficult people and had been able to overcome their idiosyncrasies. She thought she could take at least a week of it. She looked more intently at Irma, who turned her head and returned her look.

"What are you thinking of?" Irma asked.

"James," answered Emily.

After that, neither of them spoke, each lost in her own thoughts as they bowled slowly along the road to Rye. The trip took almost two hours, and it was with a feeling of relief that they finally arrived at the door of Bella Vista.

"This is Bella Vista," said Irma with pride as they drew up in front of the huge, square, white stucco house with its red tile roof and dozens of small barred windows.

Emily had been so absorbed in her own thoughts that she had not even realized that they had come into the grounds.

"Good heavens, it is a palazzo," she said, thinking that would please Irma. It did; Irma almost smiled.

"Fifty-two rooms," she said, "including, of course, the staff's quarters. You are right; it is a copy of a villa near Florence. Sloth, Koppett, and Wrangle were the architects, but Carrere and Hastings speak highly of it."

Morgan, the English butler, greeted them at the door. He looked glum as he took Irma's coat, but when Emily held out her hand and said, "I am Mrs. Codway, Mr. Shrewsbury's sister, and this is my personal maid, Miss Elsa Lichtbaum," he bowed and replied, "Welcome to Bella Vista, madam." This was obviously a lady who knew how to treat people. He liked the look of the personal maid, too; a real professional, he thought, not at all like the rough-and-ready person that Mrs. Shrewsbury had.

Irma, who had watched this exchange, disapproved. She thought it cheap of Emily to start hobnobbing with the servants and, considering the education James had given her, she should have known better. "Mrs. Codway is to be in the blue room," she said to Morgan, "and the maid in the room Mr. Shrewsbury used for his secretaries. And is lunch ready?"

"Yes, madam," responded Morgan. "Whenever you are."

"Well, we will be down in half an hour." Irma started up the stairs. "Come, Emily. I will show you to your room." She led Emily along a long corridor past many closed doors to the end where a door was half open.

"Don't unpack too much, Elsa," said Emily as she closed the door on the departing Irma. "Just the necessary things. We are only staying here for the night, I hope." Elsa nodded. She felt sorry for her lady. Mrs. Shrewsbury was not the sort of person *her* lady usually had as a friend.

### CHAPTER TWO

# EMILY DREAMS OF CARLO AND MR. PONDEROSA MAKES A DECISION

WHEN EMILY CAME DOWN THE DOUBLE MARBLE STAIRCASE FOR lunch, she found Irma waiting at the bottom. Without her hat, Irma looked surprisingly better. Her dark gray hair was thick and strong, and though severely brushed back, managed to soften her face; also without her gloves her hands were snow white and almost childish. Emily smiled and said, "I hope I didn't take too long. I hate to keep you waiting."

"That's all right," responded Irma. "But we must go right in. Lunch is ready."

Lunch was served at a large round table which stood on a cold marble floor in the elliptical dining room. The walls were hung with tapestries, which depicted bloody battles, and the fireplace was supported by stone warriors with a huge, almost life-size horse and rider above it in stone. The two women were seated at opposite ends of the table and could hear their voices echoing in the vast room. Irma asked if Reggie Beekman was a relation of Lady Chatwood. "No, heavens no," exclaimed Emily. "She's just having a walk out with him."

" 'Walk out?' What's that?" questioned Irma.

"An English expression for an affair," replied Emily, as she tried to break through the sticky white sauce which covered the fish.

"Does Lord Chatwood know about it?" queried Irma, as she closely watched Emily's smiling face. Was Emily making fun of her?

"I suppose he does, but he pretends not to. He is giving Molly her head," replied Emily blithely.

"Her head?"

"Well, I mean, she is a bit like a young racehorse. I think he feels that when the race is over she will come back to him."

"You mean when she gets tired of Beekman?" said Irma, beginning to catch on.

"Exactly," said Emily. "It would be a pity if she doesn't, because they are considered a perfect couple in London. Everyone adores them."

Irma sniffed and rang the bell for the next course. There was silence while they were being served. Then Irma asked another question. "Were you and Ben a perfect couple?" she asked.

Emily looked directly at her from across the table and burst out laughing.

"Everyone said so," she said. "Ben was *the* love of my life." And a wistful expression came over her face.

Was she longing for Ben or just putting it on? Irma wondered. If Ben had been the love of her life, why did she seem so interested in that Italian prince? She must have been flirting with him on the *Aquitania* from the way he looked at her. Was it possible for a woman over fifty to have a flirtation?

This was a new thought and Irma reflected on it for the rest of the meal. Whatever Emily was doing, it certainly agreed with her. She was blooming.

After lunch Emily went to her room intending to read, but instead thought of the trip over on the *Aquitania*. She, Molly, Carlo Pontevecchio, and the old Duc de Chienloup had had a table together. Emily had expected that Molly and Carlo would hit it off and that she would be left with Chienloup, which would have been proper. Carlo, after all, was twenty years younger than she was. But things had worked out differently. Molly, who insisted that she was fed up with George Chatwood, her husband, and supposed herself madly in love with Reggie Beekman, began flirting outrageously with the senile and amorous *duc*. When Emily, after watching her tango with the old boy, told her she was going a bit too far, Molly only laughed. "It doesn't mean a thing to me," she said, "and it seems to mean so awfully much to him. He doesn't know if he kisses my arm or my ankle, just so he is close to me. Besides, he has promised to give me a masked ball at the Château Chienloup. He is going to have all the woods lit up and says he will teach me to ride a wild boar. I want to try everything once—my mama always said, 'Don't die guessing.' " Whereupon, Molly pirouetted for a moment, then dashed away onto the deck in search of the *duc*.

From then on Emily, who felt that she had done her duty, decided that she was free to see as much of Carlo as she wanted. So Emily and Carlo walked around the deck, a routine of two miles a day, played shuffleboard, took chances on the ship's pool (never winning, which Carlo explained was a good sign), and danced every night. Carlo danced the tango divinely, far better than the old *duc* and, as they were almost the same height, they looked into each other's eyes as they slowly did the sensuous steps. On deck they talked of many things: Mussolini, Maurice Chevalier's songs, Josephine Baker and Helen Morgan at their nightclubs, of Irving Berlin and Cole Porter, of Henri de Montherlant's novels, of D'Annunzio and Mistinguett and Yvonne Printemps, the philosophy of Orage and the portraits of Bernard Boutet de Monvel, whether Lonsdale was better than Coward, of Gertrude Lawrence and Beatrice Lillie, and the magnificent Gladys Cooper. They talked of everything, except themselves. Looking back, Emily felt that they had floated with the ship and their eyes said more than their voices; a shipboard flirtation that would probably end at the sight of land. Emily sighed. It had been great fun.

IRMA, in her room, was not so relaxed. Emily had stirred her up and she could not rest. She called her office and then Wendell Ponderosa. "I have just found out that my portfolio is down another one percent," she said. "The Magnum Bank says that they have been taking your firm's advice. What right has your firm to dictate to the bank?"

Wendell Ponderosa kept his voice low and calm. "No right at all, Irma. Except that the bank came to us. We talked it over together and came to a decision together."

"A very poor one, I must say," said Irma. "From now on I would like to be advised before you make such decisions behind my back. Do you hear me?"

"I hear you perfectly," said Mr. Ponderosa softly. "Is that all, Irma?"

Irma realized that she had gone too far. Wendell Ponderosa was no underling. He was a powerful lawyer, respected in every circle of New York life. She knew that in spite of her high-handed manner she could not afford to offend him. "I am not feeling well," she said, letting an apologetic note creep into her voice. "I feel dizzy all the time."

"Have you had a checkup recently?" inquired Mr. Ponderosa. "An E.K.G. or some blood tests?"

"E.K.G.!" exclaimed Irma. "What makes you think I need one?"

"Well, a touch of dizziness, one always fears something," ventured Mr. Ponderosa, not at all worried about frightening her a bit.

"I haven't had a checkup in ten years and I haven't a doctor. I wouldn't go near the one that James had." She paused and remembered that James had died of a sudden heart attack. Stress had caused it, the doctor had said afterwards. She, Irma, was now under such stress and had been ever since James's death. This went through her mind. "Do you know of a doctor?" she inquired.

"I do indeed," Mr. Ponderosa said heartily. "Jack Robinson, the best in the land. I will send you his address. In the meantime, try to rest."

Irma hung up, and decided that she certainly did not want a heart attack. She rang for Harold, the first footman, to bring her tea and two Huntley & Palmer biscuits as usual.

Mr. Ponderosa put down the phone, sat back in his swivel chair behind his huge desk, and looked thoughtfully out of the window at the Statue of Liberty. He was not interested in what he was looking at but in what was revolving in his mind: the seventy-five-thousand-dollar retainer that Irma paid the firm was an impressive sum. He could foresee that, with her aggressive nature, she might easily need extra advice. He could envisage no end of lawsuits. It was important that she stay with the firm, which meant at least that she not risk her health. She would certainly not calm down with Emily around. He had seen at once the jealousy and envy on her face when the prince came up to say good-bye. Irma must have read more about Emily's glamorous life than she had admitted and was about to erupt. But how to calm her down? It was then that he remembered years ago when just such a question of losing a valuable client had come up. He was a young man then but had solved it personally, and he still recalled with discomfort the hysterical elderly widow whom he had had to deal with. But now he was older and must find a boy to do a man's work. He pulled the desk pad toward him and, selecting a sharp pencil from the silver cup, hummed to himself as he began to jot down the names of younger members of the firm.

### CHAPTER THREE

# EMILY MEETS JOE AND IRMA READS GOSSIP COLUMNS

EMILY, HAVING BEEN IN BED BY NINE THE NIGHT BEFORE, WAS up early the next morning. And so, after her breakfast, she had gone out for a walk in Irma's sedate and well-kept garden, with its neat turf paths and straight, narrow beds filled with tulips and hyacinths, as impersonal as a seed catalogue. However, it was nice to be out on a spring morning, and so she walked along the paths until she found a stone bench under a blossoming dogwood fairly near the house. As she sat there in the soft spring air enjoying the distant view, she saw a young man descending the stone steps from the terrace and coming toward her. He was nice looking with reddish-brown, rather long hair and a friendly face, but was dressed absurdly in baggy trousers, a trench coat buckled tightly around his waist, and pointed, bright brown shoes. He smiled as he came toward her. He looked familiar, but she couldn't place him.

"Aunt Emily," he said, "Morgan told me you were out here. I'm your nephew, Joe. I don't think we've seen each other for ten years, but you are prettier than ever."

Emily jumped up and gave him a hug. "I'm so happy to see you. You look so much like your father when he was young."

"Do I?" Joe was pleased. No one had ever said that to him before.

"What's all this about?" demanded Irma, who had just come out of the house. She gave Emily a sharp look. "What are you saying?"

"I was telling Joe how much he resembled James. Don't you agree, Irma?"

"I see absolutely no resemblance at all," answered Irma. "If he looks like anyone, now that I see you together, I think he looks like you." By which she seemed to mean that she found them equally distasteful.

Emily sensed the innuendo and Joe looked embarrassed, but Emily smiled and, putting a hand on Joe's arm, declared that she was very pleased that they shared the Shrewsbury blood!

Irma had had enough of this. "What brings you here, Joe?" she asked as she seated herself beside Emily. Joe sat down at their feet, disclosing bright red socks as he stretched out his legs. Irma, who had expected him to be in deepest black for at least six months, glared.

"I hope you don't mind, Mother, if Aunt Emily hears."

"Go right ahead," said Irma. "Say all you want, but I have to make some telephone calls. Then we are going to your father's grave—so what is it?"

Joe remained silent and seemed puzzled. Emily thought he looked pathetic. As he and Irma remained silent, Emily said, "What is wrong, Joe dear? You seem worried."

"*Worried.*" Joe repeated the word with emphasis. "Of course I'm worried. My father left me a house but not another cent. I am trying to write, but I am so worried and mixed-up that I just sit at my typewriter and can't think of a thing but how I am going to be able to live. I've come here to ask my mother for some money so that I can have a little peace of mind." He looked up at Irma while he played with a blade of grass.

"You must know how I hate to do this, Mother. I know that you have educated me and have given me an allowance and I have lived off that, always hoping that I could make a name for myself as a writer. I was just beginning to get known a little—then Father died. *Smart Set* and *Pictorial Review* have published several of my articles. Now I have the house. But nothing else. And no time to pull myself together. Mother, could you lend me some money? I'll pay you back." He looked straight into her eyes as he said this.

Emily listened, horrified. It was the last thing she expected. James had been good to her. Why couldn't he have been good to his son? Then, looking at Irma, she realized why. Irma, that dreary, dull woman, must have wanted her husband all to herself. As this horrid idea went through Emily's mind, Irma surprised her by rising to her feet. "Stay here," she said to Joe. "I'll go to my office and write you a check." And she walked briskly up the steps to the house.

Emily and Joe looked at each other as if they had suddenly been tossed up on a beach after a shipwreck. "I am sorry to have to say all this in front of you, Aunt Emily," said Joe. "And I certainly did not enjoy having to do it, but I am at my wit's end. I reckoned I had nothing to lose by coming. Mother already thinks I'm a mess. My parents have never had much use for me," he added bitterly.

Emily was about to speak, but Irma, returning sooner than expected, went directly up to Joe. "Here," she said, "is one hundred and fifty dollars in cash. I had it in my purse. Mr. Ponderosa, I believe, gave you something as well. You have perhaps forgotten that. Anyway, here is the money—and now I am going upstairs. As we have been delayed, I think that we should go directly to the cemetery. So good-bye, Joe. Emily, I will meet you at the car in five minutes." And she left them.

Emily put her hands on Joe's shoulders. "Poor boy," she said, aghast at Irma's stinginess. "This is all too terrible. I am sorry for both of you and your mother. But may I see you again? I will be coming into town soon and want you to lunch with me. Will you?"

Joe kissed her on the cheek. "Thank you, Aunt Emily. I'd love to." So back he went to New York, and Irma and Emily went to the cemetery.

When they met in the hall, Morgan was waiting for them. "A message for you, madam," he said, presenting a folded piece of paper to Irma on a silver salver. Irma opened it and turned to Emily.

"Mr. Ponderosa wants to know if he can come to dinner tonight," she said. "He also wants to bring someone else. Some man. I can't read his name. What's that you've written, Morgan?"

Morgan looked annoyed. "I wrote it down as Mr. Ponderosa told me, madam," he said. "Mr. Hopleg. Mr. Ponderosa said that it was most important."

"Well, I can't imagine what it is," said Irma. "And I certainly don't want him tonight. I did not sleep well last night and I am exhausted. Joe's visit is quite enough for one day."

"Oh, come on, Irma," said Emily, thinking anything was better than dining alone again with Irma. "We need something to cheer us up and I would love to see Wendell. He's a charming man. He did a lot of business with Ben. Also, if he says that it's important I'm sure it is."

Irma looked at Morgan. "Have we any food in the house?" she asked.

Morgan hesitated, knowing the quality of it. "I think we have enough, madam," he answered. "The cook is in town for the day, but I think that the second cook and kitchen maid could make do."

Mrs. Shrewsbury, always a careless housekeeper, had grown

worse since J.S. had died; until Emily arrived, she had been eating on a tray. This gave the staff a chance to take turns going into town to work for a caterer at twenty dollars a night. Morgan dreaded to think how the household would fall apart if Madam took to wanting guests. In spite of the delightful interlude of Mrs. Codway's visit, he still intended to hang on for only another six months before taking over as steward at the Deepdale Country Club on Long Island, where the gentlemen in their cups were heavy tippers.

"I think it would do us both good to see Wendell Ponderosa. Do let him come. Just as I said, Ben used his firm for quite a few deals and, if he says that it's important, I'm sure it is," persisted Emily.

Irma felt that it must be so, too. Although she suspected Emily of simply wanting a man around. What could Wendell want? Something about the Fifty-second Street house or a letter leaving more to Emily? "Call Mr. Ponderosa," she said to Morgan, "and say that we expect him and his friend at seven sharp."

Irma had mixed feelings about seeing Wendell Ponderosa. They had had two telephone talks that morning, neither of them pleasant. The second was precipitated by an account she had read in a society column about the trip over on the *Aquitania*. It appeared that Emily had been the belle of the ship, sought after by everyone, particularly by two great European aristocrats, the Duc de Chienloup and Prince Carlo Pontevecchio. Now that Emily had arrived back in New York, many parties were being planned to entertain her, among them one at the home of Mrs. Brevoort Beekman. In fact, Irma read, all of New York's top society were clamoring "to open their doors to the beautiful and fascinating Mrs. Codway and her friend Lady Margaret Chatwood, daughter of the Earl of Bottomley." She and James had never read these columns, but she had taken to them in her widowhood and had become an addict. She pretended that they were about absurd, stupid people who hadn't a brain in their heads. Nevertheless, she was curious about them: what they did and where they went. She had money, but was there something else? Over the telephone she had tried to say in a light, almost laughing tone something about these ridiculous people. How, she asked Wendell Ponderosa, did these silly people ever get to know Mrs. Brevoort Beekman, who was "old money" with the largest house on Fifth Avenue.

"Charity begins at home," Wendell had said enigmatically.

"What do you mean by that?" she had demanded.

"Well," said Mr. Ponderosa, lying back in his swivel chair and speaking softly and clearly into the phone, "it begins at home, dear Irma, because by giving to the pet charities of these people, you then have the key that will open their houses. The more you give, the more you will get from them."

Irma was shocked—she and James had worked hard for their money. They had married in their early thirties because they had recognized the naked desire to make money in each other's eyes. It had certainly not been a love match; but as time passed their marriage became a habit. It was a partnership, as simple as that, equally beneficial to them both. But was it? She had wondered ever since James's death about that house on Fifty-second Street, even more so when she read in the gossip sheets the sly remarks about staid married men being seen in New York at the best restaurants with ladies not their wives, particularly in August when their wives were safely in their marble Newport "cottages" or their beachside shingled palaces in Southampton. When James, from time to time, had been in New York without her, what had he been up to? Irma worked herself into a frenzy at the thought. Wendell Ponderosa, when she asked him, had not been helpful. He knew nothing about the house except that James had told him he had taken it over for a bad loan about twenty-five years before he died. That to Irma was the final insult. He had kept the place a secret for years until suddenly he let Joe live there after Princeton—but who had been there in between? She had now read of the philandering old Mr. Brevoort Beekman; had James done the same?

With these unpleasant thoughts, Irma took Emily off to view James's grave. The headstone was not yet in place, but the site was impressively surrounded by a double hedge of cypresses. Irma, immediately after James's death, had insisted on giving him the same privacy he had wanted while he was alive, and this pleased her. She had been the perfect widow. Somber in her black, working at their partner's desk at the office, proudly saying "James would have wished this" or "James would never have done that." In the office, behind her back, they claimed she was worse than Hetty Green. But what if James had been two-timing her all those years? Wasn't she entitled to something too? She didn't know what—but she felt reckless. She had her money, but now she wanted something more.

She was startled to turn and find tears in Emily's eyes. "If James had not been so good to me, I would never have met Ben," explained Emily. "My life would not have been the same."

Irma, who had put on her mourning hat to go to the grave, pulled the black veil over her face. "I am furious that the headstone is not yet in place," she said. "Let's go home. I want to call up the man in charge of the cemetery, and then after lunch we should rest before dinner."

Emily nodded. Irma seemed stranger than ever, as if she was annoyed by Emily's feeling.

Irma, on the other hand, wondered how much longer Emily thought she could fool her with this constant show of emotion. To Irma, Emily looked smug—and Irma wished she knew how to put her in her place.

### CHAPTER FOUR

# CHARLIE HOPELAND COMES TO DINNER AND IRMA DECIDES TO SEE A DOCTOR

WENDELL PONDEROSA HAD EXAGGERATED A BIT WHEN HE SAID it was urgent that he see Irma Shrewsbury at once. Actually, what he wanted to see her about was to introduce the boy he found to do a man's work. He had chosen young Charlie Hopeland, and he wondered what Irma's reaction would be to him. He wanted to see for himself, and so he invited himself and Charlie to dinner. Irma Shrewsbury was too valuable a client for Battle, Ponderosa, and Huddlefield to lose. He could foresee that with her arrogance and bad temper, her legal affairs might soon become profitably complicated, but she had already hinted that she might leave if she did not have a member of the firm constantly dancing attention. Charlie Hopeland was a smart young fellow, and Wendell hoped that Irma would not despise him at a glance. If she did, he would have to find someone else to take his place, and a second choice would be less likely to work than a first.

As the two men sat under the brilliant lights of the fake Louis XIV chandelier in the drawing room of Bella Vista waiting for Irma to appear, Mr. Ponderosa looked nervously at Charlie and noticed for the first time how very good-looking he was—not the sort of looks that were generally admired in Mr. Ponderosa's circle. Charlie was an "Arrow Collar ad," with his Grecian profile, deep-set eyes, and golden wavy hair —good-looking, but not quite a gentleman.

Wendell Ponderosa, in spite of his odd name, was an old New Yorker, a Groton and Harvard man, a member of all the best clubs, and, in his younger days, for three years a squash racquets champion. Charlie Hopeland, on the other hand, came from Denver, had gone to public school, to Dartmouth on a scholarship, and then to Harvard Law, where his record had been brilliant. That was how he ended up at Battle, Ponderosa, and Huddlefield.

Hopeland was now in his early thirties, unmarried and a very hard worker. A most acceptable bachelor, he was constantly being invited for summer weekends at Newport and winter ones in Aiken. He played tennis, golf, and bridge, danced beautifully, and was exactly what a hostess wanted. By now he was a member of the Opera Club and the Racquet and Tennis Club—the firm had seen to that—and Mr. Ponderosa knew that he was ambitious to rise in the firm. He supposed that he was socially ambitious as well.

Charlie was not "top drawer" but, Mr. Ponderosa suddenly thought, neither for that matter is Irma Shrewsbury. For all her money, Irma certainly never had, nor ever would have, any great social standing.

As Mr. Ponderosa had told Irma, New York in 1928 was socially a small and inbred group, and a newcomer could achieve reluctant entrée only by giving enormous sums of money to the causes that the elite were interested in. In return for that, the donor would receive an invitation to dinner once a season or an invitation for an evening at the opera—opera boxes being owned, at that time, by the old New Yorkers and impossible to obtain otherwise. To be seen in the front of a box in the Diamond Horseshoe meant a lot in 1928.

Irma had had neither the inclination nor the time for such endeavors. James, though, had wished a certain position for his wife and had put the screws on a man whom he had let in on a few deals and had asked him to make his wife (who was president of the Colony Club) put Irma up for membership and to get two other friends of hers to second her. The man's wife had reluctantly agreed and rounded up the seconders and letter-writers, all vouching what a fine member Irma Snood Shrewsbury would make, though none of the members had ever met her and hoped they never would, except when she had to meet them all once for tea before being duly elected. It had been a dismal occasion. Irma was not interested in the club, nor in the fact that it had been founded by Miss Anne Morgan, daughter of J.P., and two of her friends, and was decorated by Elsie de Wolfe. For their part, the members were not interested in Irma. However, she appeared harmless to them, and all of them knew of J.S.'s power in the business world.

A smile was playing over his face at these recollections when Irma and Emily came into the room. Mr. Ponderosa and Charlie jumped to their feet and walked forward to greet them.

What a contrast there was between them. Emily, so slim and youthful in a dress that seemed about to slip off her smooth white shoulders. It is said that at middle age a woman either loses her pretty face or her good figure. But Emily had kept both. And to Mr. Ponderosa she seemed a portrait by

Boldini in her clinging tea gown, her upswept hair, her pearl and diamond earrings, the flower at her bosom, and her charming, piquant profile. Just to look at her filled him with pleasure. Poor Irma, meanwhile, looked like a starved raven in her long-sleeved black dress and black satin stole, far more threatening than the mouse she had been when J.S. was alive.

Mr. Ponderosa introduced Charlie to them, and they all sat down.

"Wendell," said Emily, "it has been so long since you stayed with Ben and me at Cypress Point; but you haven't changed a bit. I recognized you at once on the pier. How do you do it?"

Mr. Ponderosa smiled. He had put on thirty pounds since he last saw Emily and his hair had turned white, but he liked to think that he looked the same.

"And you, Emily," he answered, "are better looking than ever."

It was Emily's turn to smile. She knew that she was no longer the striking beauty that she once had been, but she also knew that she looked better than most women her age, and her face-lift gave her even more assurance.

"That's straight from the Blarney Stone," she said, falsely modest. "But I like it."

Irma had turned away during this exchange and asked Charlie Hopeland if he would like a glass of sherry.

"I would love it," he answered, his heart sinking a bit at the thought of the long evening without something stronger than sherry.

Mr. Ponderosa came to his rescue. "I think that Charlie and I would each like an old-fashioned, Irma," he said, "if that's all right with you."

"I will have one, too," said Emily.

"And I will have sherry, as usual," said Irma, speaking to Morgan.

Morgan took the order glumly. Old-fashioneds meant a slice of orange, a cherry, and a lump of sugar with bitters. Why couldn't they drink their whiskey straight, the way they did in the old country? Harold, taking his cue from Morgan, looked grim as he handed Morgan the glasses.

Irma knew that Wendell would not talk business until after dinner, which meant that she would have to make the best of it for the next hour. And who was this good-looking man that he had brought with him? What did he do?

"Are you a relative of Mr. Ponderosa's?" she asked.

"No, ma'am," he answered her, smiling. "I am only a junior member of the firm."

This startled her. What was up? Why had Wendell brought another member of the firm? Was it for Emily? The way Emily and her friends behaved, this young man would be Emily's dish. She would like to have questioned Wendell then and there, but she didn't want Emily to know anything about her business affairs. They had just finished their drinks when relief came in the form of Morgan, who announced nervously that dinner was served.

It may have been the effect of the old-fashioneds or maybe the excellent champagne (Morgan was fond of champagne and had decided to serve it); at any rate, strangely enough, the dinner was almost gay. The food was wretched: warmed-over lamb, mashed potatoes like glue, and canned peas, but Morgan and the two footmen served it on silver dishes, as if it were nightingale tongues.

Emily was an agreeable dinner partner, gay and eager to please. Mr. Ponderosa wished to put Irma in a good mood and was as suave as could be. However, it was Charlie Hopeland who really made the evening. He spoke to Mrs. Shrewsbury in a quizzical, gentle, slightly teasing way that seemed to put her completely off her guard.

Mr. Ponderosa had been riveted, when, while he was talking to Emily, he suddenly heard Charlie say, "Now come on, Mrs. Shrewsbury, you don't really believe *that?*" Mr. Ponderosa was about to inject himself into the conversation but, turning his head, he noticed that Charlie was leaning toward Mrs. Shrewsbury and smiling, and that she, incredibly, was smiling back.

Mr. Ponderosa turned back to Emily, who gave him a wink. "There's nothing like young blood," she whispered, "particularly when it looks like *that.*"

"Do you find him so good-looking?" he murmured, feeling slightly jealous for no reason at all. After all, it was *he* who had chosen Charlie.

"Yes," answered Emily, "if one doesn't mind a lack of distinction. He's not my type." Mr. Ponderosa sighed.

"What are you two whispering about?" demanded Irma.

"Wendell," said Emily, smiling at him, "was asking me about some of the Codways and I was describing their very good-looking youngest son." She emphasized "good-looking" in case Irma had overheard her talking.

Irma looked down at her plate. It seemed to her that she had been right that day on the pier. Emily had grown silly. She was almost flirtatious with Mr. Ponderosa and, just now, the way she had looked at young Mr. Hopeland, she seemed to want to flirt with him too. It was undignified, she thought, especially since he seemed such a nice, quiet young man.

"Let's have coffee in the drawing room," she said, rising from the table, "and if you can go without your cigars, won't you two join us?"

"For the pleasure of your company, I am sure that Charlie and I will gladly forego our cigars," said Mr. Ponderosa gallantly. He dearly loved his cigar, as she well knew, but he also wanted to get back to New York before midnight.

Charlie knew all about Mr. Ponderosa's cigars that were

specially aged for him at the Racquet Club, and Charlie knew there were two in the leather cigar case in Mr. Ponderosa's pocket. This, therefore, meant that Mr. Ponderosa would get down to business quickly. Charlie was far from retiring. He knew that he was the brightest junior member in the firm, which was why he had been brought out here, and he had no trouble surmising that the firm did not want Mrs. Shrewsbury's annual retainer of seventy-five thousand dollars to leave. Mrs. Shrewsbury was very important to them, and she must be up to something that worried Mr. Ponderosa. Charlie was sure of that. During dinner under his flippant manner (which, incidentally, came naturally to him) he had been sizing up Mrs. Shrewsbury and agreed with Mr. Ponderosa. Obviously, she was up to something and would be extremely hard to handle. Charlie was not feeling nearly as confident as he appeared and had made up his mind that he'd wait for a signal from Mr. Ponderosa to see what was expected from him.

They grouped themselves again on the garish golden chairs under the dazzling chandelier surrounded by Bouguereaus and Ziems on the brocade-covered walls, while Morgan and the footmen passed lukewarm coffee and liqueurs. Mr. Ponderosa took a sip of brandy and shuddered. It was horrible, raw and sharp and obviously green. It seemed to him barbaric that such stuff should be served at Bella Vista. Morgan obviously knew better, but didn't care.

"I think that I'll change my mind and have some of that champagne we had at dinner," said Mr. Ponderosa.

Morgan spoke to the footman, who appeared almost instantly with a bottle of champagne.

"Is there something wrong with the brandy?" demanded Irma. "James got it through a friend of Bumper's who owns a distillery." (Bumper had been J.S.'s personal secretary.)

Morgan exchanged a look with Mr. Ponderosa. The brandy was obviously bootleg and brand-new. Mr. Ponderosa smiled at him. Morgan was exonerated. What Mr. Ponderosa had taken for sourness was really humiliation at having to serve anything so unworthy as this American-made stuff.

"I found it a little strong," said Mr. Ponderosa. Then, seeing the look of annoyance on Irma's face, he added, "Excellent, of course, really excellent, but as one grows older, one hasn't quite the head one had when one was younger."

Charlie Hopeland hid a smile. He had seen Mr. Ponderosa consume every wine at a dinner party, then top it off with several brandies and whiskey and sodas. The stuff must have been awful.

The sparkle that had sustained them through dinner was gone. It was Irma's fault. She sat there stony faced, looking idly around the room, seemingly wrapped in her own thoughts; one foot tapped the floor and she shrugged nervously. Emily sensed that something more than Irma's normal reticence was behind this, and she looked inquiringly at Mr. Ponderosa.

"I think," Mr. Ponderosa said, "that when we have finished our liqueurs, and if Mrs. Codway will excuse us, that you and I, Irma, might go into the library. There is something that I must say to you."

"But do let's just go out on the terrace for a moment," said Emily. "There is a full moon, and I would love a breath of air."

"I am certainly not going out," exclaimed Irma. "It's far too chilly."

"Then you come, Wendell. And please call me Emily," said Emily. As she swept through the French door, she added, "We will only be a minute." Mr. Ponderosa followed rather reluctantly. Could he trust Charlie?

When they had gone, Irma looked at Charlie and said,

"Emily likes her own way." Then, picking up the champagne bottle which was in a silver bucket on the table beside her, she filled her glass and handed the bottle to him. "We might as well finish this," she said. "It won't keep. Where's your glass?"

Charlie took the bottle and filled his glass. These rich old women were way beyond his comprehension. It was all right for Mr. Ponderosa, who had known them all his life, but how could he, Charlie Hopeland, the basketball captain of Benjamin Franklin High School, ever expect to fathom them? He certainly couldn't imagine his mother or his aunts sipping champagne with a stranger. It was all so crazy that it made him feel slightly crazy too. He looked at Mrs. Shrewsbury, who was looking intently at him. What did she expect? He raised his glass in a toast.

"To better times ahead," he said and could have bitten off his tongue. The firm would certainly lose a client, but strangely enough, Mrs. Shrewsbury raised her glass, her lips parted in a slight smile.

"Better times," she echoed with a sparkle in her eyes, and they drained their glasses.

"You know, Mrs. Shrewsbury," said Charlie, his blue eyes looking straight at her, "I think you're a wonderful woman. You have such courage and, if you won't mind my saying it, I am sure that Mr. Shrewsbury must have been just crazy about you. You must have helped him enormously. You look so frail, and you're so courageous. I admire you so much. You really must take care of yourself and not overdo."

Irma looked down and then up, a gesture which in another woman might have been coquettish. Goodness, she thought, how young and innocent this young man is. James would have made mincemeat of him. But she liked him. Old men often fall in love with young girls. If Charlie had been a young girl, would James have set him up in Fifty-second Street? The thought brought her up short, for the roles were now reversed. This young man was paying her compliments. Suddenly, and to her complete surprise, she felt twenty years younger. She was Irma Snood Shrewsbury, after all, not just James's wife and, what's more, she also had all of James's power. She smiled at Charlie.

"Mr. Shrewsbury was a wonderful husband," she said. "I owe everything to him." It satisfied her to say it.

Charlie Hopeland caught the drift of her words. The old girl is human, after all, he said to himself. Then aloud, "Now I suppose you will do all sorts of interesting things, carrying out Mr. Shrewsbury's ideas and your own," delicately emphasizing "your own."

"Yes," said Irma. "I have many plans. First, of course, I wish to carry on just as Mr. Shrewsbury did and I wish to run his business."

"It's going to be very hard, you know," said Charlie, boyishly earnest. "It's really going to be tough. The firm will try to help you, but gee, Mrs. Shrewsbury, now that I know you, I just hate to see you work so hard. It might be too much for you."

"Why?" said Mrs. Shrewsbury, adjusting her black satin stole around her shoulders. "What else could I do?"

"Well," said Charlie, "there are so many other things that a lady like you could do. You just *can't* work every day, all day. I think that you ought to take a trip—go to Paris, London, Egypt. Have some fun." Irma hung on his every word.

At this moment, Mr. Ponderosa and Emily returned (having enjoyed a smoke on the terrace and a quick talk about Irma and Joe). Mr. Ponderosa seated himself next to Mrs. Shrewsbury.

"Come, Mr. Hopeland," said Emily. "Let us go into the library while Irma and Mr. Ponderosa have a talk."

Charlie got up and followed her out of the room, smiling apologetically at Mrs. Shrewsbury as he did so. She, in her turn, looked at him thoughtfully. "That partner of yours seems a nice young man," she remarked to Mr. Ponderosa.

"Very nice," he agreed, letting her think Charlie was a partner. "He has a future in the firm. I wanted you to meet Charlie before I go to California next week. I wanted to be sure you approve of him."

"Are you going to be gone long?" she demanded, changing the subject.

"About a month, because after California, I must go directly to Paris. I do not like leaving you, Irma, without someone you can depend on. This is a very difficult time for you, adjusting to life without James—you are looking a little peaked."

"Are you suggesting again that I am *not well?*" Irma quavered a bit.

"No, no, no." Mr. Ponderosa shook his head vigorously. "But I still think that you should have a checkup. I have a checkup with my doctor every six months myself. You know the old saying about an ounce of prevention." Mr. Ponderosa gave a hearty laugh. "It's true. My doctor keeps me in excellent shape. I'll give you his name if you like."

Irma, looking him over, thought he certainly was a little portly but in very good shape. "Well, I'll think it over," she said. "In the meantime, what else have you on your mind? Surely you did not come here just to introduce me to that young man."

Mr. Ponderosa drew his chair closer. "In a way, yes. I wanted you to meet him; but the truth is, Irma, in view of the fact that you are not feeling well and that I am going away, I thought that perhaps even if you did or did not see a doctor, you should wish to make a new will. Your last will, made before James's death, is out of date now that you have inherited everything. I wondered if you wished to set up a trust or if you would wish to leave large sums to organizations or charities."

"Like what?" queried Irma defensively. It was just what she had feared.

"Well, the Visiting Nurse Service or the Y.W.C.A., the Metropolitan Museum, the Museum of Natural History, or set up a foundation for Joe to run."

"Heavens!" she exclaimed. "For *Joe* to run? You must be out of your mind, Wendell!"

"Well, it would carry on the Shrewsbury name," ventured Mr. Ponderosa, although he did not think much of the idea himself. "These are just my suggestions, Irma, but you definitely should make a new will, and if I am not here, Charlie could help you with these matters. Naturally, you need not show him your will, just discuss certain points. He could be, in effect, a legal secretary. Then we could discuss things on my return."

Irma rang the bell beside her chair. She had had enough of his advice. "I will certainly think about it. I like Mr. Hopeland, but he seems a bit young. I will think about that, too. However, I muct go to bed now. Call Mrs. Codway," she said to Morgan, who appeared as she rose from her chair.

Emily and Charlie came to the door and said their good-byes. As Emily and Irma ascended the stairs together, Emily said, "I think that I may go into town day after tomorrow, Irma. I have a great deal to do and also wish to spend a night in town."

"I suppose you find it dull out here," said Irma, who did not like to be deserted so quickly in this cavalier manner. "I was expecting you to be here when the headstone arrived."

"Oh, I'll definitely be back for that," Emily declared. "I won't be in town more than two nights. Reggie has planned to show Molly what New York is like and I'm included. You can get me at the Ritz, as you know. I also have to make arrangements to go up to Boston to see the Codways."

"Good heavens, you seem to want to be all over the place," said Irma. "And Emily, the light switch is by the door. Will you turn it off when you get to your room. We have our own generator and I don't like to be wasteful."

Irma had a bad night. She did not like the fact that both Charlie Hopeland and Mr. Ponderosa seemed to think that she looked bad. When she was brushing her teeth and looked closely at her face in the mirror, she noticed for the first time how pale she was and how many wrinkles she had. She suddenly thought of Emily and her face-lift. It would be a crazy thing to do. But why should someone like Emily look so young when she, who was not much older, looked like her grandmother. She stared at herself until she felt dizzy and tottered to bed.

The next morning at 8:30, she rang Wendell's office. A young female voice said, "Mr. Ponderosa's office."

"I would like to speak to Mr. Ponderosa," demanded Irma.

"I am afraid that he cannot come to the phone. He is in conference."

"Tell him it's Mrs. Shrewsbury," said Irma, annoyed.

"I am sorry, but I cannot interrupt. It is a call from overseas," said the voice.

"Tell him to call back. Say Mrs. Shrewsbury wants to speak to him." Irma was getting angrier by the minute.

The young lady on the other end of the line was also annoyed. "There is a time change," she said, speaking slowly as if to a retarded person. "Six hours' change in time. It is impossible for me to interrupt him." Then, thinking that this old bitch on the other end of the line might really be important, she said, "Is there anyone else in the office you would care to speak to?"

Irma had an inspiration. "Yes, Mr. Charles Hopeland." Although all the girls in the office were half in love with Charlie, he was a long way down from the august Mr. Ponderosa. The old girl was not as important as she pretended to be, the secretary concluded.

Charlie answered his own phone, and Irma, after complaining about Wendell's secretary, told him of her dilemma. She did not feel well and thought she needed a checkup. Did Charlie know the name of the doctor recommended by Mr. Ponderosa?

Fortunately, Charlie did—Jack Robinson. Would Mrs. Shrewsbury like him to make an appointment, and if so, when? Irma said as soon as possible. Charlie said that he would call Dr. Robinson and ring her right back.

Irma was just drinking her grapefruit juice when he called back saying he had the appointment for 9:30 the next morning, and gave her the address in the East Sixties.

"I am sure it will be all right," he ended cheerfully. "If it's convenient could you give me a ring, Mrs. Shrewsbury, and let me know what he says?"

Irma hesitated, then said, "Charlie, you have been so kind to me. How about lunching with me at the Japanese Garden at the Ritz afterwards? They say it is all the rage. It would cheer me up to see a place like that."

Charlie almost dropped the receiver. "I would like nothing better," he said, though he worried about being seen there with Irma. What would Mr. Ponderosa say? Charlie decided to tell him as soon as Irma was off the phone.

"That's fine then," said Irma. "One o'clock at the Ritz." She smiled as she hung up. What a comfort that young man was going to be! She hoped that James, wherever he was, knew that she had found someone who *really* appreciated her.

Charlie, when he told Mr. Ponderosa, was much relieved. Mr. Ponderosa laughed and patted him on the shoulder. "You are doing fine, my boy," he said. "You have a great future if you keep on like this. We need the human touch in dealing with our clients. It is not all in the law books, as you will find out as you go along."

And so it was that both Emily and Irma went to New York together.

### CHAPTER FIVE

# TWO LUNCHES AT THE RITZ

WHEN THE TWO WOMEN DROVE INTO TOWN EARLY THE FOL-
lowing morning, they hardly spoke. Irma was still worried
about her health in spite of Charlie's optimism. She had
again had a poor night. What's more, Joe's unexpected visit to
Bella Vista set her thinking of him. She had never wanted
to have a child. All she had ever wanted was to make money
with James. The child was a mistake from the start, and
they had made certain that it would never happen again. On
looking back, she thought they had given him too much
pocket money, particularly at Princeton—but it had been a
way of buying him off and at the time suited them very well.
Now she tried to shut Joe out of her mind. Then her
thoughts turned to Wendell. Why was he in such a hurry to
have her make a new will? Did she look so ill? Had Dr.
Robinson already said something without even having seen
her? And as for the will—it was *her* money. James had left
it to *her*. In many ways, she had not only helped him ac-
cumulate it, she had really made him do it. James owed it to
her. After all, why did she have to bother about what
happened after she died? The only fear she had was that she

might die suddenly, and without a will, it would all go to Joe, a fool. She must talk more with Wendell about that. Could Joe really sue? Perhaps if she gave him enough to pay the taxes on the house he'd leave her alone. Now, as they drove into town, these thoughts crowded in on her. What she really wanted was to live forever and keep her money to herself. Perhaps Dr. Robinson could keep her healthy. She was furious with her heart for trying to thwart her.

At Dr. Robinson's office Irma got out slowly, helped by the chauffeur. She felt weak and drained. Emily, who had been silent all the way in, suddenly spoke. "Good luck, Irma dear. I am sure that Dr. Robinson will find out what is wrong and will help you." And as Irma walked to the door, Emily called after her, "See you day after tomorrow." Emily always sounded so cheerful. But this was not a moment to be cheerful. She was glad that Emily was going to the Ritz instead of returning with her to Bella Vista that night.

The waiting room was jammed, and the other patients looked at Irma as they sat listlessly in their chairs. They seemed united in wanting to show how long they had been there and how they resented a new arrival. Irma, however, hardly had time to sit down before a smart-looking young nurse with a neat white cap and her class pin on the breast pocket of her uniform marched up to her and inquired, "Mrs. Shrewsbury?" When Irma nodded, she said, "Come with me," and led the way down a corridor to a door which she threw open and announced, "Mrs. Shrewsbury, Dr. Robinson."

Dr. Robinson rose from behind a vast desk with a green-shaded light on it and came forward with his hand outstretched. "Please come sit here, Mrs. Shrewsbury," he said, pointing to a chair by his desk. As she seated herself she found they were face to face.

Dr. Robinson drew a large sheet of paper toward him and

took out his gold fountain pen. "Now, Mrs. Shrewsbury," he said, "I have to ask you some questions." He proceeded to interrogate her in a way that Dr. Graves, James's doctor, would never have dared to do. But Dr. Robinson had such an air of authority that she was completely carried away by his audacity. Dr. Robinson himself was aggressively healthy. His cheeks were round and rosy, his eyes clear and sparkling, his hands strong and beautifully manicured. As he wrote down Irma's answers, he smiled benignly from time to time, showing a row of sparkling white teeth. At length he touched a bell and rose from his high-backed leather chair. "Miss Knowital will take you to a dressing room for an E.K.G., and I will come to examine you after that."

Miss Knowital, the same nurse whom Irma had seen originally, herded Irma into a tiny dressing room and gave her a gown. "I will be back for you in a few minutes," she said. "In the meantime, take off everything, but you had better bring your purse with you."

Dr. Robinson and his assistants put up with no nonsense. Every test and X ray was done many times over with always a long wait in between during which Irma sat in her white shift in the tiny dressing room wondering if it was heart, lungs, or arteries that had disintegrated. She felt that her days must be numbered and wondered if she had time to make a will. She was also afraid that she would be late for lunch. At long last, as they led her back to the cubicle after a particularly tiring session, Miss Knowital said, "Now you may get dressed, Mrs. Shrewsbury, and the doctor will see you in his office." Irma put on her clothes with trembling fingers, the more so because now that at last she could make people dance to her tune as she had so often seen them dance to James's, the last thing she wanted was to die. And then she thought of Charlie, even now on his way to the Ritz.

The door to the doctor's office was open, and Dr. Robinson stood up and smiled as she came in. "Good news, Mrs. Shrewsbury!" he exclaimed. "Please sit down."

Irma sank into the chair and gazed at him with the sad look of a dumb animal. "Good news," she repeated, wondering if he was a sadist.

"Indeed, yes. Everything—lungs, arteries, and heart—we have gone over you with a fine-tooth comb and the only thing we can find is a very slight—an almost infinitesimal—heart murmur. It comes, I believe, from the stress after your husband's death, the sorrow and worry, coupled with the formalities you have had to go through and the business leadership which you have had to assume." (Mr. Ponderosa had given him a brief rundown.) "It has all been a tremendous burden to bear, more than a lady like yourself is accustomed to."

Irma could have told him differently, but instead she said, "So I have a clean slate and can continue as I am?"

Dr. Robinson held up one hand. "No, dear lady, not quite. There is nothing to fear, nothing that can't be cured, but you should set yourself a slower pace for a while. Rest, take things easy, and perhaps, best of all, go abroad—Baden-Baden or Evian or Montecatini and take a mild rest cure. That would be best of all." Dr. Robinson laid his glasses on the table and looked at her with his shining, healthy eyes. "If you just take a little care of yourself, Mrs. Shrewsbury, you can live to be one hundred. But you should take care." With his left hand, Dr. Robinson pressed a button and Miss Knowital appeared at once.

Dr. Robinson held out his hand, and Irma took it listlessly. "I am all right," she asked. "I mean, there is no immediate danger?"

Dr. Robinson smiled and patted her hand. "Certainly not,

or I would not mention going to Europe. You simply need to change your pace, and do feel free to call me anytime. I will also send you a prescription for a mild sedative and the name of a good friend of mine in Harley Street—a cardiologist—should you need a doctor abroad."

Irma shook his outstretched hand and walked out, not bothering to speak to Miss Knowital, who, looking brisk and fit, escorted her to the door.

Well, that was that. She was all right; but she was not all right. A little murmur of the heart he had said was nothing, but was that true? Should she have another opinion before she left for London? Was she likely to drop dead in a foreign street?

But when she got to the Ritz, and saw Charlie's smiling young face, she felt better, particularly as he rushed forward with outstretched hands and said, "I can tell by your face that you're O.K. You look better already." He took her hand and they walked into the Japanese Garden.

The Japanese Garden of the Ritz was unique. It consisted of two winding open corridors, sheltered from the sun and rain by overhanging roofs of Japanese tiles; a low balustrade separated these corridors from the planting and the stream that coursed between them from one end of the garden to the other. Dwarf Japanese red maple trees, a few dwarf pine trees, and azaleas were all very low so that those at the tables could see the stream with its bed of colored pebbles and the ducks, usually followed by fluffy yellow ducklings, who either sailed majestically down the stream or sunned themselves on the mossy banks.

The maître d'hôtel knew it was special, as did all the habitués. Where else in New York could one lunch or dine outside under the sky and yet be well protected by the sturdy walls of the Ritz from any intrusion of the gaping public?

Knowing all this, the maître d'hôtel was indifferent to the people advancing toward him.

"I want a table for two," said Irma.

"You have a reservation?" he asked coolly. He had never seen these people before and he had a memory that only "Royals" are supposed to have.

Charlie felt slightly embarrassed, but Irma drew herself up. "My secretary called," she said. "*I* am Mrs. Shrewsbury, widow of the banker."

The maître d'hôtel looked at the book on his high desk and saw the name. It was not one that he recognized in the financial world. He bowed before Morgans and Schiffs, Bakers and Whitneys. *They* came often to the Ritz, but Shrewsbury did not ring a bell, so he beckoned to a captain and said in a low voice to him, "Table eighty-four."

Irma and Charlie followed the captain quite cheerfully, not knowing that eighty-four was down at the very end of the garden—a place for those with money and no class. Socially, it was Outer Siberia.

As they were seated, the captain said, "The specialties today are sweetbreads *sous cloche* or quail *en gelée.*"

"Lamb chops for me," said Irma, "and that's all."

Charlie, however, threw caution to the wind and ordered both sweetbreads and quail to be followed by strawberries Romanoff. The captain who had shown them to their table, seeing they had lost all interest in him and that, therefore, no tip would be forthcoming, muttered something in French that was not very complimentary and moved away.

Charlie and Irma, however, were quite oblivious, seated not by the stream but on the little balcony against the wall. They never bothered to look at anything and began to talk at once.

Charlie was very protective and masculine. "You have had

a terrible morning," he said in a low confidential voice, leaning across the table to take her hand. "I want to make up
for it now. How did the doctor find you?"

Mrs. Shrewsbury withdrew her hand and wiped a tear
from her eyes with a handkerchief. "He says I am O.K.
except for a tiny murmur, but it has all been such a strain."

"Oh, try to forget it," said Charlie. "Let's have some fun."
He began to recount to her some of the amusing things that
had happened to him in his life. Perhaps unconsciously
emphasizing the stupidity of *young* women.

They ended up by Irma's tasting each dish of Charlie's
lunch and laughing as she did so. The very idea of lunching
with Charlie was so new to her that she soon forgot Joe, the
will, and even Dr. Robinson. Charlie, for his part, was carried
away too. His family always said that Charlie could talk to a
stone, and it was true. At times, he became almost intoxicated
with the virtuosity of his conversation and now with the
thought of B.P.&H. in the back of his mind, ideas of partnership and commissions danced through his head—bigger and
better than sugarplums, as he poured over Irma a Niagara
of compliments and innuendos!

EMILY, after settling in to one of the pretty, small suites
at the Ritz, had decided to splurge. She went to Herman
Patrick Tappé's at 9 West Fifty-seventh Street. Tappé had
made her clothes for years, and she had gone to him every
time she passed through New York City. After consulting
with Tappé himself and buying a few new outfits, she
left in a cheerful mood.

So while the merry lunch was taking place at the Japanese
Garden, Emily was walking down Fifth Avenue on her way
back to the Ritz for lunch. As she came to Fifty-third Street,
she was astonished to see Prince Carlo Pontevecchio coming

toward her, looking very elegant with a cornflower in his buttonhole, a bowler on his head, and a slender rolled umbrella in his hand. He tipped his hat and fell into step beside her. "I thought you were in Detroit," she said.

"I was, and just returned last night," he answered in his Oxford accent. "I tried to call you, but you were not at the Ritz."

"I am there now. I just came in," said Emily. "I have been staying in the country with my sister-in-law until this morning."

"What luck to run into you," he said, "and I think that we are meeting tonight at Reggie's. I found a note from him when I returned." He looked at her appraisingly. "You are looking more attractive than ever. That suit is most becoming to you." He took her arm.

Emily was pleased. "You say that you are dining with Reggie?"

"Yes, I accepted when I heard that you would be there, and I gather he has planned quite an evening."

Emily laughed. "Reggie is indefatigable. I can't keep up with him."

"You know," he said, as they walked along arm in arm, "we have met several times at people's houses—in Paris and London and Rome—but I never had a chance to talk to you. You were always the center of a crowd—you are what the British call 'a life-enhancer.' Then when I saw your name on the passenger list of the *Aquitania* I thought, Now at last I am going to be able to talk to her." He looked down at her. "And what happened?"

Emily laughed.

"We talked a lot but we were never very personal. You did not even flirt. But—enough," said Carlo, pressing her arm against him. "We are going to meet tonight again in a crowd, when we really should be alone. Are you lunching with someone?"

"No, I'm not." Emily was as pleased as he seemed to be.

"I want you to tell me that you would rather talk to me than anyone else. Especially that old lecher Chienloup who was chasing you all over the ship. Tell me you want to be alone with me, Emily."

"How alone?" queried Emily.

"I will not be greedy," he assured her. "It's simply that I feel we should know each other. I think it would be good. Don't you?"

"Yes," murmured Emily, who began to feel that she was quite out of practice at this game, if it was a game.

"Then come with me." He squeezed her arm again as they walked briskly down the avenue. "Let's go to the Ritz."

They, of course, went to the Japanese Garden and had a table near the entrance, close to the stream. For Emily it was a heaven-sent meeting. She had been feeling a bit low and now here was Carlo—charming, masculine, intelligent, and talking in that delicious Oxford-Italian accent as they sat surrounded by the enchanting garden. Again, they began by talking politics—Hoover and how long the booming stock market would continue, the rise of fascism in Italy, Mussolini, the German economy, the Fabian Society in England, and the future of America. Emily was optimistic about the future, but Carlo was not. He had been with American business-men for the last few days. He told her that seventy-five per cent of them were optimistic but the other twenty-five percent whom he respected the most for their intelligence predicted a market crash within a year. Too many people buying on margin, they had said. Not enough real money. Whole estates could be wiped out. As he talked about the bad times ahead, Emily was wondering what she should do with the Codway money. Sell everything and put it in gold? She had heard of some people doing that.

Carlo, noticing her quiet and slightly perturbed manner, changed the subject. "But let's forget all that—let's talk about ourselves," he said. "You know how attracted I am to you. I know that you are a widow, but what else? What is your life?" He put a tone of such real interest into this question, quite different from his usual tone.

So much so, that Emily, incurably romantic, was moved. She told him of her marriage to Ben and her life with him and, as usual, even though three years had passed, the tears came to her eyes as she spoke of Ben. "Life can never be quite the same for me," she said softly.

Carlo put his hand on hers and there was a tear in his eyes too. "I understand very well," he said. "That is what happened to me. I, too, lost my beloved wife a year and a half after we were married. She died in childbirth."

Emily squeezed his hand. "How very sad for you. But the child? The child is all right?"

"Yes. Thank God I have a little daughter."

"That must make you happy. I envy you. I have no children."

"It is a great help, but it is also a great care. I must be away so much and I worry about her happiness."

"I can well understand that," said Emily sympathetically. "It must be very hard for you."

"It is," he said. "Very hard. I sometimes wonder how much longer I can do it alone." He emphasized "alone" lightly.

Emily looked at him, again in sympathy, but as he looked back at her, there passed between them a vibration. They said nothing and looked at each other. Carlo took her hand and held it.

"*Cara*," he said.

Emily smiled happily. Then she looked down at her watch, horrified to find that it was half past three, the waiters were clearing the tables, and the place was half empty. "I must go to the hairdresser," she said. "Dear Mr. Charles is waiting for me in his salon upstairs." As she stood up, she saw Irma going out the door with Charlie Hopeland. "Good heavens, look," she said to Carlo. "Do you see that couple?"

Carlo looked; it was the old lady he had seen on the dock. "Yes. Who is she?"

"My sister-in-law," said Emily, "and I find it extraordinary to see her here, particularly with that young man."

Carlo found it extraordinary that she was a relative, but he politely said, "Is that her grandson?"

"No. A young lawyer she's just met. She happens to be a very rich old lady, and I don't trust that young man, although I can hardly imagine her being taken in by him. She is extremely shrewd and suspicious."

Carlo laughed. "I would watch out if I were you. These old ladies are sometimes very lonely and susceptible."

Since Emily did not want to catch up with Irma, they walked out slowly. Carlo was staying at the Ambassador and unfortunately could not take Emily to Reggie's as he had a business cocktail party to attend. "Do not let us forget today," he said as they parted. "It has been a very special one for me."

"And for me too," said Emily. "I'll see you later."

Emily, as she was wafted up to the hairdresser's in the deliciously scented lift, wondered if she could fall in love. Beneath all that talk at lunch had been an undercurrent that she had been missing for some time. Carlo had been putting on a show for her—and she for him. But was he really in love with her? He seemed so serious. She had held on to herself because it might be just a game. By the time she stepped off the elevator, she decided not to have a love affair but a flirtation. He had just said that she had not flirted on the *Aquitania*. She thought that she had. She must be out of practice.

She was glad that she was dining with Molly and Reggie tonight. She might even stay over until Thursday afternoon. No need to hurry back to dreary Bella Vista.

After the hairdresser, Emily returned to her room and threw herself on the bed, fully dressed, and thought of Ben. Thank God she had appreciated what she had had. She had loved every minute of that wonderful life and she also knew that there still must be other happy times in store for someone as naturally optimistic and wonderfully healthy as herself; no need to play duenna forever to Molly or other younger women.

At that moment, the telephone rang. It was Wendell Ponderosa to tell her Jack Robinson had spoken to him. "He had taken every test and finds only a slight murmur. It is simple stress. I think that he suggested a trip abroad— perhaps a light cure at Baden-Baden, if you would take her there."

Emily groaned. She felt dreadfully sorry for Irma, and she was certainly not going to desert her if she really needed help. On the other hand, was she going to be linked to Irma for the rest of their lives? The idea was not appealing.

"She has no one but you," said Mr. Ponderosa persuasively. "I could send Hopeland over with her, just for a week or so, which would help you. I'll suggest it to Robinson, then I can meet her later. In any event, I'm going to Paris soon. I'll be at the Hotel Palais d'Orsay in Paris if you want me."

Emily laughed. "You will certainly get a call from me. I don't know where I will be, and I don't at the moment know if I could stand Baden-Baden alone with Irma. She is really not my responsibility. However, if I should find some other place where there would be other people I will let you know, but I'm very reluctant about Irma. Wendell, I wanted to speak to you about something else. Do you trust Charlie Hopeland? I thought him a bit pushy. I saw them at lunch today looking very cozy."

It was Wendell's turn to laugh. "I'm not surprised. Charlie can be very amusing. But don't worry. He'll never overstep where the firm is concerned. He's ambitious, but he's also sensible."

He sounded so confident that her fears were allayed. So, after lying down for another half hour, she began to think again of Carlo. He obviously wanted to start a flirtation. The thought of it tired her, so she closed her eyes and was soon asleep. When she awoke, she telephoned for Elsa and began to dress. She looked at her shoulders and her bosom as she took her dress off. She was not ashamed of her figure. It was still fresh and unwrinkled. I should not waste these last good years, she thought. Carlo is right. Life is short. Why be alone? Someone else ought to know what I look like undressed. She decided to wear her most alluring dress for the dinner at Reggie's—a clinging, pale green beaded dress from Worth, which showed off her figure seductively but discreetly. "Bosoms should be seen by appointment only," Ben had always said. She put some perfume behind her ears and a long string of pearls that disappeared into her décolleté.

CHAPTER SIX

# REGGIE GIVES A
# DINNER PARTY AND
# FRANZ AND OLGA
# APPEAR

REGGIE LIVED IN HIS FAMILY'S VAST BROWNSTONE HOUSE ON the corner of Fifth Avenue and Fifty-second Street. He had his own suite of rooms there, but his mother was taking the cure at Saratoga Springs and his father was off on his yacht, so he had the house to himself.

As Emily was led through the square front hall by a footman in handsome livery, she remembered thinking when she had been there years ago with Ben that it was not exactly a place where one could have a good time. The huge malachite vase in the middle of the hall (Reggie had told her once that it had come from the Demidorf Palace in Leningrad) was funereal, but when she was ushered into the library, all had changed. The red brocade curtains, the huge cane chaise longue by the fireplace piled with red velvet cushions, the great deep sofas, the immense silver vases standing on the floor filled with American beauty roses, and the silk-shaded lamps, created a warm glow. It was supposed to be French, but it was really American in spite of Lord Duveen's European efforts. The tables were crowded with huge, silver-framed photographs signed boldly with names that went from Royals through Serenes and right down to Dukes and Marquises— some still alive, others long dead. Emily remembered Reggie's mother, Mrs. Brevoort Beekman, sighing and saying, "Dear Dom Pedro. He meant so well." Mrs. Beekman loved them all—British, European, and middle European—but Reggie was an anglophile. For him there was no royalty but the British, and no real sport except in the British Isles. Salmon and grouse in Scotland, hunting with the Pitchley or the Quorn, racing at Ascot and polo at Smith's Lawn, although he didn't really mind polo at Meadowbrook out on Long Island with the Bostwicks and Tommy Hitchcock. He still much pre-ferred Smith's Lawn and the noble Lords. His suits were made at Anderson-Sheppard, his shoes at Peel and shirts were from Turnbull and Asher. He knew the nicknames of all the English dukes. In London he belonged to as many clubs as possible from White's and Brooks to Boodles, the Turf, and the Beef-steak, and as the one European gesture, he belonged to the Travellers Club in Paris. In spite of all this, "deep down where it counts," as a friend of his once said, Reggie was nonetheless American.

It was hard to imagine why, except for his affection for his timid and withdrawn father, who spent three quarters of his time on his yacht and who cared nothing for all this worship of alien customs. He was in his wife's shadow at home, but on the *Dragon*, dressed in club regalia, he was totally relaxed and walked as a man, not as a neglected and rejected husband. Once, when Reggie was quite young, he had taken him to a dinner of twelve at a charming house on Riverside Drive. A beautiful young lady dripping with jewels was the hostess and the other guests were yacht club members—each accompanied with a dazzling, pretty, and very, very refined young lady.

The food was delicious and served by footmen, one to every other chair. Reggie thought it attractive, but a little dull—too much like home, only even more stuffy. However, what stuck in his mind was what his father had said in the car on the way home. He was just lighting a cigar (no cigar smoking was allowed in that house) and Reggie thought for the first time that his father looked happy. "My boy," said his father, "remember this evening. Such a house as you have just seen may be a thing of the past. If they continue the income tax and the gift tax, the whole thing will be smoked out." Reggie thought this cryptic at the time, but later realized what his father meant. These very refined young ladies were the mistresses of the yachtsmen. It had, at first, horrified Reggie, but as time went on he was proud of his father. It showed that he was not just a henpecked husband but a person with spunk and dignity. This episode they never mentioned again, but it had served its purpose. Reggie felt that a duke could have behaved no better.

When Emily came into the library, Reggie, who was standing in front of the fireplace, came over at once to give her a kiss. "So happy to have you here, dear Emily," he said, giving her hand a special squeeze, which she felt meant that the last time she had been there it had been with Ben.

Molly, who was lying on the chaise lounge, a champagne glass in her hand, said, "Darling Emily, do have some champagne quickly and drink to my success. I'm going to be the Virgin Mary. Isn't it the tops?"

"Molly won over six contenders," volunteered Reggie. "She is terrific. Molly, show Emily what you did."

As Emily took her champagne from the footman's tray, Molly got up, stood against the rose-red curtain, wrapped a scarf over her head, cast down her eyes, and raised her hands in prayer. She looked exquisitely beautiful, but, thought Emily, very dumb. "Do you have to say anything?" asked Emily, sipping her champagne and trying to look impressed.

Molly shook her head. "Nothing," she said. "Not a word, and I get paid three guineas a week for six weeks and my fare over and back. Isn't that marvelous! I am sure George will be furious, but after all, I am starting a career. I might end up in Hollywood with my own swimming pool and my own hairdresser."

"It's a jolly good start," said Reggie. "And I think Franz Kramer must have fallen for Molly because he is coming to dinner tonight."

"I wouldn't be so sure. He's bringing a girlfriend," said Molly, making a face. "We never saw her in London or Paris."

"Oh," interposed Reggie, "I forgot to tell you, Emily, that Carlo Pontevecchio is coming too. Kramer wanted to take us to Jack and Charlie's, but I thought it would be more relaxing to dine here. We might go on to the Savoy or the Cotton Club or El Morocco."

"Perhaps all three," said Molly. "After all this *is* my first trip to New York and you told me about those marvelous— what did you call them—flapjacks at Child's for an early breakfast. I am all set for making a night of it."

Emily was about to say, Count me out of some of that, when Franz Kramer and a Miss "Somebody" (the footman garbled her name) were announced and walked in.

Franz Kramer was a small, dark-haired man on the plump side with a completely round face pierced with darting eyes.

Molly jumped up and, as he kissed her hand, she said, "Franz, you have changed my life. I am so keen to start at once."

"Not until autumn," he answered. "But we might start rehearsing in Austria in August."

Molly clapped her hands. "How divine. I can miss the grouse season."

During this exchange, Reggie had spoken to the lady with Kramer and introduced her first to Emily, then to Molly, mumbling her name, which he knew no better than the footman. She was about thirty, slim, with dark hair parted in the middle and rolled into a bun in back. Her eyes were heavily darkened with kohl, and her expression seemed to say that she was there against her will. Listlessly, she shook hands and drifted over to look at the photograph-laden tables. Obviously, she resented Molly, who was looking especially beautiful in a white and pink beaded dress with a headband to match, and was in a mood to spoil the evening. Carlo Pontevecchio arrived just then, and so did the caviar.

Reggie, although he sized Miss X up as being one of those disagreeable anti-American Europeans, nevertheless played the part of a good host. He brought her a glass of champagne himself and, as she only seemed interested in the photographs, led her from table to table explaining who they were. "My mother is very gregarious," he explained, trying to play down such a deluge of Royals. "She has friends everywhere."

"Ah, so," said the young lady, picking up a photo and looking at it carefully. "These are all the daughters of the Tsar, these girls in the sailor suits."

"Yes. My mother went to Russia once years ago on my father's yacht."

"Poor things," said Miss X, putting the photo back. "They got so little help from you people. I am Russian. I cannot bear to look at such a picture. It makes me too sad."

Goodness, thought Reggie, what an evening we are in for. He ordered some more champagne for the others and a double martini for himself. Franz was chatting away with Molly, who by now had assumed her original theatrical pose while attempting to use her gold swizzle stick to take the bubbles out of the champagne. Carlo and Emily had seated themselves on a huge red pouffe near the fireplace. Thus, it was up to Reggie to amuse Miss X. "It must be pretty tough on you," he said, "thinking back on all those good old days." He knew that he was not much of a conversationalist except with his own pals, but he did his best.

Miss X opened a great silver box on the table and took out a cigarette. She put it between her lips and waited for Reggie to light it, then inhaled the smoke deeply. "Holy Russia," she said. "To leave it is like leaving one's mother. One is lost. What point is there to life? Death is better."

Reggie was alarmed. "Shall we join the others?" he suggested.

She smiled. "Why not? Franz is a fool, but he can make me laugh sometimes. I can see that you recognize him as a fool, but also that you do not like me."

"Oh, come now," said Reggie. "That's not fair. We have only just met and I am delighted that you are here tonight."

She smiled again. "We will join the others, but what is the use? After seeing that photograph of those martyred girls I am sick. Yes"—she rolled her kohl-rimmed eyes at Reggie—"yes, sick. Holy Russia is dead."

Franz Kramer happened to look toward them at that moment and called to her, saying something very rapidly and loudly in Russian. She answered him with a word or two, then took Reggie's arm. "We go dancing after dinner?" she queried. "A tango I like very much. We dance that, yes?"

Reggie felt like saying no, but his good manners, which were his greatest protection, simply made him smile and say, "Perhaps, yes."

As dinner was announced, who should walk in but Mr.

Ponderosa, dressed in a business suit. He looked startled for a moment but quickly recovered his aplomb as Reggie, exchanging a look with the butler, who had come to announce dinner, put on an extra plate, rushed up to greet him.

"I am afraid that I have come on the wrong night," said Mr. Ponderosa, looking at the assembled group. "I will simply stay for a moment, then go to the club."

"You certainly won't do that," said Reggie emphatically. "Of course I expected you." He seemed so sure and at the same time so concerned that Mr. Ponderosa saw at once Reggie had forgotten that they had planned to have a drink and go over some legal papers together and then go to the Knickerbocker Club for dinner. The club did not allow any business documents to be brought to the table, which is why they were to have met first at home—also the very correct Knickerbocker Club was "dry."

"Bring Mr. Ponderosa a drink," said Reggie to a footman —the butler having scurried off to order a place at the table. "What will you have, Mr. Ponderosa?"

"A dry martini," said Mr. Ponderosa over his shoulder as he held out his hand to Emily, who had come over to him. "How nice to see you here."

"I didn't know you knew each other." Reggie was surprised and pleased. He could seat Mr. Ponderosa next to Emily at the table. "Now I want you to meet my other guests." And he took Mr. Ponderosa over to the Russian, whom he introduced as "Miss er-er."

Mr. Ponderosa bowed and Miss er-er said, "The name is Nitzkoff—Olga Nitzkoff."

"Kinsky?" queried Mr. Ponderosa, who was getting a little deaf and who had once had a client, a Prince Kinsky.

Olga flashed her eyes and shrugged her shoulders. "A distant cousin," she murmured as she moved closer to Reggie. She was about to put her arm through his when Franz

Kramer came up and gave her a look that stopped her. "How do you do?" he said. "My name is Kramer and I am a producer in the theater."

"Ah," said Mr. Ponderosa. "You have a play coming here?" Looking him over, he wondered if Reggie was a sponsor. If so, he felt inclined to tell him to go easy.

"Not yet, but we are looking at theaters and trying to decide which one will be suitable. We need a very large theater, as it is a very large play which I have adapted."

"If you need any help with contracts, Mr. Ponderosa can help you. He is the best lawyer in town." Reggie smiled delightedly at being able to bring Franz Kramer and Mr. Ponderosa together.

"So—" Franz nodded "—thank you very much. At present I do not need such help." And he turned to Molly who came up with Carlo.

"I thought that dinner was announced, wasn't it? I am longing to get started on our evening." Molly did a Charleston step.

"Yes. Just now." Reggie made a gesture toward the door. "But first I want you to meet Mr. Ponderosa—Lady Chatwood—and right behind her, Prince Pontevecchio."

Mr. Ponderosa, after shaking hands with Molly, smiled broadly at the prince. "I have had the pleasure of meeting your father when he was here several years ago." Carlo smiled as they shook hands. They understood each other at once. These amenities over, dinner was announced again, and they crossed the vast hall to the family dining room, which was smaller and more simply furnished than the "state" dining room. It was a French room paneled in gray with overmantels attributed to Boucher—cupids playing gaily with knowing looks on their faces. The table could stretch to hold eighteen or twenty, though it was tonight reduced to seven, and therefore seemed like a toy in the room. The service plates were silver gilt, as were the knives and forks, and the white orchids in the middle of the table filled a silver gilt swan.

The conversation was at first general, which was Emily's idea because Reggie touched her with his foot under the table when they sat down and murmured something about a "crashing bore." She did the best she could, but Franz wanted to talk to Molly, thereby leaving Carlo alone, and so she ended up talking to Carlo, thus leaving Reggie to Olga and his wine.

They resumed their general conversation of the morning—politics, travel, books, people; but there was a difference. They were friends now and perhaps something more. They both knew it and enjoyed it. Emily was not sure of her next step, but it was a game that during the last few years without Ben she had learned to play well. Carlo was not a newcomer to the sport either; so they talked and talked and what they said meant very little. It was their eyes that spoke.

Reggie broke the spell by kicking Emily under the table again. "Turn and talk to me," he whispered. She turned reluctantly as Carlo obediently turned to Mr. Ponderosa. "You have been talking to Carlo for two courses. You must talk to me whether you like it or not."

"What about Mr. Kramer's friend?" asked Emily in a low voice.

"Frightful," whispered Reggie. "She hates America, thinks we are all barbarians, no better than the Bolsheviks. She's a fearful snob, too, talking about prince this and duke that. I have a feeling that she didn't know any of them."

"Hush," said Emily. "She and Mr. Kramer have stopped talking and are looking at us. We are all going to the Ziegfeld Roof after dinner, aren't we, Reggie," she said in a loud voice, "or is it some other place?"

"I don't know," answered Reggie. "I thought that the Ritz Roof might be nice. No drinking there, but we can drop in at the place on West Fifty-second Street first for some coffee and a drink, then the Ritz. Then the Cotton Club or the Savoy. I'll keep the car, and we can have some wine in the cooler."

Molly heard him and clapped her hands. "That's a good start," she exclaimed. "It is just what I imagined New York to be, but I want to see Harlem most of all."

"This not having drinks in public is quite absurd," Franz Kramer said. "The whole nation is being treated like naughty children and I understand that the control of liquor is being run by gangsters."

"You are absolutely right," agreed Mr. Ponderosa. "No one believes in this law. No one respects it and so we have become a nation of lawbreakers."

"It's hard to foretell where this total lawlessness will lead you. You will become hardened to crime," predicted Franz with a sardonic look on his face.

"I would not want to live in such a place in twenty years," interposed Olga and she shuddered.

"With a change of president, we may have repeal of the law," said Mr. Ponderosa, who by this time was counting the moments until he could leave and go home to read *The Decline of the West* which he had almost finished.

Emily imagined that Olga would say "too late," but she kept quiet and Carlo interposed that what he, like Molly, really wanted to do was to hear some authentic Negro jazz. He had been told that it was extraordinary and that to go to the Cotton Club or the Savoy in Harlem was an experience never to be forgotten. It seemed a good idea to Reggie and Emily, who thought it would really change the tempo of the evening. So after dinner when Mr. Ponderosa left they went first to the speakeasy on Fifty-second Street for coffee and drinks (at Molly's insistence).

Usually, one had to have a meal, but Reggie was well known there, so they accepted him gladly after he had rung the bell and they had approved him through the peephole. Emily had never been in a speakeasy and was surprised to find it a perfectly correct, ordinary restaurant inside and absolutely jammed with people drinking every imaginable drink from sherry, vodka, and gin to old brandy. The crowd was varied and full of people whose faces she recognized— Marlene Dietrich, Kay Francis, Heywood Broun, Brooks Atkinson, a few publishers (Reggie pointed them out to Molly); and the rest were lawyers, bankers, and rich suburbanites out for a night on the town.

Soon after that they left and went to the Ritz Roof, but found it dull, so they departed quickly and went up to the Cotton Club in Harlem to hear Duke Ellington. It was jammed with both black and white people, the men dressed in sedate business suits or dinner jackets and several in white tie and tails. The trumpets and saxophones were doing improvised solos. The piano players were jumping on their piano stools; and the dancers were swaying and stomping, alive and vibrating, infectious. No drink was really needed here. The music called, sweet and hot, and the bodies on the dance floor responded. Molly took to it eagerly, dragging Reggie with her, and so did Carlo and Emily; but Franz and his girlfriend found it difficult to start. The chemistry between them seemed to have evaporated. This was not Franz's idea of what the evening should be; so, breaking in on Molly and Reggie, he said, "I understand that in America, one does something called a 'cut-in.' That means a change of partners, yes? We change, all right? I have Molly. You take Olga."

Molly, only too glad to be with her future boss, blew Reggie a kiss, then threw herself at Franz, doing a mad step of her own as he seized her around the waist. Reggie found Olga in his arms, surprisingly supple and sinuous, just as the mood of the orchestra changed. It was melancholy. It was a wail of despair and frustration. The dancers were locked in each other's arms, slowly swaying as the lights turned low. The music seemed hardly to breathe and the dancers barely moved. Reggie and Olga stood in one spot, holding each other close, swaying back and forth. Reggie was a good dancer, full of rhythm and by now full of drink; so he held Olga tightly and swayed, as the saxophones and clarinets sobbed. As he did so, he felt her coming to life in his arms. She pressed against him, her legs tight against his, her eyes shut. She was as smooth and soft in his arms as wax. As their faces were almost touching, he ventured a light kiss on her cheek. She did not open her eyes, only pressed a little closer. Reggie gave her a more spirited nuzzling kiss, upon which she opened her eyes and shook her head. "Too fast," she murmured. "First time. No good."

Emily, who was swaying not far away with Carlos, had seen the whole scene and was irritated. Reggie is a sitting duck, she thought, for that Russian. He'll think she's exotic. Emily suspected that the whole thing was a put-up job. Franz Kramer had probably brought her over from Austria for just such a purpose because he thought that he would get a fat commission if he could marry her off to Reggie. Or, if Reggie's mother made too much of a row, perhaps it might be arranged that Reggie could set her up in an apartment.

Emily was truly fond of Reggie; his naïveté was part of his charm, but she saw trouble ahead with this pretentious Russian. She glanced over to see where Molly was and found her clasped tightly in the arms of Franz Kramer, but she was looking at Reggie with an expression of such despair on her young face that Emily felt if Franz had not been holding her so tight, she would have fallen to the ground. Her marriage to George Chatwood had been called the "love match of the year," but the glamour of it soon wore off for Molly. She quickly lost interest in country life, shooting parties, and hunt balls. She also did not want a child. George finally seemed not to care what she did or where she went as long as she was there once in a while for one of his shooting or fishing parties. On the surface they appeared the ideal couple, but they began to live separate lives and were both unhappy.

On their safari in Kenya, Molly had told all this to Emily. "Reggie means my whole life to me," she had said. "I am mad about him." Emily was enraged to see Molly's sad little face looking at Reggie with the Russian in his arms.

Carlo, noticing that Emily had grown rigid and was not even in step with him, looked down at her and said, "What is the matter? Are you tired?"

She shook her head, then changed her mind. "Yes, I am tired. It really is getting late. Let's dance over to Reggie and suggest going home."

When they reached Reggie he was nibbling gently on Olga's neck, and Carlo, who saw what had annoyed Emily, immediately came to the conclusion that she was jealous. He slackened his hold on her and said stiffly, "Perhaps *you* had better explain to Reggie that you want to leave."

Emily gave Reggie's arm a shake. "Reggie, let's go home. It is very late and I have a lot to do tomorrow."

Reggie shook his head. He had had enough to drink to make him obstinate and lose his usual good manners. He did not want to be pried from the entrancing Olga. "Take the car and send it back," he said over his shoulder. "I'm not going yet."

"Shall I ask Molly?" queried Emily.

"Do anything you like." Reggie was annoyed. "Just take the car, go home, and tell Whitelaw to come back and wait for me here." And he returned to Olga, who had never released her hold on him during this exchange but who now, seeing Emily's face, threw back her head, closed her eyes, and said, "It has been many years since I have been so happy." Whereupon Reggie guided her quickly into the thick of the crowd.

Molly, when Emily approached her, said she could not leave without Reggie. "This music is so hypnotizing," she said bravely, "I couldn't possibly leave it now. Could you, Franz?"

"Never," he said emphatically. "I never knew I could dance like this. That is, if you call it dancing." And he laughed.

Emily turned to Carlo. "You could stay. I have Reggie's car. I don't mind a bit going by myself."

It was Carlo's turn to laugh. "Who will I dance with? No, I will come with you."

The cars were clogging the street outside but Whitelaw, Reggie's night chauffeur (he had another one for the daytime), was used to Reggie's ways so he was close to the door and seemed delighted to take them home and return.

"The Ritz," said Emily to Whitelaw.

Carlo helped her into the car, and when they were settled in and the glass between them and the chauffeur was firmly shut, Carlo turned to her and said, "So you are in love with Reggie."

Emily was surprised and annoyed. "That's absurd. Whatever made you think that?"

"The way you behaved when you saw him dancing with Mademoiselle Nitzkoff."

Emily laughed. "You are totally wrong. I want him for my friend Molly. She needs a good, solid, decent man who will be kind and affectionate and nice to her."

"You consider Reggie such a man? To me, he seems a pleasant fool."

Emily took offense at this remark. "You have only just met him on *Aquitania*. How can judge him? If you don't like him, I, in my turn, don't like that Miss Nitzkoff nor Mr. Kramer. I think that they are a pair of adventurers. Anyway, they have spoiled the evening."

Carlo looked at her skeptically. No Italian woman would have been so concerned about another woman's affair. Emily was far too attractive to be without a lover. He looked at her smoking in a very nervous way, putting the cigarette quickly in and out of her mouth.

"I am leaving for Chicago day after tomorrow," he said, "after that a day or two in London, and home."

"And I am going back to Rye," responded Emily.

By this time they had arrived at the Ritz and Whitelaw was opening the door of the car. Carlo jumped out and walked into the Ritz with her. She was so pretty and appealing as he looked down at her to say good-bye that he was sad to see her go up to her suite alone. She deserved something better than that ass Reggie. "Shall I come up with you?" he asked.

She smiled, rather wanly, he thought. "Thank you, but my maid is there. I am quite all right."

He kissed her hand in a perfunctory way and said, "Good night."

The elevator door was open and the attendant was standing there. "Good night," Emily answered as the elevator door shut. It was only when she was in her room that she realized that he had never mentioned lunch the next day. It upset her and that night she slept poorly.

Carlo walked slowly up Park Avenue to the Ambassador. Was he wrong about Reggie? He could not forget how determined she had been to leave the Cotton Club, with or without Reggie. It was a pity because he had not in years met a woman who attracted him so much. He took the bottle of champagne his valet had bought from the hall porter, which was in a silver bucket in his sitting room, and poured himself a glass. *E sempre cosi*, he thought. I am an unlucky man.

### CHAPTER SEVEN

# EMILY DECIDES SHE NEEDS A CHANGE

THE NEXT MORNING, WHEN THE WAITER BROUGHT IN EMILY'S breakfast table, there was a small bouquet and a note lying on top of the *Tribune.* She gave the waiter the flowers to put in water, then opened the note. "Dear Mrs. Codway," it read. "I am so sorry but unfortunately I find that I must leave today for Chicago instead of tomorrow. I am very disappointed not to be able to lunch with you but hope that we may meet again at some future time—perhaps in Rome, if you come there. Sincerely, Carlo Pontevecchio. P.S. I shall not forget our lunch in the Japanese Garden."

There it was, just like that—cool and polite and yet a definite rejection. Italians, she thought, are always running after young women. Someone my age bores him, and surely he's using Reggie as an excuse. The P.S. might mean something, but she was no schoolgirl to take comfort from a straw. She felt very sorry for herself until she remembered that Ben had said self-pity was the most ignoble emotion. Ben would certainly not have been proud of her foolishness. She sighed. I am behaving like a sixteen-year-old, she

thought. It is a tempest in a child's teacup and most unworthy
of a woman of character. What on earth did Carlo mean
to me anyway? She remembered an older friend's advice:
Sleep with no woman and damn few men. It is better to be
done with the whole thing than to have become involved,
and I must remember that I have already had more out of
life than most people.

Still thinking of Carlo, she poured a second cup of tea and
started to read the paper. Suddenly, it occurred to her that
she was free for lunch. She thought of Joe Shrewsbury
and looked him up in the phone book. He answered himself,
and she asked him if he could lunch with her. He accepted,
and when she suggested the Ritz he suggested the Algonquin,
which he thought she'd like more. So they agreed to meet
there at 12:30. She was about to take a bath when Molly
called, depressed. Apparently Reggie and Olga had danced
until 4:30 A.M. For what seemed a very long time, Molly
could not find them on the floor at all.

When she had said to Franz, "It's very late. I am wondering where Reggie is," he had told her they must be somewhere and then said that he saw them coming in the door.
Molly thought they must have gone to the car for a drink. In
any event, it was a disaster. After they had left Franz and
Olga at the Hotel Royalton, Reggie was so drunk that the
chauffeur and the night watchman had had to put him to
bed. Molly was in tears. "I have never seen Reggie like that
before and it upset me. It must be the dreadful stuff they
drink here," she said. "He was never like this in England or
on the Continent."

Emily agreed with her that it was a frightful thing for
Reggie to do and asked, What did Franz and Olga do? Molly
said that Franz was helpful, but that Olga just sat in the
car and never spoke. "Reggie was falling all over her in the

most disgusting way," said Molly, "but she did not seem to mind a bit, and neither did Franz." They had dropped Olga and Franz off first and by that time Reggie was either asleep or passed out, Molly couldn't tell. The chauffeur took it very calmly, hoisted him up the stairs and into the elevator, while a footman took Molly's coat and showed her to her room.

"Reggie is still asleep," Molly said, "and Carlo can't come tonight, but we already have another couple and Reggie, when he wakes up, can find another man." Anyway, Molly said that she would absolutely die if Emily did not come, so Emily said yes, and then they decided that Emily would come to Reggie's around teatime to see how things were.

When Emily hung up she felt that there were worse things than being lonely. She felt less depressed that Carlo had evaporated. Life was easier alone, and then she thought again of poor Molly, so happy to be playing the Madonna and now torn to pieces by a miserable evening. Emily smiled to herself in the mirror as she put on her lipstick. She began to think that the less involved she was in life, the happier.

The Algonquin was just beginning to fill up when Emily arrived. She could recognize Anita Loos and Bob Sherwood, who were already at the Round Table, and the usual would-be writers were congregating in the lobby to gape at their more successful fellows. George Jean Nathan and Ernest Boyd passed so close to Emily that she could hear Boyd utter the name Firbank and she was envious. She longed to know such people, share their brilliance, know what they took to be important. She wondered if she could hold her own with Bob Sherwood and George Jean Nathan and Woollcott and Mencken, but she would probably never meet them. Down with love, and up with the intellect was her mood. Just then she heard, "Hello, Aunt Emily," and turned to see Joe standing before her. He was dressed, she thought, like a gangster and had gone so far as to affect black leather gloves and a hat pulled down so that she could hardly see his face. Emily put her face up to be kissed, and he bent down to kiss her with his hat still on. He had tied a red silk scarf around his throat.

"I am so glad that you were free for lunch," she said. "I wanted to talk to you alone."

"We have a lot to catch up on," Joe said as they were seated at their table.

"Let's start with you," said Emily. "Tell me what you are doing with your life and what you want to do. But first please take your hat off." As she said this, she looked at him critically. He was dressed outlandishly, but he had an attractive face. His brown eyes were full of life and intelligence, his reddish hair was curly (like mine, thought Emily), his skin clear. When he smiled, his face lit up. His manner of speaking was a bit intense, but she felt that came from naïveté and nerves.

He put his hat and coat on an empty chair at the table before answering her question, then lit a cigarette and blew a circle into the air. "Do you really want to know? It's not very interesting."

"Of course I want to know," Emily said. "I want to know what is wrong that you seem to be on such bad terms with your parents. Your father was always so kind to me. I would have thought that he would have been proud of you. So what is the trouble?"

Emily was not surprised by his answer. "My mother. She was jealous. She wanted my father for herself. She kept me away from him so that I never really knew him. In the end he was as irritated by me as she was. I never knew what it was to be welcomed at home. I was always off at boarding school or camp and when I was at home, I was left to the servants. The chauffeur was supposed to be in charge of me, but he was drunk most of the time. So in return, as a sort of unconscious reaction, I suppose, I tried to be everything they so disliked."

"That's sad. I am sorry to hear it. But tell me, what do you like to do? What are you doing now? What are you planning in the future? What is your aim in life?"

"You know my father left me nothing."

Emily nodded. "Yes, of course. I was at Bella Vista when you came there. All you have is a house." She felt like adding, "And that generous one hundred fifty dollars," but refrained.

"That's right." Joe lit another cigarette, having scarcely finished the first. "The playboy, the boy who wanted to be a writer and has not had much success, has to put his nose to the grindstone if he wants to live in that house. You ask me what my aim in life is—I don't know how to answer you. Just now, I am not sure I will always want to write, but I do know that I can't do without eating—" he paused "—at least one meal a day. I'm not bad at playing jazz on the piano. I thought that I might try to get into a café or a nightclub. I'd really like to play up in Harlem, if possible. That's where the top men are, but I am not sure that I'm good enough. If I can't do that, I can play in a speakeasy. There are endless possibilities." He laughed mirthlessly. "I don't intend ever to ask my mother for money again. I've thought of bootlegging. There's lots of money to be made there and it is becoming quite acceptable."

Emily shook her head. "Not that. Have you got any special friend?" She was appalled by the dreariness of Joe's situation.

Joe's face lit up and he smiled broadly. "Annabelle," he said. "You'll like her. She's nifty."

"What does she want?" asked Emily, hoping for some good news.

"Nothing," rejoined Joe. "Nothing. Just me."

"That's marvelous." Emily spoke loudly for lack of enthusiasm. "Are you going to marry her?"

Joe looked shocked. "Annabelle doesn't want to tie herself down, even though she says I am her life. She's a cigarette girl now, but she wants a career. She paints and she plays the clarinet and she can act. She says she's too young for marriage."

"How old is she?" Emily was feeling slightly antagonistic toward Annabelle. Joe certainly did not appear very happy. She had taken Molly's side against George Chatwood but now she was all for Joe.

"Twenty-two." Joe sighed. "She is a great girl. You would love her. She has such spirit and works so hard. She can't decide whether to be a painter or a musician or an actress."

Emily repressed a sniff. "I think that she should make up her mind. She seems a bit all over the place—you, the painting, the clarinet. She should help you get a job or you could be a team."

Joe shook his head. "No, she wouldn't like that. I forgot to say that she has a good voice too. You ought to hear her sing 'Love, Oh Love, Oh Careless Love,' and 'I Wish I Had Someone to Love Me.' She is absolutely terrific." Emily felt that she could do without *that*. So having finished her frugal lunch, she thought she would make the move to leave. "Joe," she said, folding her napkin and opening her purse. "Here in this envelope is a one-thousand-dollar check. It won't keep you going forever but it may help you avoid making a decision so quickly that you'll regret it. It comes to you with my love. You are, after all, my only blood relation. Even though I would like you to call me Emily, I am indeed your aunt. I wish you well and admire your grit. But stick to some one thing. Try to decide exactly what you want, and go after it even if it takes time and hard work."

Joe looked embarrassed. "It's very dear of you. I don't know how to thank you. I will remember what you say and try to live up to it. I know that I sound rather hopeless, but seriously, I do intend to make a good living, one way or another, and I certainly intend to be able to pay you back! In fact, to be truthful, I want to make money more than anything. I don't know how just at the moment, but I am sure I can."

Emily kissed him on the cheek. "Bless you, and don't forget, you can always call on me."

Joe took her arm and put her into a taxi. "I can never thank you enough, Emily," he said as he closed the door.

Emily smiled and sat back in the cab. "You don't need to," she said. She turned and looked out of the rear window of the cab as she drove off. What a pathetic figure he was, dressing like that. The poor wretched young man. She felt truly sorry for him. In a way she felt that James's having cut him out of his will was probably good for him. He was faced with a real challenge and perhaps he could meet it. Maybe he really would turn out to be "somebody." She wondered about his Shrewsbury blood and remembered Ben speaking of "good blood" and "bad blood" in a family line, as opposed to the Codways who were "well bred." What was it the Shrewsburys had? Shrewdness! Surely Joe must have inherited some of his parents' shrewdness. Who knows, if not for Ben, she might have been singing in a nightclub herself like Annabelle. She had often been told that she had a "heart of gold." Well, if she did, it was about to sink her and she had better be careful. After all, she had not come to America to find herself saddled with two people whom she had not seen for years and who meant less to her than so many of her friends.

These dreary thoughts filled her mind until she reached the door of Elizabeth Arden. For the next two hours during her facial and body massage, she lost herself in the chitchat of the people who were administering to her.

When Emily arrived at Reggie's at teatime, she was shown upstairs to Molly's little guest sitting room. Molly threw herself into Emily's arms the moment the door was closed. "I have had positively the worst day in my whole life," she whimpered. "Even George would never have behaved so badly." She put her head on Emily's shoulder and said, "I wish I'd not come to America. I am so frightfully upset and you are my only friend here."

Emily kissed her and patted her shoulder. "Let's have some nice, strong tea," she said.

Molly poured it out with shaking hands. "Do you know I haven't seen Reggie or heard from him all day long. Not a word. Here I am in his house, and not a sign from him. It's downright rude. I have never been so insulted." Molly put down her teacup and wept copiously into her lace-trimmed handkerchief with its embroidered crest.

"Perhaps he's too ill to talk after last night," suggested Emily.

Molly shook her head. "No. He's had his masseur and his barber and his lunch. He's sleeping again, the beast."

"Well, you needn't stay here. You can come to the Ritz with me," Emily said, reaching over to give her a kiss.

Molly didn't answer.

"What about Franz? Have you heard from him?" continued Emily.

"Yes. He called this afternoon to ask if dinner was on tonight, and I said as far as I knew it was. So he said that he and the frightful Olga would be here a little before eight. I am beginning to wonder if I want that wretched part. A great deal of the fun was because I could be with Reggie. Reggie said that he would be waiting backstage every night with a dozen red roses. I won't have him near me if he brings that horrible creature along with him." Molly blew her nose defiantly. "Even that old Chienloup seems better. He just sent me a cable saying 'How is my opalescent kitten?' "

Emily did everything to pacify her, but she, too, thought that Reggie had behaved atrociously no matter how drunk he may have been. He certainly should have sent some word to Molly.

"Who are these people we are dining with?" asked Emily. "What sort of people are they? Racing friends, hunting friends, tennis friends of Reggie's?"

Molly shrugged her shoulders. "Bores, I feel sure. Just bores."

At this moment there was a knock at the door, and to Molly's "come in," a footman entered with a note on a silver salver. He presented it to Molly, who thanked him wanly, then opened it as he left the room. "From Reggie," she said. "He begs my forgiveness, says he is so ashamed to have behaved like a cad, getting drunk and being a bloody bore. He says that he loves me and will I try my best to forget his dreadful behavior, that it will never happen again." She folded the note and put it back in the envelope. "I am not going to forgive him right away," she said firmly, "even though it is a dear note. It will take me some time before I can forget how horrid it all was."

"You are right," said Emily. "You must be firm. You want to be an actress. Why not put on an act."

Molly nodded. "I'll put that beast Reggie through his paces and if he throws me out, I'll come to the Ritz. No one can treat me the way he did. After all, Daddy is the premier earl of England."

"Well said," answered Emily, clapping her hands. "Now I must go and get dressed. I will order a car from the bell captain at the Ritz and meet you at dinner."

Molly jumped up and kissed Emily. "Thank you for being such a dear friend, and I will send Reggie a note telling him to get an extra man."

"I can drop out," said Emily. "I am really rather tired."

"My God," exclaimed Molly, "don't do such a thing to me. We must go through this evening together."

And so Emily went back to the Ritz, thinking she might have a double martini in her room. The evening was not promising. She decided then and there to go back to Europe as soon as possible. But where? Suddenly she remembered that some friends had told her of a charming little castle in Portofino, near Genoa. On an impulse she looked up the address in her notebook and immediately sent a cable to a Lady Carter in Portofino, who she understood was the agent for the so-called Castello Brown. She would take it if it were free, invite a few friends, and regain her equilibrium. At this moment, the wild animals of Kenya seemed far better behaved than the people she had been seeing in New York. But she didn't want to revisit Kenya. Better to sit in a small castle overlooking the Mediterranean and "invite her own soul." What was odd about her decision was that it had not even occurred to her that Italy was Carlo's country.

### CHAPTER EIGHT

# REGGIE AND MOLLIE ARE RECONCILED AND CHARLIE IS CAUGHT IN IRMA'S NET

EMILY ARRIVED LATE THE NEXT DAY AT BELLA VISTA AND, strangely enough, was glad to get back. They had had a cocktail at Reggie's the night before and then had gone to the house of Reggie's friends, the Alfred Buxtons, who were pale copies of Reggie: not quite so rich or sure of themselves although they spoke knowingly of the difference between salmon fishing in the Rogue River versus the Restigouche, or if the dove shooting were better in South Carolina or Florida. Mrs. Buxton wore enormous crystal and diamond clips and a huge single pin in the bandeau around her hair. She spoke with a strong English accent, but lost it during the cocktail hour when her voice returned to the Middle West, despite the *"magnifiques"* and *"tout* Paris." After her first half hour of silent laughter Emily had had enough of them. So when dinner was over, she begged off. She had a good excuse, as the extra man, a cousin of Alfred Buxton's, had a frightful cold and only wanted to get home as soon as possible.

Molly had called her early in the morning and recounted the rest of the evening. Reggie had danced most of the evening at the Cotton Club with Olga and, when they got back to the house, followed Molly up to her sitting room and gave her a big hug and a kiss. Molly gave him a large push, but he clung to her. "Fortunately, he was not drunk, or he would have fallen down," Molly said. "I really gave it to him."

"I know I have behaved terribly," he whispered in her ear, "but won't you forgive me? I was drunk last night."

"But not tonight," Molly said, disentangling herself. "You were still dancing in a disgusting way with that horrible woman. Even the people at the Cotton Club noticed it."

Reggie let Molly go and sat down on the sofa. "Well, I have never met anyone quite like her," he explained. "It's really not my fault. She is very aggressive."

"Aggressive," shouted Molly. "That's clear. And you are remarkably passive. Just imagine how you'd feel if you saw me acting that way. I am finished with you. You bore me. You are just a stupid American pretending to be British *and* a lady-killer, and you are neither."

This remark infuriated Reggie. "Well, it's you who brought Mr. Kramer and Olga Nitzkoff into my life. They are *your* friends—not mine. Any bad habits I've picked up are probably because I don't know how to behave with people like that. A lot of fun you will have being stuck with them when you get that part in the rotten play. *If* you get it. I think Franz Kramer has had enough of you."

Molly, in relating this, told Emily that she had burst into tears and said that she was far from home, had come to America because she thought Reggie really and truly loved her, and here he was treating her like someone off the streets. At this point she admitted to Emily that she had become hysterical and was so blinded by her tears that she never realized that Reggie had his arms around her and was murmuring in her ear, "Darling, darling, please don't cry." He was like the dear old Reggie, she told Emily. The rest of the scene was left to Emily's imagination but this morning the room was full of flowers and an adorable note from Reggie which she had in her purse. But what should she do? Reggie or Kramer and Co.? It was a frightful situation. Emily counseled her not to see Mr. Kramer unless he was really serious about giving her the part in the play and at the same time not to give in to Reggie so easily.

"He's having it all his own way," said Emily matter-of-factly. "I think he should be taught a lesson. You give in far too easily. One of you has to be strong." But Emily had no illusions. She was convinced that they were equally stupid, fond as she was of dear silly Molly.

"Oh," said Molly, "to change the subject. I forgot to tell you something. At the Cotton Club when I was dancing with Mr. Buxton and we passed the band, I noticed a white man hanging over the piano and singing, and beside him a mad-looking girl with red stockings with huge rhinestone clocks up the sides, dancing an absolutely crazy dance by herself. She was singing 'Drizzle, drizzle, the party was a fizzle, but oh, what a night for love,' while holding the man's hand, and a whole crowd was hanging around them. Guess who the man was?"

"Who?" Emily felt she already knew.

"Your nephew, Joe Shrewsbury. Mr. Buxton went to Princeton with him. He spoke to him and Joe Shrewsbury invited us to come to his table. He had that whole group with him. It was his party. Isn't that odd?"

"Very," said Emily laconically, and stupid as she thought

Molly to be, Molly got the message: No more talk about the Shrewsburys. They said good-bye and we will meet soon, sooner, soonest.

IN thinking it all over again as she returned to Bella Vista, Emily thought that dreary old George at Chatwood Hall might be better for Molly than Reggie. Molly was far too susceptible and childish to be on her own. Much better for her to settle down and have a house full of babies and nannies. Emily knew, realistically, that in spite of Molly's great beauty, she would not be a success in the play even if she never had to speak a word. She probably could not sustain a pose for long. Emily was devoted to Molly, but at the moment it exhausted her to be involved in such absurd antics. What she needed was a little peace. The thought of Joe and his group spending a thousand dollars at the Cotton Club so that Annabelle could sing did not lighten her mood. She was even beginning to look forward to seeing Irma, grim as she was. She was at least down-to-earth. Absorbed in her thoughts, she was astonished to find herself at Bella Vista.

When Morgan opened the door, she gave him a smile and said, "Morgan, I'm a bit late. It's nice to be back. What time is dinner?"

Morgan looked mournful as he said, "Eight o'clock, madam, and there is company."

"Oh, really? Who?"

"Mr. Hopleg." Morgan's evident disapproval seemed to ring through the hall.

"Mr. Hopleg. Who is he?"

"The young gentleman who came with Mr. Ponderosa. He has been here since lunchtime."

Charles Hopeland. Good heavens. What on earth is he doing here, thought Emily, alarmed. However, it was much better than being alone with Irma, and soon she would find out what he was up to.

"Cocktails at seven-thirty," intoned Morgan, "in the library," as if cocktails in the library were the last thing any sane person would want. The Shrewsburys had hardly ever used the library. It was far away at the other end of the house from the dining room, too far to go before their rapid and frugal meal. But now the houseman had been taken away from his radio to dust and clean the room, and Mrs. Shrewsbury had wanted the big orchid plant in the hall to be carried in there. Since this plant had never been moved before, a gardener had to be called who left a track of mud in the hall to be cleaned off. The whole household was upset by these unexpected demands and, as a result, Morgan had had a further talk with the Deepdale Club. Unfortunately, they had not yet decided to fire the present steward. So, feeling that he must make the best of a bad thing in the household in order to keep peace, he had put all his energies into soothing the staff and had no patience left over for madam and her guests.

"Thank you, Morgan. I may be a few minutes late." Then Emily dashed upstairs.

CHARLIE had not taken the 4:15 but had by Irma's request arrived in time for lunch. Under the eyes of Morgan and Harold, Irma had not said much at the meal, but afterwards, walking in the garden surrounded by dogwood and tulips, they had sat on a wrought-iron bench. It was there that she really opened up. She talked of her years working so hard with James, how being obsessed with the idea of making a fortune, they had had no time for anything else. She was glad that they had succeeded in achieving what they had set out to do and was proud of their accomplishments. What

James wanted, James got, she said. They never thought of failure.

Life with James had fascinated her, and even after James's death she felt that she could continue. In the first couple of months she *had* carried on, but now, suddenly, the fervor had gone. She no longer wanted to make a lot of money but just to hold on to what she had. Without James there to encourage her, to say well done, she was depressed and, she added in a low voice, lonely.

Charlie was overwhelmed by this flood of confidences and seized on the first idea that came into his mind. "What about your son, Joe?" he asked. "Can't he help you?"

At this, Mrs. Shrewsbury exploded. "Joe," she said, "is the most ungrateful, impossible young man that a parent ever had to contend with. He never showed any respect for his father's wisdom and judgment. He was rude to his father. He's hopeless—a ne'er-do-well. No mother could have a more unfortunate experience." And she added, "There is nothing of James or me in his character."

Charlie was for once at a loss, but as Mrs. Shrewsbury's hand was close to his on the bench, he took it and pressed it warmly. She returned the pressure, gazing off into space. Charlie, having once taken her hand, did not know how to get rid of it, so he continued to hold it as they sat there, both of them silently staring straight ahead. At last Irma rose, dropping Charlie's hand. "I must show you the fountain," she said. "It's down the path quite a way. James was so proud of it. It spouts higher than the one in Geneva and is the only one in this country."

The rest of the afternoon passed peacefully as they walked slowly around the garden, viewing the peacocks and the deer in their enclosure, and the orchids in the greenhouse. By 5:30 Charlie was worn-out and glad to escape when she told him that she had work to do and would see him at 7:30 in the library. Once in his room, he felt that he was at a crossroads in his relationship with Mrs. Shrewsbury. Should he treat her like one of his aunts, cajole and comfort her? Should he assume the role of family lawyer or—Charlie's heart beat an extra beat—was the old girl making up to him? It was a terrifying thought. He had been ambitious, anxious to please, perhaps even wanting to lure her away from Mr. Ponderosa. But he had not, in his wildest imagination, thought of anything else. No, that was not quite right. He would not mind at all being the golden boy, the favorite nephew—an amusing and light relationship—but his instinct told him that a press of the hand from Mrs. Shrewsbury meant more than a kiss on the mouth from an ordinary woman. He took a hot shower, followed by a cold one. Then he tried to work on some legal papers, but he was unable to concentrate and was relieved when it was time to go down to dinner. Better to face the facts than to suffer what his mind was conjuring up. He was delighted when Morgan told him that Mrs. Codway was in the library. He had not known that she was coming and sighed with relief. She was a snob, he thought, but anything was better than being alone with Mrs. Shrewsbury, and he greeted her warmly.

She, for her part, being in a bad humor at having found him there, reacted coldly to his effusiveness and decided to say nothing about having seen them at the Ritz. Irma fortunately arrived at this moment and gave Emily a peck on the cheek; as she did so, Emily noticed that Irma had on bright red lipstick. Oh, dear, she said to herself.

"I won't have my sherry tonight," Irma said to Morgan. "I'd like to try an old-fashioned."

Emily laughed. "You're running wild, Irma," she said jokingly.

Irma reddened slightly and said, "You drink them all the time. I am only following your example. Do you mind that?"

"Of course not. I only hope that you will like it as much as I do."

"What are you having, Charlie?" asked Irma as Harold appeared with a tray.

"I think I'd like a gin fizz, if that's all right."

"Did you know that gin is supposed to make people amorous and quarrelsome?" said Emily, looking at him with a twinkle in her eye.

Ordinarily, Charlie would have laughed, but under Irma's gaze, he hesitated.

"It's only true of women, so you're safe," Emily added. She could see that Irma was getting more annoyed by the minute.

Charlie lifted his glass, which had just arrived. "Amorous, but never quarrelsome. Your health, Mrs. Shrewsbury."

Irma raised hers. "Thank you, Charlie. I need that. My health is poor."

Emily, excluded, and knowing from Mr. Ponderosa that Irma's health was good, took a sip of her drink. Charlie Hopeland, she concluded, was slicker than she had imagined, an aggressive toady.

Thus the atmosphere at dinner was strained, the more so because Irma did not want Emily there either. Charlie, meanwhile, felt reprieved. There he was wrong, for as the conversation lagged, Irma's glances became increasingly provocative. She leaned toward him from time to time, speaking in a whisper so that Emily on her other side could not hear. Whether it was the old-fashioned and now the wine, she wasn't sure, but Emily caught Charlie's eye and could see that he was both embarrassed and obsequious as he affected an admiring manner toward Irma. You may think you're sophisticated, thought Emily, but you're not—not anywhere near it. You will have an unfortunate end.

Preferring not to watch these two absurd people, she thought it better to change the subject. "Tell me about the doctor," she said, pretending not to know. "What did he tell you, Irma?"

Irma said that Dr. Robinson told her to rest, perhaps go abroad, and see a famous London cardiologist. Emily, appearing concerned, said that she had heard of such a man but did not know his name, but that it was certainly a good idea to have a second opinion. The sooner the better.

Irma volunteered that she thought so too, but that she couldn't leave for at least a month. She had so much to wind up.

They discussed hotels in London and limousines for hire, shops, all the things that Irma would need in London. Emily thought it wiser not to mention any of her own friends, but she urged Irma to take someone with her. Irma did not respond, but her glance rested lightly on Charlie before she asked Emily what *her* plans were.

Emily said that she was going to see the Codways, in fact was leaving for Boston the following day, then going to Switzerland to stay with friends, and perhaps Italy for a bit. She might rent a villa there for a month. "There is a book called *The Enchanted April*, all about this little castle. It sounds so delightful that I thought I might rent it." Then Emily launched into a description of the book.

While all of this was going on, Charlie sat silently eating his dinner, but then he felt the weight of a foot on his instep. He looked at Mrs. Shrewsbury, but she, sipping her red wine, seemed engrossed in her conversation with Mrs. Codway. He moved his foot a little to see if it was an accident, but as he did so, the foot followed his. My God, he said to himself. Then he remembered an old Chinese proverb that someone had told him: He who rides a tiger must never get off. Was that to be his fate? He realized in despair that he had started off on the wrong "foot" with Mrs. Shrewsbury that first evening, then again at the Ritz. But he had treated the whole relationship as a sort of game, hoping to promote himself with his firm. He looked at Mrs. Shrewsbury, but she seemed intent on listening to Mrs. Codway reciting her plans. Then, when Mrs. Codway fell silent, he heard her say, "I definitely think that I will go to London," and Mrs. Codway replied, "I don't think you should go alone with a heart condition, no matter how slight. You should have someone with you."

At this point, Mrs. Shrewsbury tapped her foot twice and Charlie turned to find a very satisfied expression on her face. "You are quite right, Emily," she said. "I will not travel alone. I will certainly take someone."

Charlie lost his appetite. Emily, in spite of herself, felt sorry for him and asked just what he was doing at Battle, Ponderosa, and Huddlefield. Charlie threw himself into a long description of his activities, describing but not revealing the names of his clients, particularly on an important merger of two prestigious banks. He spoke well and even managed a few amusing anecdotes. Emily's opinion of him rose, but so apparently did Irma's as, with elbows on the table and a drink in her hand, she hung on every word he uttered.

It was a tour de force on Charlie's part, but when they were back in the library, he let Morgan practically fill a tumbler full of that terrible brandy for him and drank it down although his throat was on fire. Both Emily and Irma shot questions at him, but he coughed so much he could not talk. So Irma was left to talk with Emily, who soon announced that she was dead tired and had to get up early. Charlie remained silent as she rose to go to her room. She kissed Irma good night—a gesture that Irma surrendered to reluctantly. Then, with a glance of sympathy at Charlie, she left.

There was a silence in the room, and then Irma spoke. "Charlie, I think that I want you to come to London with me. I need a man to look after me. I always had my James before."

Charlie, who had just regained his speech, waited a moment to gather his wits. "That's wonderful of you, Mrs. Shrewsbury," he said, clearing his throat. "But much as I would love to, I don't believe that I can get away from the firm. We are very busy just now."

Mrs. Shrewsbury shrugged her shoulders impatiently. "That's easily arranged," she said as she again thought back to James's slogan; If you see what you want, get it. "I'll certainly double or triple the retainer. Surely Mr. Battle would agree to that. It would only be for a month or perhaps five weeks. I think I need a change and, come to think of it, as I can't leave before a month, you might even be able to finish the work on that merger." With this remark she got up, pulled her habitual shawl around her shoulders, and said good night, just as calm as you please without the slightest hint of what had been going on under the table.

Charlie went to bed but slept very little. Suppose Mr. Battle *did* give him leave of absence after being bribed by Mrs. Shrewsbury? The idea of a month with Mrs. S. alone was appalling. So was the whole relationship with Mrs. S. He wanted a partnership but not at such a price. He tossed and turned and slept only as dawn began to break.

Emily in her room was equally wakeful. Molly had apparently received a very nice letter from Carlo explaining at length why he had not been able to dine. The letter was so beautifully written and so old-world in its politeness that it was fun to read. "He really is a pet," Molly had said. This was like rubbing salt in a wound. Emily found that she was becoming more bored and depressed each day and knew the sedate Codways would not cheer her up. Maria Codway, the widowed sister-in-law still in the old house on Beacon Street, with Julia Codway and their brother Henry on Louisburg Square would be soothing but not stimulating. They would not change her mood. She needed someone more vital. So she tossed and turned, remembering in her restlessness that though she had settled on forty-nine as her official age, if the truth were known she was almost sixty. The clock was moving fast, and she was wasting these precious years. Should she seek serenity or try to retain her youth? Could she be happy without a serious relationship with a man? These thoughts kept her awake until almost dawn.

As for Irma Shrewsbury at the other end of the house, her thoughts were less complicated. She could not quite explain it to herself, but for the first time in years she was attracted to a man. She wanted to keep him near her and, if she had to triple Battle, Ponderosa, and Huddlefield's fee, she could afford it. Unlike her houseguests, she fell asleep immediately and didn't wake till dawn.

### CHAPTER NINE

# STARTING TOWARD EUROPE

MOLLY CALLED EMILY EARLY IN THE MORNING. APPARENTLY plans had changed. Reggie's mother was coming back from her cure at Saratoga, Reggie's father had just returned from a trip through the Caribbean, and they were giving a large dinner. This meant that Molly had to leave because Reggie had never asked his mother's permission to have a houseguest. Molly was annoyed that Reggie couldn't have told his mother that the daughter of the Earl of Bottomley and the wife of George Chatwood was his guest. "Silly old fool," exclaimed Molly, speaking of Mrs. Brevoort Beekman. "I daresay papa wouldn't have the old trout in his house."

"Well, you can't blame Mrs. Beekman," Emily said, "if Reggie never mentioned your name or even the fact that you were his guest."

Molly sniffed over the telephone. "Well, anyway, I met Mr. Beekman for a moment last night, and he was extremely nice to me and kept patting my hand and smiling at Reggie. He seemed awfully pleased to see us together; so as his yacht is going over to Cowes for the races and he is joining it later, he has offered the yacht to Reggie and me to cross the Atlantic in. It is really frightfully nice of him. It has eleven cabins and baths, and an immense crew, so we shall be absolutely wallowing in luxury."

"That's marvelous," exclaimed Emily, who was glad to hear some good news from Molly at last. "When do you start the crossing?"

"Day after tomorrow, although I am moving on board tomorrow as I have no other place to stay. Mr. Beekman has promised me a yachting cap with the name of his yacht on it: the *Dragon*. Isn't that adorable of him? Reggie seemed very pleased and kissed me right in front of Mr. Beekman, who I thought would disapprove, but he just kept on smiling. One never knows how Americans are going to behave!"

"No, I daresay not," said Emily dryly, as she began to get a glimmer of Mr. Beekman's behavior. Mr. Beekman's West Side establishment was well known. Ben had told her about it with disdain. "Typical New York nouveaux riches," he had said. Mr. Beekman probably would be pleased to have Reggie following in his footsteps. "I suppose he just wants Reggie to have some fun."

"That was last night," Molly continued, "but this morning at dawn Reggie called that dreadful Olga and Franz Kramer and asked them to come too; naturally, they jumped at it."

"Well, have you changed your mind?" asked Emily. "I don't think that sounds like much fun bottled up on a yacht for seven or eight days with Olga."

Molly sighed. "I know. It may be a mistake, but Reggie was being so sweet and showed me a huge check that his father had given him, telling him to spend some of it on a present for me. I just can't back out now, can I? Besides, why have that dreadful Olga alone with Reggie on the *Dragon*?"

Emily felt like saying, You British are almost as unpredictable as we are, but, from sheer laziness, she agreed with Molly that Mr. Beekman was nice and she really had to go through with it.

"When I left London, I saw a series of diamond bowknot brooches at Garrard's, or I might get a sable coat at Revillon," Molly mused. "I had no idea that Mr. Beekman was such a pet."

"He knows what a girl wants," agreed Emily. "He has had some experience, I believe."

"Well, bless him," said Molly. "I think Reggie is jolly lucky to have a father like that. I gather his mother is a tartar."

Emily said that she did not know her well but gathered that she was very social—one of the queens of New York society. Emily, in marrying Ben Codway, had taken on some of his Boston traits. She looked down on New York. There was no one comparable to the Adamses and the Cabots and the Lowells in New York, just some old broken-down Dutch and then the nouveaux riches. The Beekmans happened to be both old Dutch and two generations away from nouveau riche. Still, Emily felt superior. She considered herself a Codway and had forgotten her own humble origins as a Shrewsbury. As far as she was concerned, she owed everything to the fact that she had married Ben when she was so young. She was a Codway, wife of a Boston Brahmin, and could mingle with European aristocracy on equal terms. Suddenly, she felt homesick for Europe and hoped more than ever that the *castello* was free. She might find serenity there.

Molly broke in on her reverie by asking when they could meet. They both wanted to but it seemed impossible. Emily was going that very day to Boston for a week or so, and when she returned to board the *Berengaria*, Molly would already be off on the *Dragon*, which was stopping at the Azores and Madeira on the way over.

"I don't dare see much of Reggie in London," explained Molly. "My papa might make a row, but I expect to slip over to Paris and perhaps we could meet you there."

Whereupon Emily said impulsively, "I have an absolutely mad idea."

"Good heavens, are you going to marry?" Molly was startled.

"No, but I am really thinking of renting an old *castello* in Portofino that I have read about in a book and that may be available. I have cabled an English lady who is the agent to see if I can have it for a couple of weeks. If I can get it, I could go directly there from London. I will try for late next month but may not be able to get it so soon." As she said this, Emily cursed herself. She was going for a rest. Asking Molly would certainly not be restful. Here was the heart of gold once more getting her into trouble. Oh, why couldn't she keep her mouth shut?

"Do make it sooner," cried Molly. "I can't leave London in June. Even old Bumpkin George likes to come up to London in June. It's pure heaven then—a party every night. Why don't you come to London with us? George would be so pleased."

Emily was astonished that Molly could even think of such a thing. She was sure that George must disapprove of her, as her role as Molly's chaperone was not a very edifying one. In any event they decided to keep in touch and said many fond farewells over the telephone. Emily hung up with relief. With Molly, it was one drama after another. Yet for all the chaos she caused, she remained beautiful, childish, almost virginal. Emily, on the contrary, was quite worn-out. They say ten years makes a generation. Well, to face the facts, she was then much more than two generations older than Molly.

She stopped these horrid thoughts by getting dressed and talking the packing over with Elsa. She had decided to cut short her visit with the Codways, then leave on the *Berengaria* or on an earlier ship if Cunard or White Star had one. She was fed up with America, and went downstairs to find Irma. She had wanted to go to James's grave for one last look, but now she felt there was no time. She had kept the car overnight and wanted to get into New York as soon as possible to catch the early afternoon train to Boston.

At the bottom of the stairs she ran into Irma. "I have been waiting for you. I understand that you are leaving directly after lunch. Morgan said your maid asked for lunch at twelve-thirty."

Emily had not expected that and was furious that Elsa had taken it upon herself to make such a demand. In fact, Elsa was cross at being left in a small hotel in New York with most of the luggage while madam went to Boston. Elsa loathed New York.

"Oh, I am so sorry, Irma," Emily exclaimed, genuinely apologetic. "I certainly never told Elsa to do such a thing. I was not expecting to have lunch because I must take the four o'clock train to Boston. I do apologize for Elsa's stupidity."

Strangely enough, Irma smiled. "That's all right," she said. "We can fix a picnic basket for you. Have a picnic basket ready for Mrs. Codway, Morgan," she added, turning to him as he stood silently beside her.

"I will tell cook, madam. Anything special?" he said, speaking to Emily.

"Oh, that's very kind," said Emily. "Just a sandwich and a piece of fruit will be perfect."

"And now, with that settled," said Irma, "Charlie Hopeland is waiting outside to take us to James's grave because at long last the headstone is in place."

Emily's heart sank. She had wanted to take a walk before her trip, if there was time, to have a last look at James's grave alone, but she certainly was not keen on visiting James's grave with Charlie Hopeland. However, Irma had been most unusually gracious about Elsa's high-handed demands and Emily felt she could not say no. So off they went, Charlie and Irma in front, Emily in the backseat. Irma gave Charlie directions, while Emily wondered how Charlie would act at the graveside. Would he stay in the car and let the widow and sister go to the grave, or would he support the grieving widow and let Emily follow behind? In fact, he did neither. When he stopped the car, they had to walk up the grassy hill to the plot. Charlie said at once that he would walk ahead so as to find the exact spot. Emily was surprised. They had gone there before, but Irma said that she was not sure, as the gravestone had just been put up. Charlie coltishly bounded off and Emily caught a strange look on Irma's face. Was it pleasure in Charlie's youthfulness or was it senile self-indulgence? Emily was ashamed of such cynical thoughts. Poor old Irma. It was probably just loneliness. She went over and took Irma's arm as Charlie on the hilltop waved. "Come, let's go. Charlie has found it," she said.

Irma took her arm without a word and in doing so, Emily felt how thin she was. A poor old worn-out arm, whereupon Emily felt her own arm by comparison and concluded that it was still the arm of a young woman. What did it matter if she was old enough to be a grandmother? She felt a tingle of joy. She was young, full of life, and there were still many, many good days ahead. As she noticed a robin, she forgot the night's grim thoughts. Joy to the world, she thought, it is wonderful to be alive on a beautiful spring day. She decided to cable the agent in Portofino again, saying "urgent" the moment she got to New York, if there was not yet an answer.

Irma interrupted this reverie by saying, "I think the head-stone is too small. I am sure I ordered a larger one."

But Emily thought it was gigantic—an angry tongue of deep red granite poking up from the earth as if James were still giving orders. Emily moved away from Irma to get a better look.

"It is a great tribute," said Charlie reverently. "Mr. Shrews-bury would have been pleased."

Irma put her hand on his arm. "I am sorry that you never knew him," she murmured. "He would have liked you."

Emily wanted to laugh. James would certainly not have cared for Charlie, nor Charlie for James. Irma was losing her grip.

"What do you think of the headstone, Emily?" Irma demanded.

"Most suitable," said Emily. "It could not be more appro-priate if James had chosen it himself."

Irma looked satisfied, and the three of them stood there in silence, looking at the disturbed earth with the vast stone looming above it. Suddenly, to the astonishment of everyone including Irma herself, Irma broke into tears. "James," she sobbed. Then, "Charlie," and she put her head on Charlie's shoulder. Charlie rose to the occasion. He put his arm firmly around her waist and patted her back.

"There, there, Mrs. Shrewsbury," he said soothingly.

Over Irma's head, he and Emily exchanged glances and, to give Charlie some credit, Emily realized that he was as embarrassed as she was. Poor Irma seemed rather mixed up. Emily thought she should step in to restore some dignity to the situation. She gently disentangled Irma from Charlie and after giving her a kiss, took her firmly by the arm saying, "Dearest Irma. We must leave. This is too sad for you." She led the still-weeping Irma down the hill and into the car.

Fortunately, the drive to Bella Vista was short because again they were silent. When they were in the house, Irma asked Emily to come with her into a little room which had been James's in-house office. They sat down on the one small leather sofa and, when a moment had passed, Irma spoke. "Did I say something strange back there at the grave?" she asked.

Emily shook her head. "No, dear. You were upset, that was all—and quite naturally so."

Irma gave her a penetrating look. She had a feeling that she had made a fool of herself, but if Emily either had not noticed it or chose not to admit it, so much the better. She felt relieved and, in a rare show of affection, she said, "I am sorry that you are leaving. I waited to go to the grave to see the new stone until you came." This did not happen to be the truth, but Irma was feeling mellow.

Emily took her hand and looked at her fondly. "Irma, that was very thoughtful and dear of you. And it was very moving for me too. As you know, I owe so much to James: the school, Ben, everything really. I owe my greatest happiness to James's generosity. I have always felt very, very grateful to James for what he did."

Irma pressed Emily's hand. "I am glad you told me that," she said. "I never really knew what you thought. We have seen so little of each other, and now you're leaving. What are your plans?"

"Well, I am going, as you know, to Boston this afternoon to see Ben's sister and mother. I shall stay there with them a few days, then return to New York to sail on the *Berengaria* a week from now. After that I will stay in London for a few days, and then . . ." Emily paused. "Well, as you know, I have heard that a little castle at Portofino, Italy, by the sea, can be rented. I have sent them a cable and am thinking of taking it for a couple of weeks."

Irma looked interested. "A castle? That sounds interesting. I've never seen one." "She laughed. "Come to think of it, I have never been out of this country, but I am going, as you know, to London to see a heart specialist. Perhaps I might come to see you."

Emily, who had been touched by the first glimpse of vulnerability she had ever seen in Irma, said, "Of course," enthusiastically, and that she would send all the addresses in Europe to Irma's secretary. It was so different from any other conversation that they had ever had, this good humor and real feeling. To Emily, who was essentially an easygoing person who liked to be on good terms with everyone, it was a relief, and to Irma, it was a new sensation. It occurred to Emily that Irma was entering into a life different from anything she had ever experienced before and that she must feel like a debutante. She needed someone more knowledgeable in the ways of the world to help her in case of trouble, Emily concluded. So on this sympathetic note they parted.

Charlie led Emily into the car and, as he started to close the door, Emily said, "Be careful, Charlie. You may hurt her." He slammed the door either because he was annoyed or because it was his habit. Emily didn't know, but as the car drove off she saw him walking slowly back into the house, his head down. A word to the wise, she thought, but was he wise? She could not make him out. What was he really up to? Working for the firm or for himself? All that money dangling before his eyes, and Irma as naive as a teenager, becoming absolutely besotted. It must be very tempting. Emily felt protective of Irma. It seemed absurd; but then she thought this was not Mrs. James Shrewsbury but a poor caterpillar half out of its cocoon.

And Molly was a moth, fluttering close to the flame. What a morning she had had between the two of them! She leaned back comfortably among the cushions. It would be nice to

see a normal family for a change. The Codways might be
stodgy, but they were civilized. She was sorry to have cut her
stay short with them. She was looking forward to it—but
even then she wanted a real change. A romantic castle sounded
as though it were just what she needed. In fact, she realized
more than ever how she missed Ben's counsel. A man friend
soon after Ben's death had called her "a confirmed bride."
"You will be married within six months," he had predicted.
She had then thought what he said was true, but here she
was over three years later, still unmarried. She had had several
proposals from men she had had flirtations with, but she had
not wanted to tie herself down. She needed a romantic relationship, not a nine-to-fiver.

### CHAPTER TEN

# INTRODUCING SYBIL
# AND MURRAY AT
# PORTOFINO

AS SYBIL CARTER SAT AT HER DESK OPENING THE MORNING mail, she hummed a little tune. It was one of those rare moments in life when everything seemed to be going her way—not just that it was the most perfect spring morning, that the poppies and daisies were blooming beneath the silver gray olive trees, and the Gulf of Genoa was sparkling beyond the villa balcony; no, all these things were beautiful, and she savored them—but best of all, on just such a day and just such a time of year, she had a lover again. She spoke the words softly: "I have a lover." It thrilled her to say it. Who would have thought in the fifty-fifth spring of her life, Sybil would still be loved? But then, why not? How was it possible to stop being in love? To be loved in return was another matter, however, and she was not sure if Murray loved her. She knew he enjoyed making love to her; but love was a different thing. She had had several lovers (Lancelot Carter went to bed only to sleep) so she knew what lovemaking was all about, but Murray was the most ardent she had ever had. Yet he never spoke of love, only sex. She would pretend that it was because he was not educated, but she knew it was because he was not romantic. She hoped that she would get tired of him and they would part in a casual, no-feelings-hurt way; but for the moment, for better or for worse, he made her feel vibrant and young and she put her doubts behind her. The day was far too beautiful and, glancing at herself in the mirror over the desk, she thought that after all she still had some good years ahead. Her skin was fresh, her reddish curly hair only touched with gray, and her figure was neat and supple.

She was Lady Carter, the widow of Sir Lancelot Carter, five years dead, in his lifetime a dullish member of the British Foreign Service. He had had a little money and so did Sybil; so she was not too badly off as things go. She had the Villa Contenta here at Portofino and a tiny flat in London, where she spent as much time as she could; but it was impossible to live in London without spending more than she could afford. So when the bills began to pile up, she took the Rome Express down to recoup. It was easy to live cheaply in Portofino, so Sybil could live economically without being what she called "sordid."

She went back to her desk and slit open the top letter with Lancelot's old silver paper knife. It contained a cable from Boston, and Sybil, looking at the signature, did not recognize the name. It was in fact a cable from a Mrs. Codway, asking if by any chance the *castello* would be free for a couple of weeks. She would take it for longer if necessary, possibly a month, if it was available.

Sybil put the cable down slowly. Things had not been going well with her finances lately. The London flat had developed an expensive leak and she had had to repair it three times. She needed the commission, but at the same time she was tempted to say no, for her life at the moment was so deliciously easy and the last thing she wanted was an unknown American to deal with. Yet her practical side made her feel that she should rise to the occasion, be executive and resourceful. She put the cable down and looked out of the window. Across the port the squat little Roman fortress called Il Castello—or Castello Brown (named after the father of Yeats Brown who had bought it originally)—crowned the hillside above the olive terraces. Two huge umbrella pines flung their branches high above the parapet, but no flag flew from the flagpole, which meant that its American owners were not in residence. Perhaps it could be had. It was far the most attractive house in Portofino with its unrivaled views, its huge, pointed cypresses rising up among the silvery olives like dark towers. The Americans who owned it now had spent money on it. There were plenty of bathrooms and pretty garden furniture, and the gardens were beautifully kept. The servants were perfect but ruined by the reckless spending of the Americans. However, Mrs. Codway was, after all, American too. Sybil picked up the phone and gave the *castello* number to the operator. Luigia, the caretaker, answered the phone and, after the proper amenities, Sybil found out the *castello* was vacant, as the Americans were not returning until August. Luigia suggested that she call Mr. Mascio, the lawyer in Genoa, and find out if it were really available. Luigia, herself, was most eager. "I want to work," she said. "I do not like being idle."

Sybil well knew whence Luigia's eagerness sprang. She and her old Aunt Angela, when alone in the *castello*, were on board wages. If it were occupied they would get full wages, the larder would be groaning with food, and all their cousins, sisters, brothers, and aunts would be employed.

Sybil continued opening her mail, and by the time she got around to telephoning Genoa, she found that Luigia had already informed Mr. Mascio. He was all set to send a cable to America, but named a rather large sum as rental, twice as much as Sybil had been told that the *castello* had been rented for before. Evidently, Mr. Mascio and Luigia were preparing for the future. In ordinary circumstances she would have bargained but, thinking that this woman who said she would rent it for a month, if she could, must be rich, she decided to let it go. Mascio might be useful to her some day, so why make an enemy of him, and anyway, she would also get a larger commission. She looked at the clock. If she wanted to get to the telegraph office to cable Mrs. Codway before it closed for lunch, she had to hurry.

She looked at herself once more in the mirror. She had on wide, dark blue jersey culottes with a white jersey top that showed off her neat figure. She added a large, dark blue straw hat that she had bought in Santa Margherita and, slipping her shoulder bag over her arm, started down the path toward the village. A gate led from her villa onto the grounds of the Hotel Splendide. The path wound down the terraces between huge daisy bushes which were just coming out and pelargoniums trailing over the terraced walls. She looked with pleasure through the terraces to the gay semicircle of houses and to the fishermen who had pulled their boats up on the cobblestones and were mending their nets as the women, sitting in a circle in their stiff chairs at the doorways, bent over their lace. Children shouted and the cats fought over discarded fish. She crossed the main street and turned right down the cobblestone road where the post office was. After a few minutes' conversation with the postmistress, she was able to write her cable to Mrs. Codway, telling her the facts about the *castello* and asking for an immediate answer. Mrs. Mascio, though delighted, had been cagey and murmured about some *inglese* who might be interested. Sybil doubted it, but nevertheless, in her own interest, she had to take him seriously. As she hurried off down the narrow street to the piazza, the church bell was striking midday and she knew that Murray would be waiting at his table at Tina's sipping his morning Fernet Branca. She was dazzled by the brilliant light of the piazza after the darkness of the narrow street and almost fell over some children who were lying sprawled on the cobblestones playing with a kitten.

"*Guardi, signora,*" they cried holding up the kitten. "*Guardi com' è bello il gattino.*"

"*Bello,*" she murmured as she looked beyond them to Tina's four umbrellas shading the four little tables. Murray was there, his back turned toward her, his nose in a book. She slipped into a chair beside him, but he never looked up.

"Good heavens," she said lightly, "that must be a fascinating book. Can't you even say good morning?" He raised his head, but kept his finger in his place in the book.

"*Anna Karenina*; it's a remarkable book."

"I read it in school," said Sybil, then realized at once by his expression that she had said the wrong thing. "But that's so long ago," she added quickly, "I really have forgotten it. You must read me special bits that you like."

"Some day I am going to be as well-known as Tolstoy," said Murray aggressively.

"I thought you never wanted to write prose again," said Sybil mildly. "I thought it was poetry from now on."

Murray didn't bother to answer. Tina arrived with another Fernet Branca for him, and an *americano* for Sybil. "Oh, you ordered for me," exclaimed Sybil, delighted and touched by his thoughtfulness. "How sweet of you."

Tina, not understanding English, was smiling happily. "*Lei piace,* milady?" she asked.

"*Grazie,* Tina, *tante grazie,*" murmured Sybil, then laughed as Tina returned to the café interior.

"I am always taking things for granted. I should have learned by now."

"You are spoiled," said Murray. "You are pretty and attractive so you always expect everyone to be doing something for you."

Sybil sighed. Murray was in one of his moods. "Well," she said with a touch of asperity, "Tina did, didn't she? *She* thought of me."

"That's because you always overtip," Murray mumbled. "You've bought her as you would like to buy everything and everyone."

Sybil felt her temper rising. "I am not *that* rich," she answered. "In fact, I am just about able to make ends meet."

Murray gave a forced laugh. "You British aristocrats, you have to have personal maids and butlers and silk sheets and custom-made dresses, and then you say that you are poor. *You* should have been brought up the way I was—in a New York slum. Three of us children in one bed and my mother out all day scrubbing floors for rich people."

Sybil sighed. This was the unattractive side of Murray— harping on having been a poor boy. About once a month he had these moods, rather like a woman having her period. She usually paid no attention to them. They were especially bad if he was reading a book that was better than one he could ever write. So she forgave him for his present bad temper, thinking that Tolstoy was very strong competition. "Well, you are not so poor now," she said lightly, sipping her *americano.* "You are still getting royalties from your last book and you have the advance on your next one, so I think you've done jolly well for yourself."

Murray took a crushed package of cigarettes out of his pocket and shook one onto the table, then offered her one. She shook her head and he lit his, while looking over the lighted match into her eyes. He had fine dark eyes and long dark lashes and a lean, sharply defined face. He could have been a film star, she thought, and she remembered how his eyes shone in the dim light of her bedroom. Paul Geraldy's verse came to her mind:

*C'est dans l'obscurité que les coeurs cause.*
*On voit beaucoup mieux les yeux quand on voit*
    *moins les choses.*

She remembered, too, their first meeting in London at the Chelsea flat of an editor of the *Daily Mail*: a Bohemian party, but even then Murray stood out—his extraordinary looks and his messy clothes. He was also different in his defiant bad manners. It amused her, and she supposed that it was typical of second-string American literary types. So they stood, drinks in hand, chatting but with an undercurrent of *entente*. Eventually, she found herself telling him about Portofino and some of the well-known eccentrics who lived there, and he said it sounded like the right place for him. "I think I'll come there," he told her.

"Why don't you?" she answered and wrote down her own address, and Tina's, where he could find a room—no bath— but clean. He arrived a month ago, and almost immediately they started an affair. He was quite unlike any man Sybil had ever known. Rude, uncouth, messy, almost dirty; but his looks and sheer animal charm overwhelmed her. To be fair, he was intelligent, fun to talk to, and sensitive in his lovemaking. What he lacked was any sense of humor.

"I can't work here. This life is too soft for me. I must get back to serious work," Murray almost shouted as he shut his copy of *Anna Karenina*.

"Do you mean that you will go back to America?" she asked, knowing that he had no intention of going anywhere.

"I might," he said, inhaling and letting the smoke come out

of his nostrils. "All of this—" waving his hand around the painted background of the piazza "—is too pretty and unreal. It's like a postcard. I can't concentrate. I need ugliness."

"You are right," she said, finishing her *americano*. "Beauty *is* distracting. It must keep one from being creative. It is so delightful just to soak it up, like lying forever in a warm bath —delicious but debilitating." She turned and looked out over the almost landlocked little harbor, as if to confirm her thoughts. Her large hat hid her face, and Murray could not see her expression. It annoyed him.

"Let's go up behind the lighthouse and make love," he said.

Sybil turned sharply. "We couldn't do that in the middle of the day. Besides, it's lunch time."

"Oh, to hell with lunch," he said. "Let's get your boat, then, and go for a swim." She did not answer at once, so he put his nose back in his book.

Sybil was quite willing to put up with a little boorishness. After all, his mother had been a charwoman and his father a lorry driver (if one could believe him). One had to give him credit for what he had been able to accomplish. He had educated himself, was well read and articulate. It was really remarkable. She was proud of him and maternal, too. It was sad that his parents were dead (died of overwork, he said) and particularly sad that his mother could not know how much he had achieved. She wondered again from whom he had inherited his intellectual curiosity. She had tried to find out many times, but he had always said that his family, though decent and hardworking, had resented his desire for education and books. They said he was lazy, a shirker. He had never gone to college, he told her, but had educated himself at the neighborhood library. He had started work at fifteen—delivery boy in a pharmacy, busboy, car washer, doing two or three jobs during the day—to earn enough to travel and above all, write. As she thought of this, her mood softened. Poor boy. No wonder he had a bad temper. He had had no childhood fun. She was overwhelmed with sadness by his life. "Murray," she said softly, "stop reading. I'm not hungry. Let's swim."

Her boat was pulled up at the very end of the rocky beach opposite the *castello*. They pushed off. Murray started the motor and soon they were far out into the bay. While Murray was busy steering, Sybil slipped out of her clothes and lay naked on one of the long, blue mattresses with which the boat was equipped.

"Go back to the shore," murmured Sybil, who was lying on her tummy. "If we get under the shelter of the rocks, we will be safe."

"*Pescecane?*" asked Murray, using the Italian for "shark."

"No, worse," answered Sybil. "Luigia spends her days at the *castello* raking the gulf with her binoculars. She tells me that my compatriots are the worst. The lighthouse keeper also keeps watch. It makes me nervous. I can't make love if I feel I am being watched."

Murray laughed. "Exhibit A. Well, I think I'll go right into this little cove here under that great big pine tree hanging out over the water." He maneuvered the little boat close to the rocks and threw out a rope to attach it to the tree as the water was too deep to anchor in. When it was securely tied, he too slipped out of his clothes and lay down for a moment next to Sybil.

"Let's make love first," he said, "then swim and make love again when we're covered with salt."

Sybil rolled over and put her arms around him. "Isn't this heaven," she said.

When Sybil returned to the Villa Contenta late in the afternoon, she found a cable waiting for her on the hall table. She picked it up and went to her bedroom without opening it, and walked out onto the balcony. The sun was just setting and the mountains across the gulf were turning a rosy pink. The bay was so calm that it reflected everything. All that moved were three dolphins. The calm and beauty swept her with melancholy. It had been an incredible afternoon, quite unlke anything else she had ever experienced. The sun and air on her body, swimming in the crystal clear water with Murray beside her, and then the lovemaking—Murray so ardent—had been so exhilarating (and, oh, ignoble thought) so satisfying to her vanity. At fifty-five, to be so desired, particularly by someone at least twenty years younger, was a joy. But, in spite of all this, Sybil felt something wrong, not morally wrong because no one else was involved and she and Murray were as free as air. Probably too free, she thought. What worried her was that she felt that she had lost her sense of discipline. She was behaving like a tramp, not behaving as Sybil Carter née Peregrine should behave. It was all wrong for her, and it was wrong for Murray, too. He would be much better off in America with his own kind. He was struggling to adjust himself to her as much as she was trying to adjust to him.

She must get away from Portofino; the winks and whispers and laughter among the fishermen this afternoon, as she and Murray beached the boat, had not been lost on her. She had become a joke in the piazza. She had tried to look haughty and offhand in her good-byes to Murray, but she knew in her heart exactly what they were thinking and, of course, they were right. It was cheap and stupid. She must pack up at once and go back to London, let the Villa Contenta, and stay away as long as she could afford to. She pushed her hair back from her forehead, a habitual gesture, and in doing so, noticed the cable in her hand. Impatiently, she tore it open. From Mrs. Codway, of course.

"House sounds perfect," it said. "So does price. Would like to come as soon as possible. Hope that you will be there to help me move in and to show me the ropes. Gratefully, Emily Codway."

"Damn," said Sybil aloud. "Damn, damn. Now I *am* trapped."

### CHAPTER ELEVEN

# EMILY IS ENCHANTED WITH THE CASTELLO, MEETS SYBIL AND MURRAY, AND HAS A SURPRISE

THREE WEEKS LATER SYBIL CARTER WAS STANDING ON THE platform of the Santa Margherita station waiting for the Paris–Rome Express. She had been sitting in one of the comfortable wicker chairs by a bed of flame-colored gladiolus, but when she heard the whistle of the train, she stood up and walked along the platform so that Mrs. Codway would be able to see her. Not many people got off at Santa Margherita, so she felt it would be easy to identify Mrs. Codway, and indeed it was, as Vuitton luggage began to pour out of the railway carriage, handled by two obsequious train employees. Then came a mousy woman, who obviously was in charge of these transactions, and after her, to Sybil's surprise, a young-looking, slim woman with a kerchief tied over her hair, in a gray flannel skirt and white silk blouse. Surely this could not be the rich American widow—but it was, because Emily, surmising that this must be Lady Carter, came over with a smile and held out her hand. "You must be Lady Carter," she said.

Sybil shook the outstretched hand and smiled in return. This was not at all what she had expected and she was delighted. Much better than the American tourists who appeared in August.

Sybil fortunately had hired a bus for the luggage and a car. Most people at that time drove in carriages as the authorities considered the road too dangerous, so the only public motorized vehicle that was allowed was the passenger bus that plied twice a day between the town of Santa Margherita and the villages of Parragi and Portofino. Portofino itself had two cars belonging to individuals, which were only used if urgently needed. Emily did not know the pressure that Sybil had used to get permission for the bus and car, but she sized her up at once as an efficient woman. "If you would prefer to take a carriage," Sybil said after the luggage and Elsa were safely stowed away on the bus. Emily looked around. Several cabbies were waving their whips and crying out, "*Qui, qui signora, il mio cavallo è molto meglio, il più forte.*" It was tempting, but Emily was anxious to settle down, as she had been traveling constantly, and so chose the car.

The drive was along a breathtakingly beautiful road between terraces of olive trees on one side and, on the other, rocks that went directly down to the sea with a view across the bay to the mountains rising in a ridge in the distance. Sybil pointed out the sights as they drove along: the *castello* of Parragi and the beach of Parragi, the only beach on the coast where, she explained, great hordes of rich Italians from Turin and Milan and Rome brought their children in August. The simplicity and peasantlike character of the place appealed to them and they felt it a good atmosphere for their children. "Very few Americans come to Portofino or Parragi, only the very nice Whartons who own the *castello*," she said. "The others are mostly English except for one big property owned by a German baroness."

Emily got her first glimpse of the *castello* as they rounded the last bend, and she gave a little cry of delight. It was just what she had imagined with its small and sturdy battlements rising up to crown the hill and the two huge pine trees on the top level flinging out their branches like dark green banners. It was a triumphant gesture and made Emily feel more than ever justified that she had decided to come to Italy.

Sybil suggested that if Emily would like it, they could get off and walk down the ramp past the church and the post office to the piazza. "It will give you a better view of the port," she said, "because you can look down on it."

Emily consented with delight, and they stood for a moment leaning on the wall, looking down at the piazza from the small terrace in front of the post office. It was as usual teeming with life and to Emily, it was fascinating; but Sybil looking toward Tina's was annoyed to see Murray slouching there in his usual place. Damn him, she thought, lying in wait to catch us on the way up to the *castello*. The postmistress at this moment could not conceal her curiosity a moment longer, and leaving her place behind the counter, came out to have a word with Sybil.

"You have the telegram?" she asked in Italian, knowing full well that she herself had given it to Sybil a couple of hours before. Sybil responded with a shock. She had completely forgotten the telegram in her purse which, it so happened, was for Mrs. Codway. As the postmistress was watching her like a hawk, she did not dare to reveal her forgetfulness. It would be all over the village in half an hour that the English milady could not be trusted. So she waited until they were in the middle of the piazza before handing it to Mrs. Codway. "I am so sorry," she said, "but in the excitement of meeting you, I quite forgot this telegram. So stupid of me."

Emily tore it open with foreboding. Who was pursuing her to this delicious retreat? It was Molly. ARRIVING PORTOFINO TOMORROW. HOPE YOU WILL DINE ON BOARD. I MAY SEEK SHELTER WITH YOU NEXT DAY. LOVE, MOLLY. Emily folded it up and put it in her purse. It seemed that she was not to find peace after all. She smiled at Sybil and said, "Friends on a yacht, stopping by. One of them may come up to the *castello*. May I ask a favor of you? Could you possibly come up to the *castello* and show me around? Introduce me to the servants and give me an idea of what their jobs are. I speak enough Italian to be able to talk a bit, but I have no idea of how the household is run or who is in charge—that is if it is not too much to ask."

"Of course, I will come up with you," said Sybil. "No trouble at all; and there goes your luggage now." She pointed to a row of men who, with Emily's luggage on their heads, were starting up a steep cobbled path that was almost hidden by one of the houses on the piazza. Emily was appalled at the number of people and the amount of luggage. The whole village was staring. The children stopped playing, the lace-makers dropped their bobbins, and the fishermen forgot their nets. Murray threw down the *Corriere della Sera* and turned to look at the procession. "I really am embarrassed," exclaimed Emily. "I had no idea that I had so much luggage or that it had to be carried up. I feel like Simon Legree."

"Don't worry, they do it every day, and you may be sure that Luigia will pay them well. You will find that she runs everything at the *castello*."

By this time they were almost at Tina's where Murray sat

watching them with bored disapproval. Sybil could imagine what he was thinking. The luggage and Emily in her chic and simple traveling costume, jangling gold bracelets, and a silk scarf on her head was certainly not a woman of the people and, even worse, she was an American. He despised foreign aristocrats, but Americans who aped them were even worse in his eyes. Sybil tried to steer Emily past him, but it was impossible, as Tina's was just at the end of the path that led up to the *castello*. To her horror, she saw Murray rise and come toward them. "Hello, Sybil," he said. "What are you doing up so early and where are you going? What about some breakfast? The same as usual?"

Emily looked at him and then at Sybil, who looked as though she had not heard him. But she had heard him all right and felt like slapping his face. Instead she forced a laugh and said, "This is Murray Kent. Mrs. Codway, an American friend of mine."

Emily, looking from the rather sedate Sybil to the young man, thought it must be a fairly recent friendship. He did not look the type to know Sybil for long. She saw at once that he was extremely good-looking with a magnificent figure, although in Emily's view his trousers were two sizes too small for comfort. Perhaps he had on one of those *faux* contraptions Emily had seen men buying in Capri, though Sybil could have told her differently.

To Sybil's surprise, Murray was holding out his hand to Emily. "Welcome. All of us here in Portofino are happy that you have come," he said with a winning smile.

Emily took his hand, just as Sybil, who had noted Emily's appraising glance, said, "Murray loves to make speeches. That's because he is a writer and if he can't write, he must start making a speech." She had meant to say, When he isn't writing, but the word "can't" came out instead, and she glanced fearfully at Murray. Was he going to take offense? His nose was twitching, a sign that he was ready for action.

Emily prevented the scene by saying, "How very kind of you, Mr. Kent, and I can only tell you that I am enchanted by what I already see. It would be difficult to be unhappy here."

On this jolly note, Sybil started up the path followed by Emily.

The path was actually a cobblestoned mule track, and at the start had houses on both sides, where in the doorways the lace women were busy turning out their mats. They knew Sybil all too well and considered her hopeless as a customer, but they called beseechingly to the newcomer. "It is too bad," Sybil remarked, "that they turn out such hideous things because the work is quite good."

Emily nodded, taking in every detail. Although an inveterate traveler, she was still intensely curious about a new scene. They soon left the houses behind and were walking between two gardens—one with a low wall, the other, a terraced olive grove with flowers beneath the trees and a view of the pink, yellow, and green houses of the little port. After a while, on the right side there was a small church with a piazza in front, and here one could look down directly into the Mediterranean. "It is a church," explained Sybil, "dedicated to the fishermen. Inside, it is filled with photos and wreaths and Madonnas given by grateful families whose husband or brother or cousin has been saved. They have a big service there once a year and the whole town turns out."

"I would love to go in, but I am very anxious to see the *castello* and meet the household."

Sybil smiled. She liked Emily's enthusiasm so she added, "That high wall we passed a little while ago is where the German baroness lives. She has the most beautiful garden in Portofino, with seven German women gardeners."

Emily nodded. Ahead of her she saw the great gray wall of the *castello* with its fat round tower. As they turned the corner of the path, there was the garden gate. "Tell me," she said quickly, "how many in the household?"

Sybil laughed. "It will be hard to find out. Luigia, with her family, runs the house, and it will depend on what you want, and I am afraid, a bit on what she thinks you can take. Sometimes there are four; sometimes ten. There is a whole galaxy of cousins, aunts, nieces and nephews and brothers in the wings. Angela, her old aunt, rules the kitchen. She shops every day, but she sometimes forgets who is best served—her employers or her relations."

"Good heavens." Emily stopped in the path. "I do at least hope that they are good-natured."

"*That* they are, except Vis-Vis—the gardener and his sons. There is a feud between them." At this moment, Luigia in a black dress with white apron, collar, and cuffs appeared at the gate, her face wreathed in smiles. "Welcome to the *castello*, signora," she cried.

The three gardeners stood behind her and bowed low, saying welcome in Italian. Emily shook hands with them all, then, led by Luigia, walked past the huge daisy plants at the foot of the *castello*'s outer wall, then under an arbor, up some stone steps, and finally up the entrance steps of the *castello* itself to a great door, which was open and where at least seven women reached out in turn to kiss Emily's hand and give her a shy smile. Emily immediately went straight down the red tiled hall to a large glass door which gave out onto the garden. When the *castello* had been built as a fort against the Moors back in the sixteenth century, this had been the parade ground for the garrison. Now, since Cecil Pinsent, the noted English landscape gardener who lived in Florence, had worked on it, it was dotted with gay flower beds and had a gravel square in the center on which a group of wicker garden chairs with bright cushions stood. Emily ran to one small point in the parapet (which was raised and just under the pine trees) and looked over down at the port. The pink and yellow and pale green houses in a semicircle around the harbor looked like a stage set. And then she went to the same little round gunpost on the gulf side, and looked down the bay to Santa Margherita and across the gulf toward Zoagli, nestled at the foot of the mountains. She cried aloud, "How unbelievably beautiful! It can't be real!"

The servants looking on thought, Just another mad foreigner, but Sybil thought, I must be more careful than ever if I go swimming with Murray.

After that Emily was shown all over the *castello* from the round tower salon on the top floor to the salon below, then to the bedrooms and bathrooms and the dining room which opened onto the garden and the bay and finally the kitchen, where she was astounded to find a wood-burning stove on which, she was told, Angela concocted the best soufflés in Italy. It was fun but exhausting because of the chattering entourage, bursting with pride to show off the *castello* (with its new American renovations) and also wishing to ingratiate themselves with the new signora. At last Sybil and Emily had a cup of tea and then Sybil departed.

Emily had found Sybil businesslike and helpful, while Sybil on her part was delighted by the prospect of a pleasant relationship. The mistress of the *castello* was an important person in that small village, and to be welcomed at the *castello* would improve Sybil's standing in the community. Murray was a folly and, though she found herself incapable of giving him up, she knew that her affair reflected a dreadful lack of character. The widow of Sir Lancelot Carter, K.C.B., should know better. As she walked down the path, she felt slightly envious of Emily, who seemed so sure of herself, so happy, so secure. If I had her money, I could be like her too, thought Sybil. But that was not quite fair. She felt sure that Mrs. Codway would never have risked a wanton tumble with someone like Murray or with anyone else for that matter. This depressed her, and she was pleased when she arrived at Tina's and found that Murray was not there, so she went directly back to her villa.

Emily, back at the *castello*, lay on a chaise longue under the pine trees and reread Molly's telegram. What a bore! She longed to be alone, to soak up the beauty of the place, not to be bothered by anyone. She remembered reading in John Cowper Powys's *The Meaning of Culture* that no man was cultivated unless he liked to be alone so as to renew his spirit, and Emily could see that she had been far too dependent on people since Ben died. She had not "invited her soul" in a long time, and this was the place to do it. She stood up and wandered around, looking at the view, listening to the cries of the children rising from the village, the fishermen shouting to one another, the barking dogs, and braying donkeys. After a while, she went up to her room, already arranged by Elsa. The pale pink handkerchief linen sheets edged in Binche lace from Rouff in Paris were incongruous on the iron bed made for a nun, draped in mosquito net, and she decided when the sheets were changed to use the heavy linen provided by the *castello* from now on. She lay down on the bed and was asleep almost at once. When she woke up it was dark and she heard Elsa and Luigia talking at her door. Luigia was urging Elsa to wake up la signora in order to see the full moon just coming up over the mountains behind Rapallo. "All American ladies like to see the moon rise," said Luigia, but Elsa stood firm. Her lady was tired and wanted to sleep. Emily stopped the argument by getting up and flinging open the shutters. Luigia was right. The full moon, that ever-beautiful miracle, was just peeping over the top of the mountain, and its light made a path that crept across the gulf so that the olive trees glowed faintly on the terrace below the *castello* and the great cypress tree just beneath her window stood out in relief. Emily quickly slipped out of her traveling costume and with Elsa's expert help put on a white crepe chemise dress from Vionnet. Then she ran down the stairs and onto the gulf-side parapet to watch the enchanted moon world.

By the time the moon was fully over the mountain, Luigia had brought her dinner on a tray. The dogs began to howl as was their custom. "*Sono tutti amorosi,*" declared Luigia over the din. Though Emily loved dogs, these howls irritated her. "When La Tillina, the dog who lives with the *contadino* next door, is in heat," volunteered Luigia, "all the other dogs come running up from the piazza. The whole path is full of them, and some dogs even jump on the bus at Santa Margherita to visit La Tillina. She is very popular." Emily laughed and, having finished her dinner, wandered over to look down on the piazza. There seemed to be a lot of people strolling about, and as she stood there, she heard a man's voice singing, "*Parla mi d'amore, Mariu.*" She listened, delighted. It was a perfect touch and seemed even to have calmed the dogs. It was such a beautiful evening, why not walk down and have a drink? She changed from slippers to low-heeled sandals and threw a shawl around her shoulders. Luigia seemed shocked but handed Emily a torch, and said the signora was not to take a key. Either she or her sister, Maria, would be waiting for her. But Emily insisted on the key. It made her feel the *castello* was hers.

She thanked Luigia and was off. The walk down, though hard on the feet, was an adventure—everything looked different by moonlight. There were mysterious dark passages with cats moving stealthily about and then suddenly the moonlight shone brilliantly and the strong scent of jasmine with which the garden walls were festooned was almost overpowering. For a moment or two she was apprehensive. After all, she knew nothing about these people. Perhaps there were brigands among them. So she was glad when she came out onto the piazza and she saw Sybil and Murray from the corner of her eye, seated at Tina's, a bottle of Grappa in front of them, deeply engrossed in each other. She had no intention of interrupting them, so she rushed past Tina's and into Nino's in the middle of the piazza, a more imposing café than Tina's, enclosed by low flower boxes and partly covered by an awning. Emily chose a table as far away from Tina's as possible, and ordered a *punt e mes* which Nino brought in a flash. He already knew her as the American lady at the *castello* who had had the good sense to pass Tina's and come to him. Unfortunately, she thanked him in Italian for the drink and this encouraged him to start talking. He told her that he served meals—the best restaurant in Portofino, he said, in fact the only *real* restaurant in town, as the Delfino served only fish and he had *everything*. Emily feared that the conversation was going to last forever, when suddenly a tall man seated himself in the back near the house. Nino rushed over to him with loud greetings, among which Emily heard the word "*principe*." As they chatted away, she sipped her drink and looked out at the moonlit piazza. A man was seated on one of the upturned boats surrounded by a group of fishermen. He had been talking to them but at this moment, he burst into a hearty rendition of "*Sole mio*." At the end, the clapping was so loud, not only from the group around him, but also from the people hanging out of the windows, that he was encouraged to sing it again. This time he put his heart and soul into it, and some of the listeners felt the impulse to join in. The piazza rang with the sound of strong male voices which, though they sang about the sun, was really a hymn to the night. Emily felt romantic and that it was a waste to be alone on such a night in such a setting. When the song stopped, she applauded appreciatively; this was echoed by the man behind her. Nino sauntered over to her table. "You like the Italian songs," he said. "The *principe* noticed that you clapped and was pleased that an American lady should like our songs."

"The *principe*," said Emily, repeating the title to please him as she felt that he meant to impress her by his clientele. "Is there a *principe* here?"

Nino smiled. "Yes indeed, a very good client of mine. He has a small apartment here, over there—" he waved toward a house on the quay facing the *castello*. "He comes here for a week or two for a good rest. He loves Portofino. His Excellency Il Principe Pontevecchio."

Emily almost fell out of her chair. "Prince Pontevecchio— is he here now?"

Nino nodded. "Yes, where else? He is just there in the corner."

Emily got up and hurriedly paid her bill. She had no intention of letting Carlo think she was pursuing him. Nervously she walked out from the shadow of the awning into the moonlight; but as she hurried to get away, she tripped and dropped her flashlight, which broke on the cobblestones. Carlo Pontevecchio, seeing only a slim woman in a clinging white dress obviously upset over breaking her flashlight, got up and came out to her. She turned toward him and he said, "Emily." He had never called her anything but Mrs. Codway before, and in his voice there was more than just surprise.

"Yes, it's me, and what a mess I've made," Emily said as matter-of-factly as possible. "It's a nuisance because I have to walk up to the *castello*, and the walls and olive trees make the park dark even on such a lovely night. Do you think Nino could lend me a flashlight?"

"Better than that," said Carlo. "I have one with me and I will escort you up the path. I know it well."

Emily protested. He insisted. As he looked at her in the

moonlight, she seemed so pretty and feminine—so helpless—
that he almost forgot about Reggie. So he took her arm and
they strolled across the piazza.

As they passed Tina's, Murray said to Sybil, "Your friend
from the *castello* seems a fast worker. She must have picked
him up at Nino's." Sybil felt a twinge of jealousy. She had
always admired the prince but had never met him. Mrs. Codway seemed to get everything she wanted.

### Chapter Twelve

# GOD REWARDS EMILY
# FOR HER HEART
# OF GOLD

SYBIL, AS IT HAPPENED, HAD CAUSE TO BE JEALOUS, FOR EMILY was about to have one of the happiest weeks of her life: one of life's rare moments when everything seems perfect, like a gambler's run of luck. In the first place, Emily and Carlo in that short walk up the path past the fighting cats and barking dogs and scurrying mice seemed to be the only human beings around in their own world of moonlight and shadow. Emily dared to reproach Carlo for his cold, even rude, note. He apologized deeply and asked her to forgive him. He laughed and said that he had been jealous of Reggie, and Emily joined him in laughing at such an absurd idea. They chatted away, old friends talking of people they knew, places they had visited, his farm, and his little daughter. They were like two boxers in the ring watching each other warily. It was only after he had opened the *castello* door with the immense key Emily had handed to him, and had kissed her hand lingeringly, while looking into her eyes, that Emily took charge. She withdrew her hand, gently thanking him a thousand times, said she was very tired from her trip and would he call her in the morning. It was impossible to make plans until Molly's arrival, a subject they had already discussed, having also agreed that it was too bad to have to deal with Molly so soon after Emily's own arrival. It would have been so much more peaceful without her.

Carlo stood at the foot of the grill door and kept his flashlight on the steps so Emily could see her way to the great oak entrance door. She turned at the top, blew him a kiss, and said, "Thank you again," and then she closed the door. She knew, of course, that he had wanted to come up and sit on the terrace, and she would have liked it too. But in truth, she was tired and felt she could easily have lost control of the situation, a situation she had no trouble anticipating, given that look in Carlo's eyes, to say nothing of what Carlo might see in her own eyes. In a way she regretted it as she went up to bed. Perhaps there would be another chance. It was a bore about Molly, but what could she do about that?

Then her lucky streak began. The next morning Angela, coming back from her marketing, brought a telegram from Molly saying that they were still in St. Tropez, would then go to Monte Carlo, and would not be in Portofino for another week. Emily laughed with joy at the prospect of a week alone in this gloriously beautiful place surrounded by the attentive and ever-smiling Doppi family (that was Luigia's family name). In the last twenty-four hours, two very young and pretty little girls had appeared, all rigged out in black dresses and white aprons, their hair in pigtails down their backs; a bent-over old woman who Luigia swore made the best lasagna in the Provincia di Genova seemed to be helping Angela in the kitchen. There was, of course, always Luigia's sister Teresa, who was in charge of the bedrooms and another sister, Maria, who was the laundress. Emily began to love them all as she ate her lazy breakfast on the terrace and decided to let them run the house and to hell with expense. Even Elsa, who at first was terrified by such casual arrangements, cheered up when they began calling her Fräulein and serving her meals on a tray.

Emily sighed contentedly, and thought of Carlo. She disliked scenes or bad feeling. She wanted to feel surrounded by goodwill and good humor and had felt incredibly romantic last night. It had taken every bit of her Codway discipline not to have fallen into his arms, but what a tonic it would be to be kissed again by a lover. Yet she knew a thing or two about Italian men, for she had visited Italy often and had several good Italian friends—women. The men, in her mind, were Indians displaying their conquests as if they were scalps. There were, of course, certain *cavaliere serventes*, men who maintained long liaisons, but even they strayed occasionally and let it be known, just so their friends could know that they had not lost their vigor. She also knew that Italian men usually liked younger women. The sight of fresh young skin delighted them. Emily could hardly blame them for that, but she was determined to remember her own worth and not be beguiled into a transient love affair.

Having decided all this and feeling very sensible, she poured herself a second cup of coffee, still thinking of Carlo. He was the best looking man she had seen in years—so slim and fit and elegant, with such marvelously expressive brown eyes and beautiful hands, especially the hands. Old Lord Portweigh had once told her that he always looked at a woman's hands; "They are what one makes love with," he had said. It would be fun to have a fling with Carlo—if things were different. She still liked to flirt, but to make a fool of herself or lose the respect of the people who worked for her was out of the question. "Not in front of the servants" was a good axiom. Emily Codway, even though she had reached "the grateful age," was not easily available. She would see a lot of Carlo because she liked him. She liked the way he looked at things; his quick intelligence and sense of humor were a delight. She felt confident that they could have an attractive relationship without going to bed—perhaps!

She got up and looked down at the piazza. It was busy as usual, and her eye wandered contentedly to the houses just beyond the beach on the opposite side of the harbor. There she noticed someone in the second story of a pink house having breakfast on the terrace. She picked up the binoculars which Luigia had left behind and focused them. It was Carlo in a red silk dressing gown, reading a newspaper. Emily quickly put the binoculars back on the table, feeling guilty; however, the temptation was too much, so she went to the wall and, leaning on it, looked back across the harbor. She had good eyes and could still see Carlo clearly. She felt almost as though she could reach across and touch him. As she watched, as though in a dream, she saw him get up, throw down the paper, and stride back into the house. Was it his bedroom or sitting room? What was the flat like? As she idly dwelt on these questions, the telephone rang and a few minutes later, Luigia rushed out in a highly excited state. "Il Principe Pontevecchio is on the telephone to the signora," she cried happily. Emily turned languidly and then, caught by Luigia's mood, walked rapidly into the house.

"How are you this morning?" asked Carlo. "I hope that you slept well, your first night in Portofino."

"Oh, I slept marvelously," rejoined Emily. "I usually hate mosquito nets, but the one around my bed seemed like a cocoon and had a marvelous effect on me. Then this morning I received a telegram from Molly. She and Reggie won't be here for a week."

"Bravo," Carlo exclaimed, his voice sounding strong and possessive. "So then you are ready for a little expedition. I will meet you in the piazza at twelve, and then I will show you some of the sights of this region. Is that all right? Would you like it?"

"I would indeed," answered Emily. "I will see you at noon." Then she went once more to the wall and saw him sitting comfortably back in his chair, reading his paper.

She met him in front of Nino's as the church bells struck twelve. The perfect week had begun. The first day they went in his boat, an immaculate thirty-foot affair, with a boatman in dark blue trousers, blue and white jersey top, and bare feet at the helm. They lay back on great white canvas cushions. They passed beneath the *castello* and looked into the cave that Carlo told her led to a tunnel which went directly into the *castello*, where people and boats hid during the wars against the Moors. Then they rounded the peninsula past the lighthouse and the *castelleto*, a tiny version of the *castello*, originally the first outpost against the enemy and now the home of an Englishman; then they were suddenly on the other side of the small peninsula and out in the Mediterranean. Slowly they passed the church which was on the path up from the village and for the first time Emily saw the home of the German baroness and Alta Chiara, the Italian home of the Herberts, whose house in England was called High Clare. Carlo was a perfect guide and described in detail the inmates of these houses and the history of the peninsula, a solid little stronghold against the Moors. Slowly, they went along the coast until they came to a largish cove on whose beach stood a crumbling monastery, known as San Frutuoso. The water in the cove was so clear that they could see a vessel lying on its side at the bottom, a British ship lost in some mercantile struggle a century ago. Carlo went in for a swim, but Emily, having brought no suit, sat back on the cushions and watched him disappear out to sea. He was a strong swimmer but she was frightened by his going so far out. The boatman, Francesco, explained that the *principe* always did this. "He is like a fish," he explained. "Have no fear, signora." At last Carlo returned, and they had a picnic lunch on a rock: cheese and bread and fruit. They drank Chianti. Carlo was full of anecdotes but also full of wisdom and wit. After lunch they returned to the Golfo di Tiguillo and made the tour past Parragi to Santa Margherita and back.

It was a glorious day, but the days that followed were equal to it. They walked to San Frutuoso, over the hills of the peninsula through vineyards and then climbed back again, ending up on the terrace of the Hotel Splendide for tea. They went to Rapallo and took the funicular up to Montallegro, then walked along the ridge to Zoagli to enjoy the magnificent view of the small towns beneath them, the sea lapping at their feet.

Day followed day. In Genoa they visited two palaces filled with Van Dykes—Van Dyke had lived in Genoa for several years and, as Carlo explained, painted the nobility. Then on to the cemetery with its outlandish tombstones. In Rapallo Emily met Max Beerbohm and his wife, Ezra Pound and Augustus John and the di Robilants, who had the most spectacularly lovely house in Rapallo. They even went on an all-day walk in the mountains behind Montallegro. These mountains, which one saw from Portofino, were the foothills of the Apennines, Carlo told her; and in the old days were hideouts for brigands. "The people of Portofino are mostly descended from these brigands," he explained. "Perhaps you have already recognized some of the traits: feuds and greed."

"In a small but funny way, yes," said Emily. "The people in the house at the *castello* won't speak to the people in the garden and vice versa. The household say the gardeners are buying eight times more manure than we need, and the gardeners say that I am feeding the whole village, and yet they have all worked together for generations." She laughed.

"How good of you to laugh." Carlo was pleased. "It *is* funny, but you must not let them get away with too much. As the French say, appetite comes with eating. The Americans who have done over the *castello* will not thank you for your generosity—to say nothing of the Italians and British who count every lira."

"Well, this is just once in a lifetime for me." Emily smiled.

"Is it?" Carlo's voice became tense. "Will you never come back?"

Emily looked away. "Perhaps, but sometimes when one is very happy, it is better not to try to recapture it."

"Then you are happy here," he said.

Emily smiled again and nodded, then looked away. They were sitting on a rock under a pine tree overlooking the foothills that descended to the sea.

"I think we should go home, Carlo. I must make a telephone call and we must not miss that last funicular."

They rose reluctantly. It had been a specially congenial and happy day. Carlo had described his life, particularly his farm in Tuscany, which was the favorite of all his places, partly because his father had given it to him outright. It was not far from Siena and had always been a patrician dwelling. Carlo and his wife used to live there most of the year and had modernized it enough to make it comfortable. He described it in detail to Emily—the terrace, the lovely gardens, the magnificent view of rolling hills and farms. He told her again of the loss of his wife and more explicitly of his little daughter whom he adored, and how difficult he found it to see enough of her. He described his father, a gentleman of the old school, and his mother, a gentle, religious soul. His father was the duca di Venturi, and he told her that the Pontevecchio family had two titles: the principe de Pontevecchio and the duca di Venturi. His father had chosen the latter, as he owned vast lands in the south and his wife came from a great southern family. They also kept the palace in Rome in which Carlo had a wing.

Emily hung on every word he said and then told him again in more detail about her humble childhood, about her marriage to the much older Boston aristocrat and Ben's death, and even about the boring Irma. They held nothing back, or so they thought; but perhaps things were colored a bit here and there as they wished to appear worthy in each other's eyes.

Because of Emily's "not before the servants," and Carlo's having to dine with some friends in Rapallo, they had had only two evenings together beneath the full moon. The first was at the *castello* on the bay side terrace. The second was at Nino's, which fortunately was crowded as it was a Saturday night. The tables all around them were filled with Italians who were shouting and singing and consuming vast carafes of a dark red wine. Since the gentry never appeared until the summer months, these were shopkeepers and clerks from Genoa and the surrounding towns. They tied their napkins around their necks and set to with fork and spoon eating enormous soup plates of pasta al pesto—a specialty of Genoa—followed by platters of fish and cheese. The crowds made for privacy, and Emily and Carlo could talk entirely at their ease, knowing that these people could not hear nor were in any way interested in them.

The piazza, however, was *very* interested in them, as Carlo well knew. Women, hanging out of their windows yelling to their children who were playing at the water's edge, stopped when Carlo and Emily passed, calling to a neighbor to "look." The fishermen and old men lounging by their boats followed the couple with their eyes, and the café owners stood still at the doors of their cafés. Even the padre hurrying along with his string bag full of vegetables and eggs (gifts from grateful parishioners) quickened his pace so as to catch a glimpse of this foreign lady and move his hand in benediction to the prince. Carlo was adored in the village. He came there very seldom, but his agent came often and saw that money was given to the church, that the needy were looked after, and that bright children were given a chance at education. Carlo's life touched every one of the several hundred residents, and they were much concerned about his future. What was this foreigner like? Was she a good woman or crazy, running after every man she saw, as so many of these ladies did, especially when it was such a man as the prince? What was money compared with an ancient title and vast lands? Was the lady gentry in her own land?

Emily, of course, had no idea what was going through the minds of the villagers, much less that they talked about her night and day; but she knew enough to surmise that she and the prince might interest them and so acted accordingly. She always smiled at everyone, never concentrated on Carlo, and never took his arm or hand unless to cross over a rough spot. This was seen and appreciated by all, but with a touch of cynicism. "Wait and see," they cautioned. "She may be playing a game." To Emily, and to almost the same extent to Carlo, they were, for that week, locked in a world of their own, exploring each other's minds and spirits and thinking of nothing else.

The night before Molly was to arrive, Emily had asked Carlo to dinner at the *castello*. He was leaving to go back to his farm and also to see his parents in Rome, so it would be a farewell party. She put on her prettiest, most becoming evening dress and sprayed Chanel No. 5 behind her ears and on her hair and on her hands. Then she went down and sat in the garden and wished on the first star she saw, something she had done all her life, a talisman. These tiny threads of continuity were what she thought held her life together. There was a cushioned swing in the garden, and she pushed herself back and forth with the tip of her slipper; it was there that Carlo found her when he arrived for dinner.

"How beautiful you look," he murmured as he kissed her hand. "You should be painted in that dress."

"Never, never, never," said Emily. "I dislike the paintings of themselves that people hang on their walls. It is a form of self-love." Carlo seated himself beside her and Luigia, who had been watching, immediately came out to ask if they would like a cocktail. "It's our last night. Why don't we have champagne?" suggested Emily, and so they did.

Angela really outdid herself: scampi in her special sauce, piccata of veal with green noodles, salad with Bel Paese, and one of her famous soufflés standing proudly two inches above the fluted white dish. They ate and talked and sipped their wine while Luigia and the two little girls whisked around them.

Eventually, they fell silent, partly because of the constant attention of their eager attendants, but also because at the back of both their minds was the thought of tomorrow. They had grown to know each other so well during this week of isolation, it saddened them both to part. At last the meal was over and they went out onto the terrace where Luigia had already put the coffee tray.

They sat down silently on the swing, and Luigia asked if they wanted more champagne. They agreed they did, so she appeared again carrying the champagne in a large glass bucket, followed by the two little girls, bringing glasses and green almonds and amaretti. When they had gone, Carlo said something in rapid Italian to Luigia that Emily did not understand. Luigia was grinning from ear to ear, particularly as Carlo was putting something into her hand. Bowing and scraping, Luigia backed away into the house, closing the door behind her. "What were you telling her, and were you giving her a tip?" demanded Emily.

"Yes, I was giving her a tip," answered Carlo. "It is often done in Italy when one dines at a friend's house, particularly after such a perfect dinner. I told her it was for herself and Angela with my thanks."

"And why did she close the door?" asked Emily. "The door is never closed."

"I told her to close it—" Carlo moved a little closer "—because I said that I had something important to tell you and wanted no interference."

"Good heavens," exclaimed Emily, moving a cushion behind her neck. "What is it you have to tell me?"

"That I love you," said Carlo, putting his arms around her and kissing her gently. Emily lay silently in his arms; so he began to kiss her ears, her neck, and the top where her evening dress ended.

Emily closed her eyes. This was delicious, but she suddenly pulled herself away. "Don't, Carlo," she said softly, "please don't."

Carlo kissed her on her mouth to stop her—and it did. Between kisses Carlo whispered how much he loved her, reciting all the things he loved about her. Emily responded with equal rapture, telling him how much the week had meant to her. Then the swing began to move and they sat up and looked at each other and laughed. "May I put you to bed?" asked Carlo, holding her hand and then kissing every finger. "I want to see you in bed."

Emily shook her head. "No, the servants," she said. "It is

not right. They would know and I would be the scandal of Portofino."

"That's absurd," argued Carlo. "They sleep like logs. Come with me. I will show you what to do." He took her by the hand and led her down the corridor, turning out the lights as they went and making her take off her shoes. As he took off his, they tiptoed past the door that led up to the servants' quarters, then up the stairs, past Elsa's room and into Emily's at the far end of the hall.

At dawn, Emily had tears in her eyes as she locked the front door behind him. Climbing back up the stairs, she nearly fell on the ruffled edge of her dressing gown. Once back in her no longer monastic bed, not even knowing why she did it, she wept bitterly and fell asleep just as the sun began to filter through the shutters.

### CHAPTER THIRTEEN

# IRMA HAS PLANS FOR CHARLIE AND VISITS THE DOCTOR

WHILE EMILY WAS BLISSFUL, THINGS WERE NOT GOING SO felicitously with Irma and Charlie. The trip across in the *Paris* had not been too bad for Charlie. Irma had led such a secluded life that to watch people dancing was like seeing a circus for the first time. She was fascinated and though appalled by the gyrations, never wanted to go to bed. Charlie, who, on Irma's orders, was only allowed one after-dinner drink, could hardly keep his eyes open, waited impatiently for her to go to bed so that he could go to the bar for a stiff whiskey.

London was not so bad because when Irma visited the cardiologist, Charlie could go off his leash and made a few friends at the Berkeley Bar, which was just around the corner from Brown's Hotel, where they were staying. Brown's Hotel was favored by Battle, Ponderosa and Huddlefield. It was said to be the hotel preferred by the landed gentry when they came to London. Irma disliked it and so did Charlie. It was an acquired taste, an old-fashioned place used by those who did not wish to spend too much but who required to be recognized. Irma, never having traveled, judged everything, including the plumbing, by American standards. She liked the dining room, which was dark and small but, since she was not recognized and liked to see people kowtow, she soon decreased the size of her tips. But even the waiters, accustomed as they were to impoverished aristocrats, were insulted—a sixpence left on the table was a slap in the face—so they moved her over to the pantry door, whereupon she reduced her tip to one every other meal. At this point, Charlie started to slip something extra into the waiter's palm as they left the dining room.

It was worse when they ate at the Savoy Grill or at the Connaught. Charlie found himself digging into his own cash and began to wonder if B.P.&H. would reimburse him. It had all started on the *Paris* when Irma gave a dollar to her room steward and a dollar to Charlie to give to his.

As the days passed, Irma grew even stingier and Charlie was horrified when after her visits to the doctor and a bit of sight-seeing was over, she said that she was tired of London and wanted to go to Paris to stay at the Ritz. "I have always heard about it," she said, "and I want to take you there and give you a good time. Ooh la la." Irma, feeling that she was really gilding the lily, grimaced. "Gay Paree. Won't that be fun, Charlie?" She was wearing a large white hat garlanded with a wreath of yellow silk flowers. The saleslady at Harrods had said that all the ladies at Ascot wore such a hat. She felt quite beguiling in it.

But Charlie cringed. What had begun as a game that he was playing for the firm was now becoming a disaster. Irma seemed not to notice he had grown less attentive. Perhaps she thought he was shy because she grew fonder of him every day. The thought of Paris chilled his bones. He had never been there himself but had imagined what a joy it would be to go there with a lovely girl by his side. He felt that after this trip he would never go to Paris again. He tried to persuade Irma to change her plans, but she was adamant. "It is something I want to do for you, Charlie. You will never forget it." Miserably, Charlie agreed.

At the end of the week, they were on The Golden Arrow, the deluxe train, on their way to Paris. It was while they were lunching on the train, eating a delicious meal as they sped through the Normandy countryside abloom with poppies, that Irma bent across the table and touched Charlie's hand. "Charlie," she said, "I want you to know that I have an appointment with another doctor day after tomorrow in Paris. He will tell me if I have to have an operation." At Charlie's horrified look she added, "Nothing serious, but you might have to spend a week or ten days by yourself at the Ritz. Would you mind?"

Charlie almost jumped from the table but quickly managed an anxious expression. "You say it is not serious, but any operation is serious." He started to say, at your age, but caught himself just in time. "I am so sorry to hear about it, but couldn't you wait until we get back to New York? Perhaps we should go home now."

Irma smiled her usual smile. "Not for *this* operation," she said. "Only here in Paris." Charlie wondered what on earth it could be. Mrs. Shrewsbury looked in the pink of condition. She kept smiling her knowing smile from under her dreadful flowered hat and hung on to Charlie on the way back to their seats as though she were unable to stand by herself.

Charlie dreaded going to the Ritz. It had been bad enough at Brown's, but what would happen at the Ritz once she started tipping? They would probably end up in the staff's dining room.

When they arrived at the Ritz, the doorman and porters were surprised to see an elderly lady and a young man with so little luggage. Irma, having seen Emily's luggage, had decided to travel light and had instructed Charlie to do likewise. She tipped neither doorman nor porter, but they surmised that she must be one of those old American ladies who gave lavish tips at the end of the visit. The assistant manager escorted them to a palatial suite facing the Place Vendôme. It was like a private house with old paneled *boiserie*, a huge crystal chandelier hanging from the ornate ceiling, and gilt chairs sprinkled between a couple of comfortable sofas done in rich brocade. There were bouquets of flowers everywhere, a bowl of fruit, and a silver bucket with a bottle of champagne.

When the obsequious assistant manager had gone, Irma turned to Charlie. "This is my surprise," she said. "How do you like it?" Charlie did not know how to answer. Had Mrs. S. gone mad? "I did it for you," continued Irma. "It is usually reserved for royalty. You have been very good to me, Charlie, and I appreciate it. I want you to know that I want to keep you in my life. I can do a lot for you; in fact, I intend to. I can push you up in the firm. I can give you tips on stocks to make money for yourself. You, in return, must be like a son or . . ." she hesitated, "a nephew to me. We can take trips together, go all over the world. I have never traveled, but now with you, we can just go on one interesting cruise after another." She stopped and looked at Charlie.

He had to say something. They were standing there face to face under the great chandelier. If the floor had opened under Charlie, he would have welcomed it. However, here he was in Paris with no chance of getting away from her and had to make the best of it for the time being. So he took her hand and kissed it and, reaching into his innermost self for strength, he smiled sweetly and said, "You are too good to me, Mrs. S.

I can't tell you how I am moved by what you say and how much I appreciate your great thoughtfulness and interest. I don't know if I can live up to it. Truly, Mrs. S., you exaggerate my qualities if you think I am worthy of all that attention. I am truly stunned."

"I knew it would surprise you. You are a modest young man. That's one of the things I like about you—and, Charlie . . ." She hesitated. "I never thought that I would need affection. James and I were always so busy these last years, we never were very—what shall I say?—personal. But now, I *do* feel the need for affection. I have all the money I want. I need something else in my life. I need someone to look after me and whom *I* can look after."

"I will do what I can," said Charlie. "You are a wonderful woman; but this is all such a surprise for me."

Irma went to the champagne bottle and handed it to him. "Let's drink to the future," she said. "Then we can unpack and get out our Baedekers, do a little sight-seeing, and come back and have dinner here."

Charlie drank to the future, but in this fancy room felt most uncertain about everything. What had happened to the old Charlie Hopeland, who could talk himself out of any situation? Once in his room, he threw back the satin cover and lay on his bed, knowing that if he wanted to he could probably marry the old girl. The poor old thing was sex-starved. But Charlie, ambitious as he was, was not ready to give up his freedom at any price. The idea of an around-the-world cruise made him shudder. Also, he knew Mrs. S. well enough now to know that once she really had him in her clutches, she would be as stingy with him as she was with her tipping. Suddenly an idea came to him. Mr. Ponderosa, was he in Paris now? Charlie jumped off the bed and opened his briefcase. He found in it his address book with the name of the hotel where

Mr. Ponderosa always stayed in Paris. The Hotel d'Orsay on the left bank, on the Quai d'Orsay, near the Foreign Office. The firm did a lot of business with the government. Charlie asked the operator to get him Mr. Ponderosa and, miracle of miracles, she had Mr. Ponderosa on the phone in a minute. "You just caught me," said Mr. Ponderosa. "I was going out. I heard through the firm you were going to be at the Ritz in the Royal Suite. Are you calling because you need some advice?"

Charlie hardly waited for Mr. Ponderosa to finish. "I need your help urgently, Mr. Ponderosa," he said hoarsely.

"What's up?" queried Mr. Ponderosa.

"Well, things have gotten out of hand," said Charlie. "Mrs. Shrewsbury practically wants to adopt me. Mr. Ponderosa, I can't take it anymore. When can I see you?"

"I tell you what," said Mr. Ponderosa, who didn't like the idea of Irma's adopting Charlie any more than Charlie did. "I was going to dine with a French lawyer friend of mine, but I will put him off. Let's say that you and Irma meet me in the bar on the Cambon side of the Ritz at seven-thirty and I will take you out to dinner, either there or at Laperouse. I'll try and size up the situation. Don't lose your head, my boy," and he hung up.

Charlie breathed a sigh of relief. Mr. Ponderosa was a rock to cling to. He then called Mrs. Shrewsbury's room and told her the good news. She did not seem as pleased as he was.

"We did not come to Paris to see Mr. Ponderosa," she said icily, "but I will be there at seven-thirty," and hung up.

Mr. Ponderosa arrived at 7:15 and settled himself in his favorite corner of the bar. He was immediately brought an ice-cold martini with an olive in it by the waiter who knew him well. The idea of Irma's making a fool of herself did not please him at all. He had imagined that she might fall for Charlie, but that she could dream of adopting him was a different matter. Mr. Ponderosa had other plans for her. He sat there musing. The place was filled with people having drinks at the end of the day—mostly Americans living in Paris, and a few French. It was too early for the predinner crowd, but Mr. Ponderosa, knowing Irma, had suggested the early hour.

He was right, because she and Charlie arrived on the dot of seven-thirty and all Irma said was, "Hello, Wendell. I hope you two don't want to drink too much as I am hungry, although I wouldn't mind a Manhattan." When she sat down and Mr. Ponderosa ordered the drinks, she became more gracious. "It's nice to see you," she added. "Charlie and I have been having such a good time. He wants to do everything to please me. I should give you a finder's fee, Wendell, for finding me such a good companion." She smiled at Charlie. "I don't want this trip to end. Bella Vista will be quite lonely."

"I am glad you have enjoyed yourselves," said Mr. Ponderosa, preferring to ignore her reference to Bella Vista. He then proceeded to quiz them as to what plays they had seen in London, what sight-seeing they had done and had they driven into the countryside? It turned out that they had done nothing.

These questions made Charlie look very glum indeed. What could he tell people when he got home? How could he explain that Mrs. S. wanted nothing but him? They had walked, they had talked a bit, and they had eaten three meals a day in their hotel, and that was it.

Mr. Ponderosa looked worried. He had had no idea that it was as bad as that. Looking at Charlie, he thought that he seemed thin and wan, whereas Irma looked almost aggressively healthy and even had lipstick on and a bit of rouge on her cheeks. As she gulped down her Manhattan, Mr. Ponderosa was appalled. Was the old girl taking to booze? Mr. Ponderosa decided to lift the burden from Charlie's shoulders for the evening. He began to flatter Irma, telling her how clever she was, how she was admired on Wall Street. "One day you might be the first woman to have a seat on the stock exchange." He said that if she started a firm of her own, people would flock to it. "They trust your vision," he told her.

Then he decided to take them to Maxim's for dinner, where they sat on a banquette near the entrance so they could see the people coming in. Mr. Ponderosa did not know them all, but he knew who most of them were, and he peppered his talk with anecdotes of each and every one. Irma, in spite of herself, was interested, while Charlie looked with longing at the pretty young women who flocked in. At least with Mr. Ponderosa there, they wouldn't think he was a gigolo.

They left just as most people were arriving. Irma said she had to see a doctor in the morning. While she was in the ladies' room, Charlie and Mr. Ponderosa made a plan to meet in the morning, but Mr. Ponderosa wanted to know about the operation. Charlie could tell him nothing. Charlie pressed Mr. Ponderosa's hand and thanked him. "This is the best evening of the trip," he said, but he might have said, the only good evening.

The next morning Irma was off to her appointment and refused to let Charlie accompany her. "I must face it alone," she told him unaware of the pun, because actually she was going to see the famous Dr. Michel Peauchic, who did face-lifts. Elsa had secretly given her the address, and Irma had written him from Bella Vista to arrange the appointment.

His office was almost as far as Neuilly, and she was nervous when she arrived. The doctor had a charming, cheerful waiting room, and his office, too, had the same quality. The doctor himself was a youngish man with a small blond beard and bright eyes. He wore a white high-collared jacket and, despite an easy smile, was businesslike. He spoke perfect English, so that Irma had no problems telling him about Emily and that she would like to have the same procedure.

He then took her into an examining room and looked at her through a magnifying glass for a few minutes, turning her face this way and that. Then he lay down the glass. "My dear madame," he said briskly, "I am afraid that I can do nothing. You should have had this done years ago. If I did something now it would not be artistic. You would have the face of a doll. Dear madame, I cannot turn you out of here no longer looking like a plausible human being. It would be quite silly to contemplate. There is nothing wrong with your face as it is. It shows your age, but you have not taken care of yourself. I have some creams that I can recommend that may help you. But surgery—no." And he got up from his chair and led her courteously to the door, where he said good-bye, and his nurse came in with a bill for 5,000 francs. Irma was crushed. She had not expected to be turned into a beauty, but she thought she could at least look a few years younger. She was, therefore, in a bad humor when she met Charlie and Mr. Ponderosa at the Ritz.

They were sitting in chairs outside the dining room and both jumped up when they saw her. "Irma," said Wendell, bending down to give her a light kiss on the cheek. "What did the doctor say? Must you have the operation?"

"No," she snapped. "He says it is not necessary."

"What is his name?" asked Wendell. "I would like to have my doctor at home look him up, just to be on the safe side."

"I have already looked him up. There is no need to do it again. Now let's have lunch." She marched into the dining room. She certainly did not want Wendell Ponderosa to find out about Dr. Peauchic.

To make matters worse, as they sat down, the old duc de

Chienloup came up and greeted Wendell Ponderosa, who introduced Irma, explaining that she was the sister-in-law of Mrs. Codway whom he thought the *duc* had met coming over on the *Aquitania.* "Ah," exclaimed the *duc* rolling his eyes. "*Quelle jolie femme.* What a *beautiful* woman—such eyes, such skin, such hair, so young. Unfortunately, I had to go to Washington so I did not see her in New York. Is she coming to Paris?" he demanded of Irma.

"I really don't know," responded Irma sourly. "We see very little of each other."

"What a pity," said the *duc.* "Such a charming woman— so full of life. I wanted her to come to Chienloup." At this moment, fortunately, his attention was diverted by two very pretty girls who were beckoning to him from another table. "Excuse me," he said lifting Irma's lifeless hand but not kissing it. "I must join my friends." He rushed off.

"What a silly old man," said Irma, looking at the menu. "I hope you don't spend your time in Paris with people like that, Wendell." Before he could answer, she put the menu down and said, "I am sick of Paris anyway. I hate the place. All anyone thinks about here is clothes and food. And I am not interested in either. I like the English way of dressing better. How soon can we get away from here? When does the next boat sail? Find out for me, Wendell." She snapped out her remarks as though she were a noncommissioned officer drilling some rookies.

"Oh, I am sure you can get passage within the week," said Wendell soothingly. "But I have another idea. I spoke to Emily this morning. She adores Portofino and the *castello.* She has plenty of room and she suggested that you and Charlie come down for a week, then sail from Genoa on the *Conte di Savoia.*" Actually, after his morning with Charlie, Mr. Ponderosa had called Emily and asked if she would have them.

Since Wendell had called just after Carlo had left, Emily was not in a mood to see anyone, least of all Irma, so she sounded slightly put out but ended by saying that of course she would have them. (Her heart of gold sinking her again.)

Mr. Ponderosa thought that being with Emily would take the heat off Charlie and might force Irma to see how absurd the situation was; he also had another card up his sleeve, one that he had not even mentioned to Charlie. As he watched Irma now, he felt sorry for her. She obviously had had a blow of some kind. She appeared upset and barely glanced at Charlie. The duc de Chienloup had seemed to annoy her more than a silly old man should have. "Irma," he said, still speaking with a soothing voice, "you are a busy woman. You may not come to Europe again for a long time. Why not see this place where Emily is. There has been a book about it called *The Enchanted April* by Lady Russell. It is supposed to be very romantic and beautiful. It would be something different for you. Then after a week there, a nice leisurely trip home on the *Conte di Savoia*. The purser, Count Passarini, is a friend of mine and will treat you like a queen."

Irma shrugged her shoulders. "I don't want to be treated like a queen. I hate people kowtowing to me."

Charlie exchanged a look with Mr. Ponderosa. "What about you, Charlie? Would you like that?" said Mr. Ponderosa jovially.

"I think it sounds absolutely great," said Charlie. "I would love to go there, and I think it would be great fun for Mrs. Shrewsbury, too. We could have a good time there."

Irma, looking at Charlie's face all aglow with enthusiasm, felt guilty. She had not seen him look like that for a long time.

"All right, Charlie," she said slowly. "If you want to go that much, I will go. As you say, it might be good for me."

"Oh, thanks, Mrs. S.," exclaimed Charlie. "You are a real brick. I think it will be good for us both. I agree with you. I want to leave Paris."

Mr. Ponderosa cleared his throat. "Well, it's settled, then. Charlie can get compartments on the Rome Express, and I will call Emily. Also, to make you even happier, I hope to join you for a day or two at the end of your visit." He laughed.

They laughed too. Charlie laughed the loudest. "It's going to be a real treat, Mrs. S.," he said.

"And the trip home," murmured Irma, thinking with a tinge of regret of the things she might have done in Paris. This trip would be twice as long. "That will be nice, too."

The air had been cleared, and they were all in a good humor. In fact it was too good. Fate had other things in store for them, for Mr. Ponderosa, a busy man, quite forgot to call Emily to tell her that Irma and Charlie were on their way.

### CHAPTER FOURTEEN

# REGGIE'S YACHT ARRIVES AND THERE IS TENSION IN THE AIR

THE MORNING AFTER CARLO LEFT, EMILY WOKE UP EARLIER than usual but did not leap out of bed as she normally did. Instead she lay there quietly, reluctant to start the day. Finally, she pulled herself together and opened the shutters. She looked down at the cypress tree and beyond to the blue water shimmering in the morning sunshine. She leaned out the window to breathe in deeply the clear, fresh air and in doing so, she saw the great white yacht lying outside the harbor, almost as far away as Parragi. An American flag flew from her stern and a small Italian flag fluttered at her mast. As she looked, she also saw a launch containing two sailors and a man in a captain's cap coming toward Portofino. She turned from the window, her heart sinking. She was in no mood to take on Molly and Reggie. There was, however, no escape. Within the hour, while she was finishing her breakfast on the terrace, Luigia came out in her habitual rush waving a letter which, she said, an American sailor had brought up. She gave it to Emily and then produced the binoculars from behind her back. "Will the signora permit me to use the glasses to look at the beautiful American ship?"

Emily said yes and slit open her letter. It was in Molly's schoolgirl hand and full of "I can't tell you in a letter," and "I must see you privately," and signed "Wretchedly yours, Molly. P.S. What about lunch on board or in port?" Emily sighed. That was that.

"O, scusi, signora," said Luigia, "I was so excited to see the big boat, I forgot to tell you the sailor is waiting for an answer."

What can I possibly say? thought Emily. I am hooked for lunch. Would it be easier to get away from them if I say to meet at Nino's—or more polite if I ask them here? She decided she wanted to get away from them. She needed her siesta and, after her wonderful night, she needed to be alone. In any event, she was trapped and foresaw a dinner at the *castello* and lunch on the yacht. If they came for dinner she would ask Lady Carter and that rather odd young man. What a dinner party that would be! Olga and Franz and Reggie and Molly—and she, poor Emily, as the extra woman. Not that she minded being an extra woman in that group, not with those men. This thought cheered her a bit. At least if she were deprived, she had had something far better than any of them. She had read somewhere that, generally speaking, most people during an average lifetime really lived about twelve hours. She had had Ben, and now she had had a whole week—alive, happy, and responsive to everything around her: the sky, the sea, the trees, the flowers, the noises, and . . . Carlo. Their night together was the exquisite culmination of the week, as they became spiritually and physically one person. She must think of herself as lucky.

She looked at her watch. It was just eleven, and she had said 12:30 at Nino's in her note to Molly. She had to get busy and order the meal at Nino's. *Lupo di mare*—rather like bass, but more delicate and a specialty of the surrounding bay and sea—followed by salad and cheese and zabaglione. She would get Luigia to order and also tell her that they might have a dinner party that night. She dressed leisurely, looking at the yacht a couple of times through her binoculars, but could see little as they had the awnings up over the afterdeck. Eventually, she pulled herself together and set off down the cobblestone path.

The clock was just striking 12:30 when she arrived at the piazza. The snappy launch with its dark blue cushions was being tied up alongside the small quai by an immaculately turned-out sailor. Some of the fishermen had already clustered around, and the children stopped playing, gaping instead in a circle, occasionally trying to aid the sailor, who remained unperturbed.

Molly was helped out of the launch first, then Olga, Franz, and Reggie. Both Molly and Olga wore culottes, Molly in white, Olga in dark blue. Molly wore an immense floppy hat with a poppy in front, and Olga wore a boy's cap. Franz was in a dark suit, but Reggie had on white duck trousers and a blazer with brass buttons and the insignia of the New York Yacht Club on the pocket. He wore a cap trimmed with black braid.

Molly and Reggie waved on seeing Emily, and Molly ran toward her, arms outstretched. She literally threw herself on Emily as she whispered, "God, I am happy to see you. All is over between Reggie and me." The others arrived just as she was kissing Emily on both cheeks. Franz and Olga were moderate in their welcome, but Reggie also kissed Emily, whispering, "It's a mess. I need your help." After these salutations and a brief glance around the piazza, and followed by two-thirds of the children, they took refuge under Nino's awning and ordered campari and soda all around.

"Tell me about your trip," said Emily, wishing to keep everything as low-key and natural as possible.

Reggie, being the captain, started first. Perfect trip over. Eight days to Gibraltar, only one bad day. Then Algiers, where they took a trip into the mountains to see the famous monkeys. After that the whole Riviera, ending up in Monte Carlo, where they had the most glorious time. All of them ran into old pals at the Hotel de Paris, so they spent their time dancing and gambling every night, all night. "Great fun," declared Reggie, looking rather defiantly at Molly. "Lots of Molly's pals."

"Do not forget the grand duke," interposed Olga. "So handsome, so elegant. A true Russian."

"If you like old men," said Molly. "He looked at bit seedy to me."

Olga pushed her drink away. "You do not recognize a real aristocrat. You British are like tribal barbarians, you like only your own people. Very narrow and stupid."

Molly lit a cigarette. "It's lucky we are that way," she said. "It keeps away boring foreigners."

"What—" began Olga, her face flushing, but Franz put his hand on her shoulder and stopped her, saying something rapidly in Russian.

"Well, anyway," said Reggie, "I thought we had a good time." Then, raising his glass to Emily, he said, "Cheerio. It is great to be here with you, Emily."

"It is great to have you," repeated Emily, thinking that it was going to be worse than she thought. "And there is my house, that little castle on the hill—" She waved her hand toward it. They all turned and looked and admitted that they had been looking at it through binoculars and admiring it.

Eventually things calmed down a bit. Reggie tried his best to put some life into the gathering, and Molly joined in (anything to be one up on the dreaded Olga). Franz, who was an intelligent man, usually talkative, said little; and Olga remained inscrutable, smiling to herself in a way that annoyed Emily. It could not be said that it was much of a party, even though Nino had done a wonderful job at producing on such short notice a truly delectable fish.

They were just finishing their espressos when Emily saw Lady Carter walking down from the telegraph office and asked Nino to tell Lady Carter that she wanted to speak to her. Sybil came over at once, looking very chic in a bright red, tight-fitting sweater and an extremely short blue linen skirt. Emily introduced her and asked her to join them for an espresso, which she did. Emily explained that Lady Carter lived in Portofino and knew everything about the entire neighborhood—where to eat, where to sightsee, where to shop. Sybil with a new audience was at her best, describing all the things to see and inventing a few more. She talked well, was funny, and knew when to stop. The four from the yacht decided that after going back to the yacht for a siesta, they would like to explore Parragi and Santa Margherita in the afternoon. Sybil agreed to get two carriages and to be their guide. Emily begged off, pleading a slight headache, but asked them to dine at the *castello*. Reggie would have none of that. "You two must come aboard for dinner," he insisted. "I will have the launch here for you at eight."

Though Emily would have preferred dinner at the *castello*, she had to accept. Sybil, on the other hand, was thrilled. She never mentioned Murray. They had had one of their rows, and she could imagine how furious he would be to see her stepping into a launch to dine on board the yacht, which was already ringed by the boats of the curious fishermen.

·  ·  ·

AT ten to eight promptly, Sybil arrived at the launch and
was annoyed to find Murray there talking to one of the sailors.
"Hello there, Lady Carter," he said, saluting her with two
fingers to his forehead, aping a peasant pulling his forelock.
"How is your ladyship tonight?"

"Very well, thank you," said Sybil acidly as the sailor
handed her down to another sailor in the launch.

Murray caught hold of one of the launch's brass stanchions
and leaned down toward the seated Sybil. "You didn't lose
much time, beauty. Do you always cast off your old friends
when you find new ones, particularly when the new ones are
filthy rich?"

Sybil shuddered. He had not bothered to lower his voice,
and she was sure the sailors could hear him.

"I am thinking that I'll take some of the crew into Rapallo
tonight. They are my style. These boys here say that they are
going to have time off, not much doing here, nor in Rapallo,
either. But just the same, where there's a will, there's a
way. I'll scratch up something for them. They have been on
the yacht almost three weeks, so they need some girls. Don't
you agree? *You* can imagine how they must feel."

Sybil was about to lose her temper when Emily appeared,
apologizing for being late.

"Mrs. Codway," said Murray in a suitably humble voice.
"Would it be all right if I go out in the launch with you?
The sailors are coming back to bring some of the crew ashore
and I would love to go along just to get a glimpse of the
yacht." He gave an appealing look and a boyish smile. "I
will sit up front and not bother you two girls."

"Why, of course," said Emily, thinking what an attractive
man he was, in spite of his too-tight trousers and dirty shirt.
"Come sit here with us. The sailors will be busy and three
in this case is not a crowd."

"Ah," said Murray. "We have a problem. Sybil, may I sit with you? Will you graciously permit me to do so?"

Sybil gave a fake laugh. "You *are* funny," she said, wishing to ruin his game. "Of course I will give you my gracious permission."

"You see, Mrs. Codway," he said, seating himself and taking out a paper and a bag of tobacco in order to roll a cigarette, "I have never been in a launch like this before. I have never seen a huge yacht. It is all a new scene for me and, as a writer, I find it very intriguing."

"The boats in Portofino don't interest you?" Sybil asked.

Murray shook his head. "They're not the same," he said. "The richness and style here are impossible to find in an ordinary boat rented out for a day. To be in a launch like this is a luxury. A boat in Portofino is a simple necessity."

"How absurd," said Sybil sharply, thinking his comparison was invidious. Was he comparing her to a Portofino boat? "You are becoming redundant."

Emily felt uncomfortable. They must have had a row, she thought. "We are almost there," she said. "Look how lovely the yacht looks all lighted up."

They had slowed down and were approaching the gang-plank. The ship was lighted from bow to stern, including all the portholes. Reggie and the ship's captain were standing at the top of the gangway and, as they came alongside, a man in a kilt joined them to pipe them on board.

As Emily stepped onto the gangplank, Murray caught her hand. "Good-bye, Mrs. Codway. Take care of Sybil. I am taking the sailors out to show them the sights tonight but hope to see you tomorrow."

"Come to dinner at the *castello*," said Emily as she started up the gangway. "I want you and Lady Carter."

"There you are," whispered Murray to Sybil as she too left.

"I will do you proud tomorrow." He gave her a bite on the neck.

Reggie, waiting at the top of the gangplank, was all smiles, particularly as Emily and Sybil exclaimed over the Scot who piped them aboard. "Heard him at Argyll's shoot last year, and he came down and joined us in Monte Carlo. He will pipe us in to dinner, too."

The yacht was magnificent, and Emily and Sybil oohed and aahed as they were shown around from the bridge to the galley, where the chef was busy with the dinner. The main saloon was done up in chintz, very English, with a large fireplace surrounded by a leather fender, the paneled walls were covered with prints of naval battles. The library was smaller with huge leather chairs and sporting prints on the walls. The dining room was all Queen Anne and could seat twenty-four. The eleven staterooms, each with bath, were done up in different colors.

"A crew of sixty-two. My father insists on night and day services so there are three shifts of the crew for the passengers," explained Reggie, as he finally led them out onto the stern deck where the other three were having cocktails. They seemed in a better humor and were enthusiasic about their afternoon with Sybil. Olga and Franz were particularly pleasant, but Molly and Reggie seemed jittery.

At dinner, Emily was seated on Reggie's right. Since Sybil and Olga seemed to be getting on well, Emily and Reggie were able to talk. "I have made a fool of myself," whispered Reggie. "I never really cared for Olga; it was just because she was so strange and exotic, and I was drunk most of the time. Besides, I suppose I sound like a cad," he said sipping his Margaux 1883, "but she kisses like a tigress."

"To kill," suggested Emily.

"Just about, and then suddenly she changed." His whisper

was almost inaudible. "She began to talk about money, and my financing Franz's show. Well, believe me, I began to get on to them. I suspect that Franz and Olga are a team. Father always said, 'Don't take a mistress unless she's clean.' You know what I mean—has no other connection. Fortunately, I caught on to them, Franz and Olga, before it was too late. At Monte Carlo, to be exact. In other words, I said I would never give them a cent, that the theater didn't interest me; but I think I've lost Molly. You will speak up for me, won't you, Emily?"

Then Sybil turned to ask him a question, and so Emily never had another word with him alone for the rest of dinner. After dinner the men went on deck to smoke their cigars and the ladies went to the stern, where a vast divan covered with cushions reached from one side of the ship to the other. Olga and Sybil sat in one corner, Emily and Molly in another. Molly took Emily's hand. "I have never been so miserable in my life," she whimpered. "Reggie behaved like a rotter. He was falling all over Olga and all over himself. It was disgusting. I was left with Franz, who, when one gets to know him, is not the person one originally thought he was. He was quite different in London. He seemed bored and uninterested in me, and I became rather bored with him. He never mentioned the play. I think that was the trouble, because without that we really have nothing in common. It was not until we got to Monte Carlo and I saw a whole group of my pals that Reggie suddenly sobered up, dropped Olga flat, and began buttering me up. Fat chance of my falling for all that after the way he has treated me. I don't care if I ever see him again."

"It doesn't sound as if he acted like a perfect ass," said Emily. "But you might forgive him one slip. He really is a dear at heart, but naive and foolish. He was no match for Olga; she swallowed him up."

"Oh, you should have seen her—rolling her eyes and shaking her bosom and saying, 'Reggie,' in that dreadful accent of hers."

"How did Franz like all these goings on?" demanded Emily.

Molly shrugged. "He didn't seem to care. He kept talking about wanting to get back to Vienna. It was all dreadful and boring. I don't know what to do. I was going to ask you a favor when we come to dinner tomorrow night but I shall ask you now. May I stay a day or two with you until I can pull myself together? I saw Sylvia Rutlander in St. Tropez, who wants me to share the villa with her. I might go there. I don't know." Molly squeezed Emily's hand. "I will only impose on you for a day or two, Emily dear."

Emily told her of course to come. Then the men joined them. Everyone complained of feeling tired and so the launch was called and Emily and Sybil left.

Olga and Franz went to their cabin, and Reggie and Molly were left on deck with half a bottle of champagne to finish.

"I say, Molly," Reggie said, moving closer to her on the divan. "Do forgive me. I have apologized for making a fool of myself. I have told you how sorry I am. I have promised never to be so stupid again. Why can't you forgive and forget? I am really not such a bad chap, you know."

"I do know that," agreed Molly, "but you don't seem to remember. The motto of my father's family—it's written right on the crest of the Earl of Bottomley—says Forgive but don't forget."

"That's dreadful," cried Reggie, "and impossible. How can one forgive and not forget?"

"My father always said it means appear to forgive because it's easier that way. But never, never forget. I will forgive you, Reggie. I will always be nice to you. I will ask you to my big parties, but I will never forget you and that dreadful, fearful, frightful Olga, entwined in each other's arms. It was sickening. So now I am going to bed." She threw her champagne glass on the deck and ground her heel into it. "That's my toast to you." She ran down the deck toward the saloon before Reggie could struggle off the divan.

### CHAPTER FIFTEEN

# MURRAY STARTS TO CAUSE TROUBLE AND MOLLY LEAVES THE YACHT

THE NEXT DAY PASSED PEACEFULLY FOR EMILY, WHO WAS arranging plants about the house, making bouquets of daisies, and writing letters to the Codways and to friends. Molly arrived about half past five, and they settled down in the swing. "I really was horrid to Reggie last night," explained Molly, "but I have been through a lot. Do you remember how I talked about Reggie when we were on safari in Kenya? I thought he was to be the love of my life, not just a walk-out. It would have been so different, married to an American and with all that money to be able to go where one wanted, not chained to those dreary old cows and pigs in Hampshire."

"Do you mind if I ask a direct question?" said Emily.

"Of course not. That's what I need."

"Well, were you really so much in love with Reggie, or was it his money and a chance to change your life?"

Molly looked away. She had not expected such a question. Then she turned back to face Emily. "It was both. I *did* love Reggie, and I *did* want to change my life, and of course being tremendously rich would have been fun."

"What about the theater? You were so anxious to act."

"Oh." Molly hid her face in her hands for a moment. "That is the worst of all. I overheard Franz saying to Reggie today that if he did not want to back the show, there would be no part for me. Franz said that was why he and Olga had come to America. I think they only came to find a backer and a theater. They saw that Reggie and I were in love and thought that he would certainly pay to give me pleasure. Can you imagine anything so humiliating and horrible? I overheard them from my cabin while they were on deck. I almost screamed." Molly burst into tears. "Thank God I brought my luggage with me here. I could not spend another night on that yacht. I wish to heaven they were not coming for dinner tonight."

Emily tried to console her, but she kept on crying and saying that her life was over and that she had a frightful headache. "Just lie back quietly," suggested Emily soothingly, "while I go and get some aspirin for you."

As she returned from her bedroom and was passing the front door, she saw the porters who carried luggage up from the square standing just outside. Luigia got to the door just as Emily did to find Irma and Charlie Hopeland there. Emily was aghast. "Irma," she cried. "How extraordinary. Where did you come from?"

"Not extraordinary at all," responded Irma. "It seems to me more extraordinary that there was no one to meet us at Santa Margherita, nor anyone to tell us how to get to this godforsaken place."

"But I didn't know that you were coming," protested Emily. "Seeing you is the first I have heard of it."

"Well." Irma sniffed. "Wendell said he would telephone, and we telegraphed four days ago, giving you the time of our arrival. When we didn't hear from you, we thought you might be off on a trip; but I knew that the house was well staffed, so we came anyway."

"I am terribly sorry, but I never got the telegram or the telephone call." Emily was annoyed. Had Irma just presumed to come whether she was in residence or not? It seemed pretty cheeky. Luigia, who had been listening, now spoke up. "The telegraph office has been closed this week," she said. "The postmistress had to go to Camogli for her aunt's funeral."

Irma snorted. "Fine place you have chosen, Emily. At the end of the world, up a cobbled path, and no way of communicating with the outside."

"The view is divine," said Emily. "Wait till you see it."

"I hate views," answered Irma, "and I am exhausted. Could I see my room?"

Emily looked at Luigia. She wanted to get back to Molly. "Show the signora and the signor the guest rooms facing the village and tip the luggage men."

Charlie Hopeland came forward to shake Emily's hand. "I am so sorry that we took you by surprise. I was worried when we got no reply, but Mrs. S. said Mr. Ponderosa had called you, and she seemed to think it was all right. Mrs. S. just today telegraphed that she was arriving, and Mr. Ponderosa must have forgotten to phone. We came on the Rome Express, but then we went to Rapallo by mistake, had lunch there, had all sorts of adventures getting here; but here we are. I certainly hope that it is not too much of an inconvenience." He added as Irma had already disappeared upstairs, "I feel quite embarrassed."

Emily began to like him better and patted him on the

shoulder. "Don't worry. I did ask Irma to come originally and I have got rooms, so it is quite all right. We have people for dinner tonight. Go ask Luigia, the maid, to tell Irma that, will you. Dinner at eight, informal."

"Great," said Charlie heartily. "I may come down before, if that's all right."

"Anytime," said Emily cheerily as she scuttled away to look after the miserable Molly.

For Charlie it was a godsend to be at the *castello*. He already felt more at ease, even though they had gotten off to a bad start. After a month with Irma, a little scene like the one he had just witnessed meant nothing. Now, at last, he was going to be with other people and could be himself.

So while Emily was consoling the distraught Molly and Irma was sulking, Charlie was whistling softly to himself as he unpacked, occasionally looking out the window high above the ground with a view of the path and part of the village. In about half an hour, Luigia brought him some tea, which he drank while lying on the bed. He could vaguely hear Irma next door talking to Elsa. Thank God, she wasn't calling on him to help, nor was there a room telephone. A happy thought was that Mr. Ponderosa would soon be in Portofino to take the burden off his shoulders. Mr. Ponderosa had promised him that!

On board the yacht, things were glum. Olga and Franz were leaving for Vienna in the morning by a roundabout train route; while Reggie had engaged a car to drive him to Paris, stopping one night at the Hotel de Paris in Monte Carlo. The yacht was going on to Cowes. As he watched one of the stewards packing, Reggie felt sad. He and Molly had been so discreet in London that they had both been looking forward enormously to being free in New York. It had seemed too good to be true. Then he had ruined it. Why? Reggie was not given to introspection and rarely questioned why he did what he did. He simply went along having a good time, not worrying about anything, knowing that for him, things usually turned out all right. Looking back now, he wondered perhaps if part of Molly's charm was that they could not see each other all the time. Their love affair had consisted of many late-night telephone calls, lunch in out-of-the-way restaurants, and an occasional night at a little inn either in England or France. Molly always arrived breathless, looking pretty, smelling delicious, and very anxious to know everything he had done since they had last met. She hung on his every word and was extravagant in her praise.

But in New York she had begun to take him for granted. Seeing him every day had made her speak out on her own instead of waiting for him to take the initiative. He found this less attractive. She had had this other couple in tow, and she seemed more interested in getting a stupid job in the theater than she was in Reggie. Thinking back on it, it seemed to him it was all her fault for being so egotistical—going on about her career; instead of listening to Reggie, hanging on the words of that second-rate producer. As Reggie thought back, it quite enraged him that he had been taken in so easily. Molly had used him to come to America and to further her own ends. As Reggie tied a silk scarf around his neck and the steward put a cornflower in his buttonhole, he made up his mind that he would remain a bachelor all his life with just an affair now and then when he felt like it. None of this being tied down and expected to do this and that. No, siree. He remembered his father saying to him, "Never marry your mistress, Reggie." How right he was. As for Olga, he reckoned that the whole episode came from being bored with Molly. Olga was available; in fact, she threw herself at Reggie. It was not an affair, just an episode, and Reggie decided that since he had been drunk most of the time, he could really write it all off. He had heard someone say that to be bored can be dangerous. It had almost been dangerous for him; but when he sobered up, he realized what a game they were all playing. Now that he had seen through them, he was himself again. Reggie, the man about town, the best shot in America, the most welcome member of ten clubs. He was someone and he must not forget it.

Having bolstered himself in this fashion, he went up on deck to the bar in the stern to have a drink before going to the *castello*.

He found Olga already there, smoking a Balkan Sobranie, lying back in a chair with her eyes half closed. Reggie asked the steward for a stinger and walked over politely, drawing up a chair in order to sit near her.

"So—Lady Chatwood has gone. She left you flat, as you people say." Olga gave a harsh laugh. "Poor Reggie. It's sad; but you were too good for her. She is a spoiled little beetch."

Reggie drank half his stinger. "She is just a good, old friend." Reggie felt he must behave like a gentleman. "We will see her tonight at the *castello*."

"Not much fun anymore, this old friend," said Olga slyly. "Perhaps because she knew that Franz would not have let her on the stage if he had not thought that you would back her." Olga laughed. "She had the talent of a cow."

Reggie stood up. "I say, Olga. You are being rather crude."

Olga stood up too. She put her arms around Reggie and stuck her tongue in his mouth. Reggie backed away nervously. "Not in front of the steward," he said, wiping his mouth off with his pocket handkerchief. "Let's go get into the launch. I see Franz coming down the deck."

Olga threw her empty vodka glass over her shoulder into the sea. "I make a wish to get back to civilization someday," she said as they walked toward the gangway. Reggie reckoned that the chief steward would not be pleased that he now had only twenty-three pieces out of two complete sets of glasses.

Sybil did not wait for Murray but went up by herself to the *castello*. She had not seen him all day and had no idea what he was doing. Her imagination ran riot with visions of Murray and the sailors carousing in squalor. Rapallo was about as wild as Eaton Square. How could Murray even find a brothel? He must have been there before. These thoughts did not put her in a very good mood, and she forced a smile on her face when she greeted Emily.

Emily was standing under the pine trees with Molly and a sharp-looking older woman in a black crepe dress accompanied by a very good-looking young man in a white dinner jacket. Sybil shook hands with the old lady, but when she shook hands with the young man, she held his hand a moment longer, then stood beside him. "Are you and your mother staying here?" she asked.

"Yes, we are staying here," answered Charlie. "But the lady is not my mother. She is Mrs. Codway's sister-in-law." How relieved he felt to be able to put some distance between himself and Irma by exploiting her relationship to Emily.

They stood talking casually until the group from the yacht arrived, and then they sat down, while Luigia and the two pigtailed little girls rushed about with drinks. As time passed, Sybil began to get nervous, particularly as Emily called out to her, "Do you think that your friend understood that it was eight o'clock?"

"Yes, I am sure he understood," said Sybil, not liking to be singled out as Murray's friend. "He must have been delayed. I would not wait for him though, if I were you."

Luigia seemed anxious and whispered to Emily. "We will wait ten minutes more," said Emily. "Then we will go in.

We have a scampi soufflé to start with. Angela is so proud of her soufflés; we mustn't let it fall."

"Pride comes before a fall," Sybil whispered to Charlie, and he laughed uproariously as though she had made the greatest bon mot in the world. His relief at having his freedom was so great that anything would seem amusing.

At this moment, Murray appeared. Emily rose to greet him and at first, in the dim light, could not see him clearly; but as he approached the garden lamps, she saw that he wore a clean white shirt but with it was wearing an extremely short pair of black bathing trunks, so short that Emily at first thought it was just a *cache sexe*. He was also barefoot. Murray shook her hand warmly. "I am delighted to be here," he said. "Particularly as Sybil told me it was to be an informal occasion."

Sybil, having told him no such thing, felt like throwing herself over the parapet. The wicked bastard. She could have strangled him before jumping! Emily did not bat an eye. She had forgotten his name so she mumbled, "I want you to meet . . . er-er-er."

Reggie stiffened and was very formal. Franz and Olga seemed not to notice his odd attire. Molly laughed as she said, "Hello."

It was Irma who flashed her eyes and gave Emily a look that clearly said she had always known Emily associated with people decent Americans would not permit to cross their threshold. These people could not even make the gossip columns, was her opinion.

Irma's look, however, was placid compared to Sybil's, especially as Emily left Murray with her and went back to Reggie. "Hello, honey," said Murray, holding on to her hand and giving her a smoochy kiss. "How's my little puss tonight? Introduce me to your friend."

Sybil glanced at him. "This is Murray Kent, who lives in the piazza," she said. "This is Mr. Hopeland."

Charlie shook his hand, but his reaction was the same as Reggie's, worst of all, by Murray's accent he knew that he was a fellow American. He said, "How do you do?" and would have continued his conversation with Sybil, but Murray was ready for that.

"It sure is nice to meet some real Americans," he said, speaking with a Southern accent. "You folks staying long? Sybil and I can show you around. Isn't that right, toots?"

Sybil froze. With all his faults, Murray could speak perfectly good English. Why then did he put on this strange accent? She stepped hard on his bare foot. "Goddamn it," he said in his normal voice. "What in the hell are you trying to do. Maim me for life?"

"No," said Sybil, "just stop you from playing your game, whatever it is. You look obscene and are behaving in character."

Charlie could hardly believe his ears. Fortunately, whatever reply Murray was about to make was drowned by Luigia, beating a gong with all her force to announce dinner.

Emily had not heard this exchange of greetings, but she gathered from their looks that they were in very bad tempers. To separate them, she put Murray next to Irma, and Sybil next to Charlie. She herself took Franz on one side, Reggie on the other next to Molly. As she looked around the table, she thought that this first dinner party was going to be a mess. Fate may have thrust these people on her, but it was her own fault to have tried to get them together and make an occasion of it. She had probably made it worse by her seating arrangements.

Murray was talking to Irma, and she was giving him all her attention. Fortunately, Emily could not hear him. "It is so wonderful to meet a real lady like you, Mrs. Shrewsbury," he was saying. "There are so many crazy women around, like that Lady Carter across the table. You know what they call her in Portofino?"

"No," said Irma with interest.

"They call her Sybil the Siren because she plays a tune to every man she sees. Just look at her now."

Irma looked, and her small but bright eyes flashed from under her drooping eyelids. Charlie was bending solicitously toward Sybil, who had tears of rage in her eyes which he mistook for wounded feelings, and which aroused his Boy Scout instincts. He was begging her not to cry and was saying that he wished that he had punched Murray in the face.

Sybil smiled through her tears and put her hand on Charlie's. "You are very dear," she murmured.

"Did you say that she is called Lady Carter?" queried Irma, noting all this.

"Yes. She is relict of poor Lancelot Carter, a decent fellow if ever there was one." Murray shook his head. "Poor fellow, it was too much for him."

"You mean that *she* was." Irma kept on looking at Charlie and Sybil.

"Yes, ma'am." Murray went back to his Southern accent. "That's what they say. Mind you, I'm not one to spread tales, but the poor man . . . well—I really don't like to say it, but they found him in bed, an empty bottle by his side."

"Bottle of what?" asked Irma, not up on those things.

"Pills. Must have swallowed the whole lot. He had suffered enough. He wanted to go. God rest his spirit."

"Enough of what?" Again Irma questioned Murray, who thought she was pretty slow. He had finished off Lancelot very neatly. Something had to be left to the imagination. However, this silly old girl was keen on the scent. He had better spell it out for her.

"Ma'am," he said solemnly, "it was her carryings-on that

got to him. One man after another. Lancelot was afraid of
scandal. He might even lose his knighthood. It was terrible.
I was a good friend of his." If Lancelot could have risen
from his grave at this moment, he certainly would have.

By this time, Irma was glaring so across the table that
Charlie noticed and, looking away from Sybil, turned to face
her. He smiled, but she scowled back and shook her head
fiercely. He was at a loss to understand what to think, so
he returned to Sybil, slightly perturbed. "I think that man
Murray what's-his-name is talking about us to Mrs. Shrewsbury. I can't imagine what it is, but she's furious."

Sybil threw a contemptuous glance at Murray. "Whatever
it is, you may be sure it's making trouble."

"Is he in love with you?" asked Charlie. "I can understand that."

"No. He's not in love with me. He's only in love with
himself," said Sybil. "But since you ask, I'll tell you. I was
lonely here. There was no one else. He is physically attractive—at least I thought so at the time—but he has been
acting worse and worse. I can't stand him anymore."

Charlie caught her hand under the table. It was heaven
for him to be talking to an attractive woman who had been
hurt by a dreadful, unfeeling man, and who was now turning
to him for comfort. After these weeks with Irma, Charlie
needed some comforting himself. So they talked during the
entire dinner and Charlie told how he happened to be with
Irma for the firm's sake, not knowing how arduous it would
be. "I suppose she fell in love with you," said Sybil.

"Well, in a way," said Charlie modestly. "She wants to
adopt me."

Sybil looked across and caught Irma's baleful eye. "I
suppose she's very rich?"

"Millions," responded Charlie, "but believe me, I would
rather beg in the streets than be tied to her for life."

Sybil pressed her knee against his. "I like your spirit," she said. "People are such money-grubbers these days. It's disgusting. There is so much more to life than possessing things. How many houses or yachts or servants or jewels or cars can one want?"

"How about books?" interposed Charlie. "Do you like to read?"

"Love to," said Sybil. "At home in my little flat in London, I can spend the whole day reading by the fire. Have you read *Lady Chatterley's Lover*? It's just out."

"I know," said Charlie. "But they won't allow it in the U.S.A. It's censored. What is it about exactly?"

"A woman, Lady Chatterley, who has a husband who is paralyzed from the waist down. So she proceeds to have an affair with the groom. That's the story in a nutshell."

"It doesn't sound so strange to me," said Charlie.

"Nor to me," said Sybil as they rose from the table. "It is the story of my life!"

### CHAPTER SIXTEEN

# CHARLIE IS AT
# STARVATION CORNER
# AND IRMA HAS A COLD

THINGS GOT WORSE WHEN THE GUESTS WENT OUT TO THE garden to have their coffee. Olga had been eyeing Murray all evening and advanced toward him as he and Irma emerged from the dining room. "Come talk with me," she said imperiously, taking Murray by the arm. "I have never seen anyone like you since I saw the Cossacks riding, hanging from their horses by one stirrup. We have many things to say together."

Murray, having succeeded in blackening Sybil's character, was now content to leave Irma. "Excuse me, ma'am," he said, bowing deeply, "but I must talk to this foreign lady. We Americans must not see only each other." Off he went with Olga to a dark spot beneath the trees.

Irma stood there, for the first time in her life unsure of herself. Emily, noticing this, came up at once, bringing Molly with her. "You are tired, Irma dear. Do come and sit down with Molly and me."

Irma did as she was bid, but after they had ensconced her

in a chair, she wanted to know where Charlie was. She did not have to ask because there he was, behind her, bending over her solicitously. "Are you all right, Mrs. S.?" he asked anxiously. "You must be very tired. You have been a brick to stay up so late."

"You were wonderful at dinner," remarked Emily, who was losing her sensitivity. "I saw you talking so animatedly with Murray what's-his-name. What was he saying?"

"He was telling me about the death of Lady Carter's husband," said Irma grimly. "The poor man killed himself."

As none of the others knew anything about Sybil Carter's past, they all agreed how sad it was. Sad for poor Lady Carter.

"Not sad at all for her," explained Irma, sneezing. "She drove him to it—quite a scandal. That young man told me he almost lost his knighthood. Did you hear of that in England?" She looked at Molly.

"Not a word," said Molly, "but then there are so many knights. I believe that Lady Carter said he was in the Foreign Service. Almost all of them get knighted if they can stick it out long enough."

Charlie stood rigidly behind Irma. He did not believe what Irma was saying. Lady Carter seemed to him the perfect English lady—far more so than Lady Chatwood, who he felt was a stupid snob. After his week with Irma, Sybil seemed fresh and young. Suppose she'd had several love affairs. So what? At this moment in his life he was not looking for a virgin. He was at starvation corner!

"Well, it's really not our business to pry into Lady Carter's past," remonstrated Emily. "However Sir Lancelot died, he obviously did not leave her well off. She seems quite hard up."

"I don't believe all that." Charlie spoke up. "I think that Kent has had too much to drink."

Irma looked at him sternly. "Don't be a fool, Charlie," she

said. "I sat next to him at dinner and he was as sober as I
am. He was a great friend of Sir Lancelot's."

Molly laughed. "That does sound odd. Somehow I can't
imagine a stuffy old civil servant and Murray Kent being
friends."

"Neither can I," agreed Emily. "Actually, between ourselves, I wouldn't trust Murray Kent as far as I could see
him."

Irma rose. "I think I am a pretty good judge of character
and I like him. Now, Charlie, I feel a cold coming on; will
you please walk me up to my bedroom? The hall is so badly
lit, I am afraid to try it alone." So they departed, Irma sneezing two or three times.

Olga and Murray under the pine tree were getting along
beautifully. Murray dropped his Southern accent and what
he considered his folksy charm, assuming instead the role of
the intellectual writer. Tolstoy and Turgenev and Chekhov
rolled off his tongue as he lightly ran his hand up Olga's
bare arm.

"You understand Russia. You know the sadness of my life.
To be away from St. Petersburg . . . Ah, if only once more I
could walk along the Nevsky Prospect. If I could drive
through the snow to my father's dacha, if I could dance once
more with my beloved grand duke. Now, what is left for me
—nothing, nothing. Happiness, love, beauty—all gone. My
soul is torn. My heart is broken." In the moment of intense
feeling, she caught his hand and put it against her cheek. "I
am a wounded bird," she murmured.

Molly and Emily had joined Sybil, Reggie, and Franz.
Reggie was sulking. He and Molly had hardly spoken during
dinner, and now he sat apart smoking his cigar, while Sybil
and Franz were getting on famously. Molly came and sat
down next to Reggie and began to whisper to him, as she

did not want Franz to hear what she was saying. Reggie cheered up a bit; after all, one could not behave like a cad. Emily joined Franz and Sybil, thereby allowing Sybil to say her good-byes and to remark that it was late—she must leave. Whereupon she left to say good-bye to Olga, arriving at the very moment that Olga had Murray's hand on her cheek, which had encouraged him to kiss her ear.

"Miss Nitzkoff, I have come to say good night and good-bye," said Sybil loudly.

Murray sat up, but Olga still held his hand. "Good-bye, Lady Carter. Sad you must go. Life is a series of good-byes." Olka kissed the inside of Murray's hand as she said this.

Sybil drew herself up stiffly, every inch the relict of Sir Lancelot. "This good-bye is not sad to me. I am very glad to say it. Good-bye to you both." She turned and almost fell into the arms of Charlie Hopeland, who, having deposited Irma in her room, was looking for Sybil.

"Let's get away from here quickly," hissed Sybil, dragging Charlie toward the other side of the garden against the wall of the parapet. Safely there, she took out her handkerchief and burst into tears.

Charlie drew her toward him so that her head rested on his shoulder. "What is it?" he asked. "Please don't cry. Can I help?"

Sybil stifled her sobs with her handkerchief. "There's nothing you can do," she whispered. "Except perhaps, if you can do it, never let that bastard come to the *castello* again. I hate him."

"I don't like him either," said Charlie sturdily. "I took a dislike to him the moment I saw him. Looks like a boor to me."

"You have sized him up properly," responded Sybil, taking out her powder puff. "Do I look a fright?"

Charlie could hardly see her in the darkness, but he told her that she looked great, in fact, beautiful.

"Some day I will tell you about Murray," said Sybil. "He is a total fraud."

"Was he a great friend of your husband's?" asked Charlie.

Sybil's tears dried instantly and she literally roared with laughter, in fact she became hysterical. "A friend of Lancelot's? How could you imagine such a thing? Lancelot wouldn't have Murray black his boots for him."

"He knew him, though." Charlie wanted to set the record straight.

Sybil renewed her laughter. "Of course not. I only met Murray this spring in London. Then he followed me to Portofino. I have only known him a couple of months. Whatever made you think he knew Lancelot?"

Charlie did not want to tell her, so he simply said he thought he might have been an old friend.

"Well, now you know. He is *not* an old friend, and never can be." Sybil, after this cryptic remark, started to move away, but Charlie caught her hand.

"I think that Mrs. Shrewsbury is catching a cold. She says that when she gets a cold, she stays in her room and drinks hot lemon juice. If she does, I'm free. Free as air. Could we take a long walk tomorrow or go out in a boat?"

Sybil tossed her head.

"Could we?" Charlie pleaded.

"We certainly can. I will call you in the morning. Now I must go."

Charlie looked around, a habit he had acquired since he had been traveling with Irma. "I am coming with you," he said. "Let's just leave without telling the others."

"I have already said my good-byes," responded Sybil. So they left, keeping as far away from Emily and the others as possible. They proceeded down that rocky and dangerous path, talking in whispers and guided in the darkness by the intermittent flashes of Charlie's flashlight.

Eventually, the others got talked out. Molly had told Reggie what she had overheard Olga and Franz saying, and Reggie told her what Franz had said to him. They agreed that it was lucky for them to be let off so easily, although Molly felt humiliated that her stage career had never been taken seriously. Reggie begged her to go on to Monte Carlo with him "just as a friend" if Molly was upset, but Molly said no. She needed to think about her future. Reggie kissed her lightly on the cheek and said it was time to go back to the yacht and where was Olga? Franz, who had seen her disappear with Murray into the dark shadows, called out loudly in Russian and did not move until after his second call. Olga answered. "Olga will join us immediately," he told Reggie, who nodded. They both knew Olga. A few minutes later, Olga and Murray walked toward them. Olga's hair, which was usually in a tight bun, was hanging loose about her shoulders. "I am a gypsy," and she sang a few bars of *"Otchi Tchornia"* as she held a long white arm out in farewell.

"Where's Sybil?" asked Murray.

"I believe she must have left," said Emily.

Murray smiled. "A willful woman," he said.

THE next morning, Irma had a really bad cold. They could hear her sneezing and coughing all down the second-floor hall. Charlie heard it in the morning when he came down for a late breakfast. "It's too bad about Irma," said Emily, who put down the *New York Herald* in order to say good morning. "She has no fever, fortunately, but she must stay in bed. Luigia and Elsa are looking after her." Emily went back to the paper. She was reading an article about Mussolini. He seemed to be doing a very good job getting the trains to run on time, looking after the poor, and keeping a strong government together; also, there was talk that he might sign a peace treaty within the year with the Vatican, which would be a tremendous step forward in the unity of Italy. Emily remembered talking to Carlo about these things and wished that he were with her now. She wondered if he ever thought of her. He was so much in her thoughts. She felt so close to him that she could not believe that he did not know it. Why had she not heard from him? Charlie interrupted her thoughts.

"Mrs. Codway," he said rather nervously, "would you mind if I went off for a walk and a picnic with Lady Carter?"

Emily put the paper down. "Of course not. Why should I?"

"I just wondered if you wanted me to hang around in case Mrs. Shrewsbury wanted something."

The only thing she could want would be you, Emily wanted to say. She had never like Charlie. She thought him entirely out for the main chance. Whatever happened on the trip with Irma had only intensified Irma's need for him. He may have pretended that it was for the firm, thought Emily, but it was really only for himself. Irma had murmured to Emily something about wanting to adopt him, which had horrified Emily. She had never thought Irma capable of being seduced so easily. Now, she looked Charlie in the face and said, sharply, "I am sure that Mrs. Shrewsbury will be quite all right without you."

Charlie did not like the tone of her voice, but then he had never liked Emily. As she returned to her paper, he finished his breakfast hurriedly and left. Emily put down her copy of the *Herald* as soon as he had left the *castello*. It seemed to her that after the many years of tranquility, she was suddenly caught up in a whirlwind. She wished that she had never come to the *castello*. No. That was not quite right.

She was enchanted with the place. She had had one wonderful week. It was only that habit she had of asking people to visit her that had been her undoing. Why on earth couldn't she have come here quietly by herself?

As she lay there, Molly came out to say that she had already walked out to the lighthouse and now wanted some coffee. "I couldn't sleep last night," she said as she seated herself, "thinking of all the things I've done that I ought not to have done, and left undone those things I ought to have done."

Emily almost fell out of her chair on hearing Molly quote the prayer book. Was she going crazy? "Heavens, Molly," she exclaimed. "Are you all right?"

"Of course I am," answered Molly crossly. "Don't be silly. I was thinking that here I am, twenty-four years old, running around all over the place, expecting to go from here to Sylvia in St. Tropez after spending a most unhappy month in New York and yachting in an absurd, vulgar yacht. What will I do with Sylvia, who is fun but totally mad? Just the same old round . . . dancing the Charleston and the tango, drinking champagne, and flirting with some silly man. What I ought to do is go back to George. That is, if he still wants me. There are worse things in life than living in a beautiful house surrounded by thousands of acres and listening to the cattle lowing and the sheep baaing."

"What about George? Do you think that you can stand him now?"

Molly flared up. "Of course I can. Thinking of him compared to the men I have seen recently, he really is a pet. Dull, but dear. He will make a very good father."

Emily was dumbfounded. Was it possible for such a change to be sincere, particularly about George being a good father? Molly had always declared that children bored her.

"In fact," said Molly, looking at her wristwatch, "I think, if you don't mind, I will just put in a call now to George. He should be in the estate office." She jumped up and ran into the house.

Emily picked up *The Well of Loneliness* by Radclyffe Hall, which had just come out and was very controversial. It had only arrived that morning in a box of other books sent down from London. She had hoped to spend hours reading in the garden, which up to now she had not been able to do. She wondered if anyone had ever had such a group of guests and asked herself if Sir Lancelot Carter had really committed suicide. Sybil did seem a bit too keen on picking up a new man. Also the fact that Murray appeared so intimate with her cheapened her in Emily's eye. As she cut the pages of the first edition of *The Well of Loneliness* she heard Molly laughing and shouting "darling" in the hall. The squeals and inarticulate sentences floated back to Emily for the next half hour. Finally Molly rushed out and threw herself down on the chaise longue. "He was adorable," she told Emily. "Absolutely divine. He said that this was the happiest day of his life, that he had known all along that if he gave me my head, I would eventually return to my stall. He says that I will turn into a wonderful mare and he knows that we will have high-spirited foals. Isn't that funny and dear? I had quite forgotten that, under that stuffiness, is such a dear, kind, understanding person. The only condition I made was that I always wanted to be in London in June and in Biarritz part of September. He said June, yes; but he would have to think about Biarritz. He doesn't trust me with the frogs, nor really with anyone, I suppose. He never said a word about Reggie. Wasn't that divine?" Molly threw her head back and laughed. "I just can't believe it. It will be fun to go back and drive around in a dog cart and have all the villagers rush out when

I go by. It bored me before, but after what I've been through with Reggie and Franz, it seems like heaven. I think that I will go down and catch that eleven o'clock bus to Santa Margherita. I want to get my ticket to London. *A bientôt.*" And she was off.

Emily picked up her book again. All the others seemed to know what they wanted. She alone was a refugee from life. Why had she become the understudy when up to now she had always played the lead?

### Chapter Seventeen

# Carlo Goes to Rome to See His Parents

WHEN CARLO HAD LEFT PORTOFINO, HE DROVE DIRECTLY TO his farm in Tuscany. It was late in the afternoon when he arrived, so he worked at his desk where he had dinner and then went to bed. The next morning, he rose early and went around the farm with the *fattore*. The spring is a busy time on a farm, and Carlo loved walking over his fields and discussing crops. He worked all day, and it was only in the late afternoon when he had changed out of his working clothes into his smoking jacket that the English governess brought his little girl, Carmela, to visit him.

She was four years old and pretty, fair like her mother with curly golden hair and large blue eyes. She came and climbed onto Carlo's knee and put her arms around his neck. "I love you, Papa," she said. "Why don't you stay here? Why do you go away so much?"

Why indeed? He could not say that he went because the house was empty and lonely. He could not tell this child that, to him, a house without a woman was like a snail without a shell. So he kissed her and jumped her up and down on his knee and fed her cakes from the tea tray and built card houses for her, which she knocked down with shrieks of delight. After half an hour, the governess came back and said that it was time for Carmela's bath.

"We must stick to our routine, excellence," she said primly. "After our bath, we have our supper. Then we play a little. If you want to say good night, she will be in bed when you go down to dinner."

"How is Carmela doing in her lessons?" asked Carlo, standing up.

"She is doing very well indeed. She knows all her multiplication tables and does addition and subtraction. You have a bright little daughter, excellence."

Camela took her governess's hand. "Sometimes I am naughty," she said. "I won't eat my pudding. Then Miss Bland makes me stay longer at my lessons."

Miss Bland smiled. "She's hardly ever naughty."

Carmela came up and stood in front of Carlo. "Why don't I have a mummy? All my friends have one. Where is Mummy?"

Carlo knelt beside her. "I told you, darling, that God took Mummy to heaven, but someday he might send us another mummy. Would you like that?"

"Oh, I would, I would," cried Carmela, who was only four and had not read *Cinderella*. Miss Bland pursed her lips. She did not like the idea of a stranger coming between her and her darling charge. What sort of a person would the prince bring back? Probably some silly girl who would immediately start producing children in order to put Carmela in the shade. Miss Bland had had to leave her last position when such a thing happened. Just then Carlo rose to his feet, and gave Carmela a kiss, and said good night.

Miss Bland smiled at him. If he was looking for a wife,

why not the woman who really cared for his child? "It makes us so happy to have you at home. It means everything to us," she said in her most refined and gracious way.

Carlo was annoyed by her always using the plural. Also she seemed to be simpering; perhaps it was time for a change. It was not good for Carmela to have such a possessive person. He gave Miss Bland a curt nod and said that he had some telephoning to do; Carmela should take her bath and he would see her in the morning.

Miss Bland disliked his tone of dismissal, but after all, what could she expect? He never stayed long enough at the farm to get to know her. As she took Carmela's hand and they left, she decided that she should buck up—try harder, dress better and, in doing so, show the prince that she was a lady, not bad looking, and a real mother to his child.

After they left, Carlo walked over to the window and looked out across the fields to the red tiled roofs of the small village. The sun was setting, shedding a rosy glow over the landscape, just touching the spire of the church where the bells were clanging in a hearty Italian fashion for the evening service. The field below the house was being plowed by a pair of white oxen, and a flock of white doves was returning to the cote by the farmyard door—a scene of utter tranquility in direct contrast to Carlo's feelings. Carlo pulled out his case and lit a cigarette. He was putting off the ordeal of telephoning his mistress, the Contessa Giovanna Malaponte. He had bad news for her and the sooner he gave it to her, the better.

Though Giovanna Malaponte was his mistress, she was not a kept woman. She was thirty, unmarried, rich and a contessa in her own right. She was also pretty, petulant, and passionate, quite capable of making a frightful row. Carlo sat by the telephone for a long time before he put the call in to her in Florence. She answered the phone herself and gave her usual cry of pleasure on hearing his voice. "Dearest," she said breathlessly, "dearest darling. Where are you? When are you coming here? What have you been doing? Do you still love me? Tell me quickly?"

Carlo hesitated a moment.

"You have found someone else? You are tired of me; I hear it in your voice. You hate me, and I have loved you so much. I have turned down so many men just to be with you. What are you thinking of doing? Tell me, am I to be cast out like an old shoe?"

"Please don't talk like that," said Carlo, preferring at that moment peace at any price. "Giovanna, I am calling to say that I am going to Rome to see my parents and I wanted to stop by and see you. Will you be there?"

"Of course, I am always here." (Which was not true, as she had just returned home that morning from visiting a relative in Venice.) "When will you arrive? I will have your favorite *osso bucco* for you. The one that my Maria makes."

"I will be there tomorrow night, fairly late as I must work on the farm in the morning, then lunch with Carmela. An early lunch."

He could almost see Giovanna pouting. "Must you stay for that child? She is so young. She does not know one day from another. Come early, and we can buy a beautiful doll for her together here in Florence."

"I am so very sorry." Carlo was firm. "I cannot change my plans, Giovanna. Good night."

"Say you love me," demanded Giovanna.

"I love you," said Carlo. "Good night." And he hung up.

Giovanna had always been jealous, but he had not minded it too much. He certainly preferred jealousy to indifference;

however, her behavior tonight had irritated him. It was going to make the trip to Florence even worse than he had expected. His mind dwelt on her lack of interest in Carmela. If Giovanna had ever had any idea that he would marry her, her indifference to Carmela ended it. In the beginning he had, as lovers do, murmured about the joys of life together; but in the last two years, his feelings had simmered down to being only a physical attraction, which sooner or later can easily be transferred to a newcomer.

Carlo sighed and called his family in Rome. They were just having dinner, so he told the butler when he planned to arrive at the Palazzo Pontevecchio. He had no idea what he would say to his family. In fact, he hardly knew what was in his own mind. Was he truly in love with Emily after only a week? Was it worth it to go against all the tradition of his family and marry a woman who was older and, what was worse, not an Italian? On his way to bed, he stopped at Carmela's room and looked at her sleeping so peacefully, one little arm thrust out across the pillow, a little angel and so in need of care and love.

He was sad when he went to his room, so he picked a worn copy of the *Divine Comedy* from the bookshelf. He had not read it since he was a schoolboy, but it appealed to him tonight. Must he, too, go through Hell and Purgatory in order to reach Heaven? He read straight through while eating dinner and then in bed, until he fell asleep. It was what he needed.

THE evening with Giovanna was not as bad as he thought it would be. He decided not to say that he was in love with someone else. He hard hardly admitted it to himself, so why end on  a bad note with Giovanna? He went to bed with her as a matter of course but felt it hardly counted anymore. He was quite proud of himself.

He set off early the next morning for Rome amid happy farewells from Giovanna. It would be easier to write her.

He drove like the wind in his Bugatti, passing everything and everyone on the road, much to the fury of the other motorists and irate farmers with their livestock. He used to drive in the races and he still loved feeling what he could get out of the car. The car was marvelous to handle, and he felt as though he and the car were one. He sang as he drove, stopped for a bite, then on again, arriving in Rome in plenty of time to go to his own apartment in the palazzo where he changed for dinner. A note awaited him, saying that his parents had their aperitif at 7:30, and would expect him then. He dawdled over his mail, then descended to the *piano nobile*—the main floor where his parents lived in lofty state.

He found them in one of the smaller drawing rooms, sitting in their usual chairs near a window on the garden. A footman was pouring out tiny glasses of sherry (a habit the *duca* had picked up in England). As they never served anything else, Carlo, after he had kissed his father and mother, asked for the same. They talked about the various properties, asked lovingly about Carmela and when she was coming to visit them.

The *duca* was immersed in the family and its continued well-being, and he and his wife were proud of Carlo. His good character, his affectionate nature, and good sense were a great comfort to them. They suffered with him in his loss, but as Carlo well knew, they felt he had mourned long enough. They wished him to remarry, a subject they had broached many times before but did not bring up again until they had finished dinner and were back in the drawing room and the servants had retired.

"Well, Carlo," said the *duca*. "You are looking very well and fit. Have you perhaps some more personal news for us which you did not care to discuss before the servants?"

"You have just come from Florence, I understand," inter-posed his mother, who had heard of Giovanna and did not like the idea at all.

Carlo, not having mentioned Florence, was surprised at how quickly the grapevine worked; however, with cousins, aunts, uncles, nephews, and nieces scattered all over Italy, his life was an open book.

"Yes. I spent a night there," he said, "but I hurried through in order to get down to Rome to you."

Carlo's father also knew about Giovanna and agreed with his wife that it would be a most unsuitable match. The girl was supposed to be very wild and bad tempered; however, Carlo had no wife and, until he did have one, the *duca* felt they had to put up with a few escapades. "You wished to tell us something?" queried his father, leaning back in his chair.

"Yes, I do—that is, in a way I do." Carlo paused. How should he put it to them? "I want your advice."

His mother drew a long breath. What a relief. The dear boy (still a boy to her) wanted advice.

"You remember I went over to New York on business just recently and while there I met a very attractive woman—an American. In fact she was on the *Aquitania* and I had met her several times in Rome." He saw his father frown and so hurried on. "I saw quite a bit of her in New York although I was only there a couple of days. After that, I had to go to Chicago, as you perhaps remember, to see about machinery for the farm. Well . . ." Carlo felt uneasy. His parents were hanging on his every word. "I never saw this lady again until I went to Portofino. She had rented the *castello* there, the little one that Yeats Brown owned, and as we were both alone, I saw her constantly that week. I fell in love. Very much in love, as she did, too, I think. I said good-bye as though it were to be forever, but I find it cannot be so. I love her very much I would like to ask her to marry me."

"Who is she, my son?" the *duca* said.

"She is, as I said, an American. A widow, very much a lady, a charming, delightful, well-educated person."

"How old?" asked his mother.

"I think she is in her middle fifties." It hurt Carlo to tell what he thought was the truth.

"Middle fifties!" exclaimed the *duca*. "If she tells you that, she is probably sixty. Good god, do you want an old woman as a wife?"

Carlo restrained himself. "The American women keep themselves very young-looking. She could easily pass for forty, but I don't care what her age is. She is the first woman that I have really loved since Teresa died."

"I agree with your father," said his mother. "You are crazy to want to marry an old woman who cannot give you children."

"I do not want any more children," said Carlo. "Carmela is enough for me. There will be no competition. Emily will love her like her own."

"She has children, this lady?" asked the *duca*.

"No." Carlo shook his head.

His mother threw up her hands and got up. "I am going to bed. You and your father can talk. I am too upset." And she left them.

His father lost no time after his wife's departure. "My son," he said jovially, man to man, "now that your mother has left us, why not have this lady as a *chère amie?* There is no need to marry her."

"There is no need. You are right, Father. The only need is for me to have a wife I love."

"What about an heir? You do not care if the family name dies with you?"

"No need to have it die. One of my cousins can take it after I go, or before, if you wish."

His father shook his head. "I do not wish to do such a thing, but I cannot understand your stubbornness."

They argued back and forth until way past the *duca*'s bedtime, but not acrimoniously. Their respect and love for each other were too great for that; but they were sad when at last they went to bed.

Carlo stayed in Rome for four days. There was much family business to be transacted, as the Pontevecchios not only owned land but also city real estate and a small bank. Father and son agreed on all these matters and they had some congenial lunches at the Caccia Club; but on the last night, alone, the three of them at the palazzo went back in earnest to the topic which was uppermost in their minds—the marriage! The more his family protested, the more valuable Emily became in Carlo's eyes. He was like a very young man again. His mother, noticing this, was moved. After all, Carlo's happiness meant a great deal to her. His father, though slightly mollified to learn that Emily was extremely well off, still wished for a young Italian woman. "There are so many beautiful young women of good family right here in Rome, my dear son. Why an elderly foreigner?"

At long last, the visit was over. Carlo kissed them both, noticing the tears in his mother's eyes. "You are hurting your father," she whispered. "He is too civilized to show it, but he is wounded."

Carlo pressed her hand. "Dearest Mama. I am very sad, too." But he did not give in.

Back at his farm the next day, the first thing he did was to sit down at his desk to write to Emily. He was Dante writing to Beatrice.

CHAPTER EIGHTEEN

# CHARLIE ROUNDS STARVATION CORNER AND FALLS FROM HIS PEDESTAL

WHAT MR. PONDEROSA HAD NOT TOLD IRMA AND CHARLIE WAS what had happened a few days before. It was after a tiring day battling with lawyers that Mr. Ponderosa walked into the Cambon side bar of the Ritz to have his usual extra dry martini. When he arrived, he found to his surprise that a young man was already seated at the corner table that was always reserved for him. He stood in the doorway until he could catch the eye of the bartender, and then showed his annoyance by standing still and nodding his head toward the table. The bartender, who over the years had grown fond of Mr. Ponderosa, was horrified by this error. He dashed out from behind the bar and, berating his new young assistant, who did the serving at the tables, went directly to Mr. Ponderosa's table and with false smiles and gesticulations blamed the utter stupidity of his assistant and begged the present occupant of the table to move to the next table if he would be so kind. The man at the table immediately gave in to these persuasions and, picking up his glass, moved it and himself to the table adjacent to the favored seat. Mr. Ponderosa then, accompanied by the bartender and his disgraced assistant, moved majestically to his accustomed place, whereupon he ordered a double martini. "With an olive, monsieur," said the bartender, smiling ingratiatingly, knowing that his client always had one.

"No," said Mr. Ponderosa, being willful. "This time I want a small onion." He pulled a folded copy of *Le Monde* out of his pocket to stop the conversation. He started to read at once. There was an editorial on a cabinet appointment that might easily influence the outcome of the case he was working on. It would be in favor of his client, and his mood was softened. When the delicious drink was reverently put in front of him, he put the paper down beside him and had just lifted the martini to his lips for that first invigorating sip when he heard his name spoken. He put down his drink and turned his large head with its mane of white hair to face the person who had called his name. It was the young man who had been at his table and was now within elbow distance of him.

"I'm Joe Shrewsbury," said the young man, putting out his hand. "I thought it was you, but wasn't quite sure if you recognized me."

"Of course I didn't," said Mr. Ponderosa, "or I should have spoken to you." He gave Joe a sharp looking-over. It was no wonder that he had not recognized him. No longer was Joe trying to look like a gangster. This was a young man in a plain gray three-piece suit, with a conservative cravat, his hair carefully brushed back from a side part. He could have passed for a junior partner in B.P.&H.

Mr. Ponderosa's curiosity was aroused. "It would be hard to recognize you," he said, laughing. "What have you done to yourself, my boy? What made you change so?"

It was Joe's turn to laugh. "A touch of success, and, like a snake I've shed my skin. Do you like my new façade?"

Mr. Ponderosa resented Joe's flippancy, but he wished to get to the point. "Far better than your last one," he said. "But what's happened? It's only a couple of months since I saw you, and why are you here?"

Joe edged closer to him. "Mr. Ponderosa, it really reads like a dime novel; I'll tell you of my metamorphosis, but only if you promise not to repeat anything I say until I say so."

Mr. Ponderosa, more intrigued than ever though annoyed that his probity could be questioned, said in a solemn voice, "How do you think I became a senior partner in my firm? No lawyer worth his salt ever repeats anything, no matter how trivial it is. Perhaps that is why we lawyers are such poor conversationalists."

"First of all, Mr. Ponderosa, I never really was the crazy fellow I appeared to be. I couldn't stand the life my parents led. They had never paid much attention to me, so I simply did what I knew would hurt them the most."

Mr. Ponderosa laughed. "So what are you doing now?"

Then Joe told him his extraordinary piece of news, and how it had changed his whole life and attitude.

Mr. Ponderosa hung on his every word and was transfixed as Joe, once started, continued to talk on and on. This was a Joe that he'd never heard before. Mr. Ponderosa turned things over in his mind. If this news could astonish him who was accustomed to the bizarre, it might turn the trick with Irma. He put his hand on Joe's shoulder. "Listen, dear boy," he said. "I was thinking of going to Portofino to see Irma and Emily. Now, after what you've told me, I am determined to go; but we must go together."

"No, Mr. Ponderosa. I really don't think I can do that," said Joe. "I don't believe Mother would care for it. I really just came to Europe to have a short holiday."

"She will care for it if you tell her what you have just told me. *That* will warm her up." Mr. Ponderosa himself warmed to his subject. "I tell you what—we will drive down there, spend the night in Monte Carlo, try our luck there, then go on that beautiful, perilous road along the sea to Genoa and Portofino."

Joe shook his head.

"Be a sport, Joe," urged Mr. Ponderosa. "Do it for me. I want to see Irma's face when you tell her your news." He laughed heartily.

Joe laughed too. The writer in him was stirred by the thought of such a meeting with his mother. "O.K., Mr. Ponderosa," he said. "You win. When do we start?"

"I have to do a few things at the Quai d'Orsay, but that won't take much time. What about day after tomorrow? I want your mother to be settled down in Portofino before we get there." Mr. Ponderosa got up. "I am dining at the Travellers Club, but I will call Emily to tell her that we are coming and will meet you at nine A.M. day after tomorrow. Where are you staying?"

"At Foyot's, on the left bank," responded Joe, also rising.

"Great," said Mr. Ponderosa. "I am at the Hotel-Palais d'Orsay on the left bank too, near the Foreign Office; so there is no problem of distance. I will engage the car and will pick you up." He hurried off and Joe was left to finish his drink and ruminate on this sudden change of plans.

Joe was not sure at all if it were the right thing to do or even if he wanted to do it, but Mr. Ponderosa's good humor and good will had overcome his judgment. He left after a second drink to go up to Nini's at the top of Montmartre, where he had a rendezvous with some girls whom he had met on the boat coming over. He had broken off entirely with Annabelle—at least she had broken off with him. The idea of being attached to a stuffy businessman did not appeal to her at all. "I don't want to sit in an opera box with a tiara on my head," she had said, "waving my hand and saying 'There is Mrs. Jones and there's Mrs. Smith, and give me some smelling salts because Mrs. Blank is wearing the same dress I have on.' No, Joe, that's not for this gal—I've still got some life in me. I want *fun*, not some robber baron's money." They had a scene after that, and she began to sprinkle four-letter words through her conversation. The Vassar and Bryn Mawr girls he had met on the boat suited him better now.

Irma had been in bed for three and a half days, indulged in every whim by Luigia and Elsa. "Open the window, shut the window. I want orange juice. Why bring me orange juice when I asked for grape juice? No grape juice here—how absurd. What a country. Just bring me more bottled water. I want a blanket. It is too hot . . ." These plaintive bleats not only had the immediate attendants half out of their wits, but the entire household was disturbed. Now, at the end of three and a half days at siesta time when no one was about, Irma suddenly decided to get up. She also wanted to find out where Charlie was. She missed him. She had not wanted him in her room because she felt that she did not look well, but now that she was beginning to feel like herself again, she began to wonder why he had never knocked at her door or sent a message. Actually, only Emily had done that. As she tied the sash of her old camel's hair dressing gown, she decided to take a look around. She looked down the hall, but all the bedroom doors were closed; so she went down the stone steps, past the window on the landing where the flowers of the giant magnolia tree were pressing against the glass, past the front door and then along the front hall which opened onto the garden.

At first she saw no one in the garden. Then she spied Luigia leaning over the parapet. She started toward her, and, as she got closer, she saw that Luigia had a pair of binoculars and was looking at something intently. So intent was Luigia that when Irma spoke to her, Luigia turned and almost fell.

"Where is everyone?" demanded Irma.

"Siesta time, signora," explained Luigia. "Everybody asleep."

"What were you looking at?" asked Irma. "I would like to see it."

"No, no, signora." Luigia's voice rose. "It was nothing, just a big fish passing by."

"I would like to see it, too. I have not seen an interesting thing since I have been here," declared Irma. "Give me the glasses."

Luigia tightened her grip. "These are very poor binoculars, signora. Very old ones, and very bad for the eyes."

Irma held out her hands. "I want them." Her tone was imperious.

Luigia gave them to her reluctantly and then, without a word, rushed away into the *castello*.

Irma took her time. She wiped the lenses thoroughly with a piece of tissue that she had in her pocket. After that, she adjusted the glasses to her eyes. Then she sought the place where Luigia had been standing, and raised the binoculars. At first, she saw only the sea, and far away a fishing boat. Then leaning forward as Luigia had been doing, she focused her sight on the rocks beneath the *castello*. To begin with, she saw only two heads and four legs lying between two beach towels. As she continued looking, she realized that the two people who were sound asleep entwined in each other's arms were Charlie Hopeland and Sybil Carter. Irma analyzed every detail. Sybil's head on Charlie's shoulder, his lips and nose buried in her hair, one of his hands lay carelessly clasped on Sybil's rounded breast. Through the glasses, Irma could see them breathing in unison. It was the hour of the siesta. Irma

threw the glasses down and, turning from the wall, let out a
piercing screech. Emily, who had a window on the garden
as well as over the sea, flung open the shutters when she heard
the cry. "Irma, what is it? I am coming right down."

Irma continued to scream so that by the time Emily got
down to her, she was red in the face, holding her breath like
a child in a tantrum. Luigia, who had run out with a pitcher
of water, at this point was throwing it over Irma's face.

Emily was horrified, but the water stopped Irma. "Oh, *la
poverina*," cried Luigia.

"*Che peccato*. What is it?" inquired Emily. "What has
happened? Did a bee sting her?"

"Look over the wall," said Luigia in Italian. "She has had
a shock. *La poverina*."

But Irma reached out feebly and caught Emily's hand.
"Send him away at once," she said. "At once, at once. Do not
let him near me. Pack his things and send him away."

"What has happened?" Emily spoke in Italian.

"La signora saw the young sir lying asleep on the rocks with
milady."

Emily almost laughed, but Irma's agony was real. James's
death had been nothing compared to this, because this time
it was of her own making. She knew that Irma's pride must be
deeply hurt. Also, Irma knew by now that Luigia, knowing
the cause of her grief, would manage to keep all of Portofino
au courant.

"Come upstairs, Irma dear," urged Emily. "Please don't
cry. I will do what you want. We will send Charlie away."

Irma covered her face with a tissue. "At once, at once," she
repeated. "Don't let me see him ever again."

Luigia tried to take Irma's arm and at the same time tried
to dry her hair; but Irma backed away from her. "You are a
nasty, dirty person," she shrieked, pulling herself free from
Luigia's hands. "Why did you tell me you were looking at a

fish? You should be dismissed from your position here. I will see that you are."

Luigia burst into tears and threw her apron over her head. "All my family work so hard. I am so very, very poor, signora. All my family are poor. How can you do such a thing to us?"

Angela came running out from the *castello* at this moment. "My poor Luigia. What is it?" she cried.

"We are all going to be dismissed," wailed Luigia. "Every member of the Doppi family. This terrible old signora will do it to us."

Angela threw her arms around Luigia. "She cannot do it," she said. "The other Americans are the padrone. They know how poor we are and how we work night and day to save them money."

"Angela is right," interposed Emily. "The signora cannot dismiss you, so stop crying. I will take the signora to her room and I will write a note to be sent down to the young gentleman on the rocks. Call Mario and get him at once so that he can deliver the letter."

All of this was said in Italian, so Irma understood nothing.

Angela and Luigia went into the *castello* in order to telephone cousin Mario the boatman, while Emily and Irma followed slowly on their way up to Irma's room.

The letter was soon written and Mario, who had rushed up from the village at a trot, was soon on his way down to the rocks. Sybil and Charlie had just put on their bathing suits and were about to pick up their towels and fishermen's dark blue pullovers, when Mario confronted them with the letter. It was addressed to Charlie, who, on reading it, blushed bright red.

"What is it? Bad news?" said Sybil, pulling her shirt over her head. Charlie silently handed the letter to her.

"Dear Charlie," it read. "I am sorry to do this to you, but Irma saw you and Sybil sleeping on the rocks. She is in a towering rage and wishes never to see you again. I am taking her up to the tower room and hope to keep her there long enough for you to come up and pack as many of your belongings as you can in a short time. Luigia will pack the rest later. I have engaged a room for you at Nino's. This seemed the best thing to do under the circumstances. Incidentally, if I were you, I would go further afield for my pleasures another time. It pays to be discreet. As ever, Emily Codway. P.S. Mr. Ponderosa is arriving here the day after tomorrow, so perhaps you should stay at Nino's until then."

"The bitches," exclaimed Sybil. "How utterly disgusting to write such a letter. That frightful Mrs. Shrewsbury must have been spying on us. They say eavesdroppers never hear any good about themselves. The same is true of spies." Mario stood by silently, enjoying the expressions on their faces. He could not understand a word, but Luigia had already informed him of the basic facts. He expected to have a fine time at the Circolo dei Pescatori that night when he went to play cards there. The other boatmen and fishermen would hang on his every word when he regaled them with what was going on at the *castello.* Sybil understood his obvious enjoyment and was torn by fury and embarrassment. Charlie could leave, but she had to stay on. She still had her Villa Contenta.

"I suppose I must go up and get some of my things," said Charlie lamely. "Will you ask Mario to wait so he can help me carry them down."

Sybil told Mario, then turned to Charlie. "I suppose it's good-bye," she said.

Charlie took her hand. "I am terribly sorry about all this," he said awkwardly. "I hate to have you mixed up in such a mess."

Sybil laughed harshly. "Nothing ventured, nothing gained," she said.

"I want you to know," Charlie continued earnestly, "how

much you have meant to me. These weeks with Mrs. Shrewsbury have really been a hell for me. You have given me a taste of heaven and have made me feel a man again, instead of a damn footstool. I can never thank you enough. I hope that we can always be friends and see each other."

"Yes, I hope so." Sybil was not sure.

"In any event, I will be at Nino's for another two days. I must wait for Mr. Ponderosa, so I hope we can still see each other here."

"Perhaps, but you must hurry now. Mrs. Codway did not seem sure how long she could keep Mrs. Shrewsbury incommunicado."

Charlie kissed her lightly on the cheek. "Good-bye for now," he said before he turned up the path to follow Mario.

Sybil stood for a moment trying to calm herself, then turned in the opposite direction, going slowly down the terraced path between the olive trees to the back *castello* gate that opened onto the end of the piazza. She had to pass Tina's, where Murray was sitting in his usual place. He waved to her, but she shook her head, whereupon he jumped up and fell into step beside her.

"What's wrong?" he asked. Sybil just shook her head and said nothing. "Come have an *americano*," urged Murray. "It will pep you up. We haven't had a good talk for a week. You've been off with that stuffed shirt and haven't given me the time of day. Let's sit down." He took her arm and dragged her toward Tina's. Sybil gave in. Besides, Murray seemed to be in one of his good moods and almost anything seemed better than being alone. She felt conspicuous under the eyes of Tina and the lace women, as she seated herself beside Murray. "That Russian," said Murray, "she was a tiger. A real zoo; but to tell you the truth, it was a fake. Nothing behind it. She had a routine. Do this, do that," he mimicked her voice.

"She sounded like a Russkie general speaking to his troops. It was fun at first, but then it was a bore. You know me, let's forget the whole damn crowd. Who are they anyway? Cheer up. Forget that s.o.b. He's just a Park Avenue gigolo."

Sybil sniffed. "I need a handkerchief."

Murray pulled what looked like a rag out of his pocket. "Now you can cry and blow your nose at the same time," he said, handing it to her. "Sybil, you know what I think?"

"No, what?" Sybil blew her nose.

"I think that you and I need a change. I'm getting stale here. Let's go to Paris or Rome or Vienna."

"Vienna." Sybil sat up. "Perhaps you want a little more of that Russian dressing. That's where she lives, isn't it?"

"Oh, to hell with that. I wasn't even thinking of her. Let's go to Budapest. Let's sit by the Danube and listen to gypsy music. Would you like that?"

Sybil shook her head.

"Well, then, what about London? Listen, Sybil." Murray crossed his arms on the table and leaned toward her. "London wouldn't be so bad. I could find some digs somewhere. I have two or three pals there. I could afford that. You could be in your flat and see your friends, but we could still be together. We know each other pretty well by now. I don't want you to go out of my life. I could write, see Bolsheviks. But we could talk on the phone and once or twice a week we could meet. How about that? Both of us free as air, but remain good, sound, old-fashioned lovers. It wouldn't be bad, would it?" He smiled beguilingly. His dark eyes gleamed.

Sybil knew that it was an act. But it tempted her. It might be amusing to lead a double life in London. The priggish Lady Carter and the wanton girlfriend of a disreputable American. And it was a way out of her present predicament. She wanted to leave Portofino at once. She hated the thought of running into the *castello* ladies. "It's not a bad idea," she told Murray. "As a matter of fact, I was thinking of leaving tomorrow. I'm fed up with it here too."

"Great." Murray clapped his hands. "Let's have another drink on that."

"All right," said Sybil, "but I would rather you came over a day or two after me. I don't want these people here to think that we've gone off together."

"Anything you say," agreed Murray. "Let's drink to your future and mine. You'll remain the great lady, and me, I'll become the great author." They clinked glasses and drank. Then they sat silently.

Sybil's thoughts were distracted as she saw Charles Hopeland walking across the piazza toward Nino's, followed by Mario carrying two large suitcases. Charlie was still in his bathing trunks. Compared to Murray, he looked pale and thin. Sybil clinked her glass fondly against Murray's. "To a great author," she murmured, as he looked at her admiringly under his long dark lashes.

### CHAPTER NINETEEN

# MORE EMOTIONS AT THE <u>CASTELLO</u>

IT WAS QUIET AT THE CASTELLO. MOLLY HAD DEPARTED FOR London, telling Emily that after all, when one really came down to it, there was nothing like being with one's own class. She longed to return to George and be the wife of the largest landowner in the county, which meant visiting the tenants, going to church every Sunday, giving dinners for crashing bores, Molly said; but nonetheless, as she also said, they would always vote the way George did. Molly was a good horse-woman and intended to make Chatwood the center for hunt meets, hunt breakfasts, and hunt balls. It has one of the "best packs in the country," said Molly; and then, of course, there were the weekend shoots when there were never less than twenty-five guns in the field. After all these activities, there would be the season in London—a weekend at Windsor, racing at Ascot, June 4th at Eton. Of course there would be children, four at least: two boys and two girls. "It is really," said Molly, her eyes sparkling, "the very best part for me to play and I was stupid not to see it before. Thank God you took me to New York, darling, and opened my eyes to how really second-class any other life would be."

Emily, although pleased by Molly's decision to return to George, was not at all pleased by Molly's notion that other lives, including Emily's own, were second-class. "It was, after all, *your* decision to come to New York, Molly," she said somewhat acidly. "I only paid for your ticket." Molly kissed her.

"Of course I don't include you, pet. You are one of *us*. You must come to stay with us at Chatwood this autumn for the shoot."

Emily was evasive. Who was Molly to look down on a Codway of Boston, particularly as Emily was now giving her a ticket back to England? "I will certainly come if I am in England," she said. "Although I rather think that I will be up in Scotland." In any event, they parted on good terms, although when Luigia came to Emily to ask if the lady really came from a noble English family, Emily guessed that Molly felt that a tip was included with her ticket.

With Molly gone and Irma brooding in her room, Emily was left to herself. Even Charlie's luggage was gone and there was no sign of him or Lady Carter. It was relaxing for Emily, but a bit of a letdown after all the excitement. As usual, she was sitting in the garden having breakfast alone when Carlo's letter was brought to her. She looked at the great crest and the postmark before she opened it. Although she had never seen Carlo's writing, of course she knew whom it was from. It was a fat, four-double-page letter. Emily settled back in her chair to read it.

It was a love letter of the most eloquent and poetic sort—full of allusions to Petrarch and quotations from Dante.

Carlo told her how much he loved her and why. He told her every minute detail of his life—even all about Giovanna. He explained where he thought his duties lay, and what he wanted to make of his life and what he felt Emily could do for Carmela. He touched on his family and said little; but he was Abelard to Heloise, Dante to Beatrice, Elizabeth Barrett to Robert Browning all in one. No romantic woman—and Emily was an incurable romantic—could ask for more. Yet Emily, when she put the letter down, was sad. This was a letter a twenty-five-year-old man might have written to a twenty-year-old girl. Could an older woman maintain such a high romantic temperature for long? For a while, yes; but even so it would be a game. There would not be much sitting by the fire in an old dressing gown with cream on one's face. Emily sighed as she reread the letter, and for the first time noticed an almost illegible postscript. "Will be in Portofino on Wednesday." Today was Tuesday. That left twenty-four hours to prepare herself, both physically and mentally. She would have to wash her hair, and do her finger- and toenails, and she must try to ready an answer for him. That wonderful week swept over her consciousness again. That was one of the drawbacks. Such bliss would be hard to relive.

Emily rose from her chair and went into the house. She wanted to ask Elsa to get out the hair dryer and curlers when she heard the telephone. Luigia was there before her. She kept shouting "*Pronto, pronto*" into the phone and seemed to be getting a very bad connection, or else there was confusion on the other end. Emily waited a moment, then started up the stairs when Luigia called her to come back.

"They are calling from the hospital in Genoa," explained Luigia excitedly. "There has been a bad accident near Nervi. The chauffeur was killed, the old gentleman in the front seat was badly hurt, and a young man hurt a little. The young man told them to call you." Emily's heart missed a beat as she took the receiver from Luigia. The person on the other end spoke poorly on a bad connection, but she managed to learn the name of the hospital where Mr. Ponderosa and Joe had been taken. She hung up and stood there a moment in a daze. What was she to do? First of all, how could she get back to Genoa? Luigia, watching and ever avid for excitement, begged the signora to let her know what was the matter. Emily, having had a moment to collect her thoughts, said that she wanted a car and chauffeur at once to take her to Genoa to the Santo Vicenzo Hospital; that a friend and a nephew had been hurt in the accident. Luigia sprang into action, telling Emily not to worry, she would find a car, as Emily slowly climbed the stone stairs to the second floor and went to knock on Irma's door.

To Irma's bark, "Come in," she entered to find her sitting in a stiff-backed chair by the window, reading the *Ladies Home Journal*. Emily was not quite sure how to break the news, but she was in such a hurry to get to the hospital that she didn't take time to soften the blow.

"Irma," she said, "there has been an accident. A bad one. I am afraid Wendell Ponderosa has been seriously hurt and Joe, apparently, has minor injuries."

"Joe." Irma leaned forward in her chair. "What is he doing here, and where are they?"

Emily sat down on the edge of the bed. "They are in Genoa. They were on their way here. Wendell called me. They met by chance in Paris and Wendell asked Joe to join him in a motor trip to end up here."

"So Wendell is badly hurt."

Emily got up. "I am afraid so. The telephone connection was poor, but the hospital said it was urgent that I come. Do you want to come too, or do you think it would be too much for you?"

Irma found these last words a challenge. She bristled. "Of course, I will come. Wendell is one of our oldest friends. James thought a great deal of him, and he has been useful to me. I must go."

"The car should be ready in half an hour," said Emily as she left the room. She was surprised and delighted that Irma wanted to go.

Irma, as she started to dress, felt strangely moved. She had begun to lose confidence in herself since the dreadful discovery of Charlie's duplicity. She wondered how older men could find happiness with younger women. Vice versa seemed impossible. She had kept the thought in the back of her mind to make Wendell her confidante concerning Charlie, whose behavior hardly became a rising member of Battle, Ponderosa, and Huddlefield. Now, whom could she turn to? She began to wish desperately that Wendell would be spared. Her experience with Charlie had hurt, but it left her wanting a partner in her life—someone to stand between her and the world. Someone to prevent her from making her own mistakes. She was frightened.

A half hour later Emily and Irma were walking across the piazza and down the little alley which led to the bus stop and the garage where the two cars allowed in Portofino were kept. One of the cars was already out, and a fisherman, but obviously the chauffeur, was standing beside it. That was perfect, but to Emily's dismay, standing talking to the chauffeur was Charlie Hopeland. She tried to push Irma to one side, but there was no way to escape. Charlie blushed on seeing them. Irma, after one look, had jumped into the car and Emily was about to follow when she suddenly remembered her postscript to Charlie. Charlie was expecting Mr. Ponderosa. Impulsively she leaned forward and opened the car window. "Charlie," she said, "we are on our way to Genoa. Wendell has been seriously hurt in a car accident. Also my nephew Joe."

Charlie lost all self-consciousness. Mr. Ponderosa was his idol and his mentor and Charlie wanted to be with him, especially after the mess with Mrs. Shrewsbury. He forgot everything else at the moment but his desire to see Mr. Ponderosa.

"I am coming with you," he said. "Mr. Ponderosa means everything to me. I would like to see what I can do for him."

Emily hesitated. She could sense Irma's fury but concluded this was a moment for magnanimity. "Get in the front seat, Charlie," she said.

He mumbled his thanks, got in, and they were off with the glass firmly closed between the chauffeur and Charlie and the two ladies. Luigia had told the chauffeur that it was a matter of life and death.

When they drove up to the hospital, they got out silently. Charlie was about to speak to Irma but after a glance at her grim face thought better of it. Since Emily was the only one who spoke Italian, she led the way to the desk. They were told to go to a waiting room and someone would come to fetch them. They sat there in a row, Charlie a little way down the line from the two ladies. Once seated, they looked around them. The room was filled with anxious faces. No one spoke; some wept silently, others noisily, interspersing their tears with cries. Most of them were fingering rosaries. From time to time a nun came up and led someone away. Emily got up once to go back to the desk to ask when they could see their friends, but was told to return to her seat. Someone would come very soon. It was nearly an hour before a young and cheerful-looking nun came up to them and asked them to come with her. She took them in the elevator to the top floor and again they were put in a small waiting room. "*Un momento*," she said, smiling, and then disappeared down the corridor. Charlie crossed and uncrossed his feet, started to light a cigarette, then seeing Irma's face, reluctantly put the cigarette back. Irma stared at the wall, while Emily looked around her. In this room death seemed almost closer, an anteroom to a morgue. At long last the same nun beckoned from the doorway. "The doctor says only one person can see the old gentleman," she said. "The doctor is in with him now." She looked at them inquiringly.

Charlie sprang to his feet before either Emily or Irma moved. "I must see Mr. Ponderosa," he said hoarsely. "He is like a father to me." He wanted to see him before Irma got to him, but to give him his due, he was truly fond of Mr. Ponderosa. Neither Emily nor Irma said anything, so Charlie went off with the smiling nun. It was the spirit of the hospital that life and death were equal, so the nuns smiled perpetually. Everything was an act of God.

Silently, Emily and Irma watched Charlie disappear into a room. What could they say? Each of them wished in her way that all would be well. Emily had never known Wendell Ponderosa as Irma had, but she liked him and admired him and enjoyed his humorous, rather cynical view of life. It was Irma now that she was thinking of, so small and wobegone, huddled up next to her. She put an arm around Irma's shoulders and found that she was shaking.

Soon, Charlie came down the corridor, followed by a nun and a doctor. All three were smiling. "This is *dottore professore* Baccigalupo," the nun said, "and we have good news. Signor Ponderosa has a broken leg and a couple of broken ribs, but there is nothing else. He was unconscious, but now he has come to."

"He smiled and he knew me." Charlie's voice broke. "He was wonderful," he said as he took out a handkerchief.

Then the doctor spoke to Emily, after asking if she spoke Italian, and told her what Charlie had already said. It had looked serious at first but now, after a few weeks in the hospital, he would be able to go back to America. Emily repeated this all to Irma, who immediately said that she would like to see him, but the doctor suggested another day. "He must be very quiet," he said.

He turned to leave when Irma said, "Where is my son? May I see him?"

Joe apparently was on another floor, so Emily and Irma left Charlie, who said he would stay in Genoa and find his own way back to Nino's to collect his things. He wanted to be near Mr. Ponderosa. Emily shook his hand warmly. For once he was behaving properly. But Irma strode ahead without a word.

Joe was sitting up in bed with a collar around his neck, eating a tortoni, and he uttered an exclamation of surprise on seeing them. "I gave them your telephone," he said, "but I never expected you here. How is Mr. Ponderosa?"

"Not too badly hurt," said Irma. "He is going to be all right. I thought I was going to lose my best friend."

"He sure is that, Mother," said Joe soberly. "He's devoted to you and Father, and is also a good friend to me. He is a wonderful old gentleman."

"Are you hurt?" asked Emily, though Joe seemed undamaged.

"Not really, just shaken up. I was in the backseat, so I only felt the impact. I've a bruise or two and a sore neck, but no more. The X rays show nothing, and I can leave almost any time."

Irma came up to him and put her hand on the coverlet of his bed. "I will come and see you tomorrow," she said, looking around the room. "It will be better for you at the *castello*. Tell me, why did you come to Europe?"

Joe smiled wanly. "I'll tell you when we have more time at the *castello*. But I hate the thought of leaving Mr. Ponderosa here. Who's taking charge?"

"Charlie Hopeland," said Emily briskly. "He's going to attend to everything. He'll stay here so as to keep Mr. Ponderosa company. After all he's a member of the firm. But we should go now. All this has been nerve-wracking. Take care of yourself, Joe." She took Irma by the arm, and they left. Emily had not forgotten that after Joe begged Irma for money it was she, Emily, who had given him $1,000. Molly had seen him at the Cotton Club. And how did he get to Paris? Did he spend the $1,000 entirely on having a good time? She had thought he had wanted it for taxes. Still, she was glad that he was all right, but she had her doubts about him now.

Irma said nothing and allowed herself to be led downstairs and out to the waiting car. For the first time she realized what a prop Wendell was in her life. She had always taken him for granted—but what a loss he would have been to her. She looked at Emily, whom she had always thought frivolous, and suddenly saw Emily's inner strength. She was not pleased. She was determined to regain her own strength. She was also determined to see Wendell again. Charlie Hopeland was not the right person to be with him, or the firm, and she would certainly tell him so. Or would she? After all, what if Wendell heard about Charlie and Lady Carter and wondered why it had upset her so? Would it be enough for her to say that such behavior was bad for the American image abroad, especially since the servants had seen everything? Was it unpatriotic for an American to behave like an animal? Then her thoughts turned to Joe. Why had he come? He looked different. What was it? "What was it?" she said aloud.

"His hair," said Emily as if she had read Irma's thoughts. "He's had a proper haircut and that makes a difference."

"Why, so he had," said Irma slowly. "What is he up to, do you suppose?" After her experience with Charlie, she was wary of young men.

"It makes him look like a businessman," explained Emily. "After all, he is a Shrewsbury."

Irma looked startled, then smiled.

### CHAPTER TWENTY

# IRMA GETS
# A SURPRISE

EMILY, WHO WAS BOTH MENTALLY AND PHYSICALLY TIRED, decided to have breakfast in bed the next morning. She was not in the mood for Luigia, who, bounding in with the tray, told her that the *principe* had called twice and wanted to know if he could come to lunch. Luigia had said that the signora was alone and it would be fine to have him. The other signora had already left early for Genoa, saying that she wanted to go to the hospital. Luigia had been able to get the same car for her. Angela was just leaving for the market so she could have fresh *fave* and some zucchini flowers to fry. All was arranged. Luigia smiling so happily implied that, with the other signora out of the way, all was prepared for the *principe*. She was very pleased with herself. She was, after all, not a nobody, but Luigia, the queen of the *castello*, and was ready for anything.

Emily sighed. At first she was annoyed but then decided there was no point in taking Luigia seriously. She looked so pleased with herself. "*Bene, bene,*" said Emily, attacking her soft-boiled egg. "What time did you invite the *principe?*"

"Twelve-thirty."

Emily looked at the clock. She had slept late. It was after ten. After Luigia left, she took Carlo's letter out from under her pillow, where she had slept on it for luck. Now she read it again. It was beautiful—a letter any woman would be pleased to receive, well written, touching. But how should she greet him and what should she say? If he really loved her, she dreaded the thought of hurting him; but could such a match be a happy one? Would the magic last? Such thoughts tormented her. To be a princess—married to one of the oldest and richest families in Italy—was not something to cast off lightly. Even if Carlo were eventually unfaithful, she was sure that he would never do anything to hurt her pride or cause gossip. If an American had written her such a letter, she would have known exactly what to do. To her, American men were an open book. She had no fear of losing an American. She was positive that she could keep one in love with her for life. But an Italian: that was a different thing. To be left alone in a vast palazzo, forced to play the part of an Italian princess when at heart she would always be an American, would be awful, thought Emily. She loved Italy. She also loved France. But the merest glimpse of the American flag waving in the breeze of a foreign country always gave her a thrill of patriotism.

Such were Emily's feelings. Whether she could stand her ground when she saw Carlo was still uncertain. She found a letter that Luigia had placed on her breakfast tray. It was from one of Ben Codway's Oxford friends, a Scotsman, the Earl of McKee, now retired from banking and living mostly in Overdrum in the Highlands, a widower who had sold his house in London and now kept only a small flat there. He was writing to say that he had been shooting at Chienloup and the old *duc* had told him about Emily and had given him her address. Also, Wendell Ponderosa, whom he had met in Paris on his way back to London, had suggested that she might like to hear from him. He was writing to ask if she could visit him at Overdrum. The garden was beautiful now. He would have a few interesting people and Emily had only to say when it would suit her, as it would give him so much pleasure to see her again. In a postscript he said how much he really longed to see her and he hoped she could stay for a long time.

Emily remembered him as a jolly man with bright blue eyes and black curly hair, turning gray. Ben was devoted to him and they had many golf games at Cypress Point. Jock McKee! She hadn't thought of him in ages; but now that she conjured him up, she remembered how clever and easygoing he was. Obviously, Wendell Ponderosa thought he was doing her a good turn in suggesting Jock write her, but it was Carlo to whom she was drawn. Jock McKee was not a man to inspire passion. Life with him would be safe but dull. She put down the letter and got up. She was glad of an alternative, but it would never be an adventure. She knew that Carlo would be persuasive. She must prepare herself for a day of decision.

IRMA had mixed emotions as she was driven at the usual breakneck speed along the winding road, but it was not the speeding car that occupied her thoughts. What worried her was why she was in the car at all. So much had happened to her in the last months. Most of all she was bitterly ashamed of her relationship with Charlie, which had been quite out of character for her. James would have driven her from the house if he had witnessed her antics. But then, that house on Fifty-second Street . . . Had she perhaps been trying to get even with that uncertainty? Why had James hidden it from her? She knew in her heart that with Charlie she had been the aggressor, that Charlie had played along only to please her, perhaps even (horrible thought) to keep her as a client for the firm. She wanted to forget the whole thing, and perhaps this was the reason she wished to see Joe. What a pity, she thought as they approached Genoa, that she could not depend on him. He was not a businessman. On the other hand, she could use the purse strings to keep him near her. With these thoughts still in mind, she entered Joe's room.

Joe was out of bed, dressed, and looking much better, although he still had the medical collar around his neck. "Just a sprain. It's only for a few days."

"Well," said Irma, who thought it best to assert herself at once, "let's go down to the desk and pay the bill."

Joe laughed. "I've already done it, Mother. All we have to do is walk out. But why don't you see Mr. Ponderosa first? I want to speak to the people who have been so good to me and say good-bye. We're in no hurry."

Irma, for the first time in her life, shocked by Joe's self-assurance, did as he bid her. A nun guided her up to Wendell's room.

He was lying with his leg in a cast, half sitting up in his bed. Beside him, a nun was handing him a glass of orange juice. He waved it away when he saw Irma, and his face lit up with pleasure.

"Irma," he exclaimed. "How wonderful to see you." He held out his hand.

Irma took his hand and looked into his face. For the first time she saw him as a person, not simply as her lawyer. She saw kindness in his eyes, and felt strength in his hand. She sat down on the chair by his bed. "Thank God you are all right," she heard herself saying.

Wendell pressed her hand before putting his own hand neatly on his top sheet. "Yes, it is a miracle," he said. "It was terrible to lose the chauffeur, a young man with a family, but

I, fortunately, am in excellent condition. I will have to stay here perhaps a week or two, then sail home from Genoa." He did not mention that Charlie was going with him. "Have you seen Joe?" he asked.

Irma nodded.

"You will find quite a change in him, Irma. He really has found himself, and he's going to make you proud of him one of these days." He spoke so sincerely and earnestly that Irma felt startled. What had come over him? What did he know about Joe? But Wendell had shut his eyes and fallen asleep; she could hear him breathing regularly. It was the reaction from the accident and the painkillers. He looked so helpless and tired. Irma felt a wave of affection. She took his hand and kissed it lightly. He woke up and looked at her with half-asleep eyes.

"Thank you, Irma," he murmured. "Come and see me again. Remember we are old friends and have been through a lot together." Then he turned his head and fell asleep again as Irma tiptoed out of the room.

Irma returned to Joe's room. He seemed quite cheery; but when they got in the elevator, Joe became very pale and leaned against the wall, beads of perspiration on his forehead. Obviously, he did not feel as well as he pretended. Irma took him by the arm for the first time that he could remember and guided him safely to the car.

The drive back was a nightmare. Joe was obviously nervous after the accident. The driver, having had a couple of glasses of Chianti, was more reckless than ever. Irma and Joe were so intent on keeping their eyes on the road, they hardly spoke. He looked like a ghost.

When they arrived in Portofino, the first thing Joe said was that he needed a drink, so they went to Nino's, who immediately brought a Fernet Branca, saying it would strengthen the blood and could cure almost anything. As Joe sipped the nasty drink, he looked up at the *castello* and asked his mother if they had to walk up there. When she said yes, Joe took another sip of the Fernet Branca and said that if they were not expected for lunch, why couldn't they lunch here at Nino's? Nino, who had been hovering in the distance, said that they had fresh scampi and fresh squid and a very small *lupo di mare*, but they both preferred pasta. Irma agreed to stay, partly because she had told Emily that she would be in Genoa for lunch, partly because she wanted to put off the moment when Joe would have to climb the path. This last fear was allayed, however, when Nino came to tell them that he had called Luigia, who was going to send down two of the gardeners with a huge cane chair on poles, and they could carry Joe up whenever he was ready. Joe was not pleased to appear such a weakling, but he had to agree. He was having a delayed shock, and wished he were back at the hospital.

Irma only toyed with her pasta and Joe ate nothing, sipping his Fernet Branca. They watched the fishermen examining their nets, the children playing, the cats fighting, the dogs chasing the cats, and the continuous traffic of the passersby from the priest in his black gown and flat hat to the pairs of carabinieri in tricornes with their swords by their sides, looking keenly for lawbreakers.

Joe was fascinated. "This place is marvelous," he exclaimed. "I might even rent a villa here someday."

Irma looked startled. She was afraid that he was delirious. "You act as though you had come into money," she said. "First of all, coming here, staying at the Ritz in Paris, and now talking of renting a villa."

"I didn't stay at the Ritz, Mother. However, I might as well break down and tell you," said Joe, pouring some wine from the carafe in front of him. "I *have* come into money."

Irma looked at him with astonishment. "That house that Father left me—it wasn't much of a house, as you know—and I never knew why he had bought it, but it has turned out to be a gold mine."

"Your father always said that he was lending it to you and I never knew until the codicil to his will he had left it to you outright," said Irma. "It was strange. Your father told me everything. I knew how every penny was spent," she said emphatically, "except that house. I never even saw it. Somehow when we went to town we were always too busy to see it. Is it nice? Are you going to live there?"

"Nice- I'll say it is," said Joe coming to life, "but I am not going to live there. Because, my dear Mother, this dear little house has done me a wonderful turn. The buildings on each side have been sold to an enormously rich company who want to put up a huge office building. I was the stumbling block. They couldn't build that building unless they owned the house. Their lawyers came to me and offered me absurd sums: $100,000, $250,000. I wouldn't touch it. I said no."

"You said no!" gasped Irma. "You must be crazy."

Joe shook his head. "The longer I held out, the more they bid. Sooo . . . ," he paused.

"So—go on." Irma was impatient to know.

"Well, Mother darling, you will be proud to know that I got five hundred thousand dollars for it. Five hundred thousand in hard cold cash."

Irma almost clapped her hands. He had acted like a true Shrewsbury.

"Joe," she said, her eyes gleaming. "You are truly your father's boy." And she raised her glass to him.

It was a thrill for Joe, too; for the first time in his life his mother was looking at him with pride. "What do you intend to do with it?" she asked.

"I am going to the people who helped Father," he said.

"Ben Slocum and the others. I want to stretch that five hundred thousand and keep on letting it grow bigger and bigger. I want to make money. Maybe someday I'll write, but I want the money first. I met some men on the boat coming over who feel that we are in for a depression and I agree with them. I want liquidity, so I can buy in when the market drops."

"I'll help you," said Irma, feeling new life coming to her. "We'll work together."

"Later, Mother," said Joe finishing off the carafe. "Just now I want to try my own luck." He thought this might annoy her, which he did not want to do, but he felt that he had to start on a new tack and be his own man.

Instead of annoying her, it pleased her. "Spoken like a Shrewsbury," she said admiringly.

Just as lunch was finished, the men with the cane chair arrived. Joe got into it reluctantly; his mother walked behind followed by a man carrying his two valises. Joe felt like a fool and it did not make things better than a crowd of laughing, singing children formed a procession behind him. When the cavalcade arrived at the *castello* door, Luigia, Teresa, and Angela were all there to greet them, Luigia insisting that Joe be carried up to his bedroom. When Irma asked where Emily was, Luigia whispered that she was with a prince, and according to Luigia, should not be disturbed. Irma found that quite inhospitable and followed Joe upstairs, a bit put out.

Joe tried to resist when his two burly carriers helped him out of the chair. They insisted on placing him exactly in the middle of the bed as though he were some miraculous work of art. When they had departed, Irma closed the door and sat down on a chair near the bed. They were both silent, Joe exhausted, Irma sorting things out in her mind. Finally she spoke. "Joe," she said, "there is something I must tell you. Something I never wanted you to know about."

Joe, who had his eyes closed, opened them wide. Was he

illegitimate? His mother's voice had the somber note of a bell tolling. "Joe, are you listening?"

"Yes, indeed I am."

"Well, I have made a fool of myself. I simply cannot understand what got into me. Loneliness perhaps; but whatever it was, it was contrary to everything I think and believe. It was terrible of me."

Joe tried to sit up, but his neck hurt too much. What in heaven's name was she about to tell him?

"Oh, come on, Mother," he said. "I am sure you exaggerate. What dreadful thing could you possibly do?"

"I fell in love," quavered Irma. "Sort of."

"There is nothing wrong in that." Joe tried to reassure her, but also himself. Had his mother become a lesbian?

"I fell in love with a much younger man. I wanted to adopt him. I was crazy, but . . . but—" She burst into tears. "He pretended to like me but he really didn't care for me at all. He was running after another woman."

Joe breathed a sigh of relief. His mother was okay. "Who is this impertinent swine?" he asked.

"Charlie Hopeland," sobbed Irma. "Now that I have told you, you must never let him near me again."

"You bet I won't," said Joe. "He's Mr. Ponderosa's protégé. Am I right?" Irma nodded as she blew her nose.

"Well, you need not leave the firm. We will just ask Mr. Huddlefield or Mr. Battle, or even Mr. Ponderosa, to take care of you or find someone else. After all, there are one hundred and twenty lawyers in the firm. Don't you worry, Mother, I will arrange it all. Now try to forget this. Everybody makes a mistake sometime."

"You won't hold it against me?" Irma sobbed.

"Of course not. We will never mention it again."

Irma breathed a sigh of relief. "I never knew before what a wonderful boy you are. At last we have found each other."

"And we have lots of good times ahead," said Joe. "I'm still interested in writing and publishing, and in all sorts of new inventions; but I must make a killing in the market first."

Irma bent down and unexpectedly kissed him on the forehead. "Tell me all about it another time. Now rest." She went out quietly, and Joe was asleep before she reached the door.

Carlo had arrived on the dot of 12:30, immaculate and elegant in dark red linen trousers and a silk shirt. He and Emily met awkwardly, not having seen each other or spoken over the phone since their last and only night together ten days before. They went in to lunch almost at once, and while Luigia and the little girls served them, they talked of Mussolini, of agriculture, of the opera at Verona—in fact of everything but what was most on their minds. Then Carlo asked after Molly, and Emily told him of the happy ending there. Emily explained about her sister-in-law, the accident, of Mr. Ponderosa and Joe's lucky escape. Joe and Irma were arriving any moment, said Emily, which made Carlo look uneasily around him. Finally the meal was over, coffee was served, and Luigia departed ostentatiously, closing the shutter door. Emily laughed. "Luigia is playing matchmaker," she said. "She is really something out of an opera."

"Not entirely," responded Carlo. "It is her Italian intuition. She sees that I love you."

Emily smiled, so Carlo took both her hands and said, "Emily, you read my letter. What have you got to say to me? Please look at me; don't turn your face away. Tell me your answer."

Emily looked straight into his dark brown, Italian eyes. "I don't have an answer. My heart says one thing, my head another."

"And what do they say, this heart and head of yours?"

"My heart tells me I love you; my head tells me I shouldn't. You're at least ten years younger than I am. You have a noble name. You should have a son to carry on that name. But there I can't help you and I'm afraid you would live to reproach me, perhaps not openly because you are too kind, but within yourself. You might eventually seek out some younger woman and that would kill me. I could not bear it. Better to say good-bye while we are still in love. Better to live on divine memories than to risk a future of ennui and jealousy."

Carlo listened—then drew Emily to her feet and, holding her close to him, kissed her passionately. Emily responded and they stood there beneath the pines for a long moment. At last, Carlo stopped kissing her. "Now you know what I think of all that silly talk of yours. Do you think that I am not old enough to know my own mind? Do you think that I am a country boy with no experience—or an old roué with a roving eye? You speak of love, darling Emily, but you intimate in the same breath that there is no such thing as constancy. Are all American men unfaithful? But this is not true in Italy. I can tell you of many happy Italian marriages. Why are you so frightened, Emily dearest? Age has nothing to do with us, nor does my name. One of my cousins can carry on. I already have a child and you will love her and be a marvelous mother for her. What else is wrong?"

"Your family," said Emily weakly.

Carlo moved back a bit. "My family will love you when they know you." This time, to Emily's ears, he did not sound so sure of himself. "I am sure that my father will agree with me the moment he sees you. My mother will, too, if you become a Catholic."

"I understand that," said Emily. "I am a Christian and could easily join the Church." She sat down on the swing and Carlo sat beside her. "Dear Carlo, all of this is hard. I have been through so much recently with Irma, Molly and Reggie, and Wendell Ponderosa's accident. I really can't think straight."

Carlo pushed her hair back and kissed her several times on her neck. "Let's not talk anymore," he said. "I have an appointment with a man at four about my flat here. I only lease it, but now I want to buy it. It's nice with a terrace garden and a wonderful view of the harbor. Can you dine with me tonight? There's an inn up in the mountains, a simple place with a magnificent view and excellent food. Let's meet at seven."

"All right," said Emily. "I'm sure that Irma and Joe will be all right alone. If not, I'll telephone you."

So they parted and Emily climbed the stairs slowly, her whole spirit disturbed. As she passed Irma's room, the door was open and Irma beckoned her in.

"Emily," she said, "I have made the most wonderful discovery. I like Joe. He has a strong streak of James, and I never knew it before. We never gave him a chance to show us what he was really like. We were always looking to find fault with him. But he's just what I need and want: an ambitious, tough, intelligent son." She paused and looked at Emily. "I'm very lucky," she added, "because I have discovered too what a really good, kind person Wendell Ponderosa is. I expect him to be of great help to Joe and me, as our lawyer and as our friend."

Emily was still too overcome with emotion to be discreet. "What makes you think he's like James?" she asked impatiently. Irma then told her about the house and the $500,000 and how Joe wanted to invest it and make more.

"I can hardly believe it," exclaimed Irma.

"It's great," said Emily. "I'm very pleased too. Now I am off to my room for a siesta."

Actually, Emily at that moment was not pleased to be talking of money when she was thinking only of love.

When she got to her room she sat down and read Carlo's letter again, put it back in the envelope; then read Jock McKee's letter. He was a link with Ben—suitable, but she did not need such a friend. No, she didn't. She tore the letter up. She could always say that she had never received it, and her thoughts for a moment turned to the rest of her group. Molly was going to do a job as George's wife; Irma was discovering maternal pride and love. She had even heard that Lady Carter had gone back to England and that Murray Kent had followed. If these people could all sort their lives out, certainly she could settle her own life. She needed Carlo, and he needed her.

CHAPTER TWENTY-ONE

# THE DUCA DECIDES

AFTER THIS DECISION EMILY SAT IN HER ROOM WATCHING the sunset and roused herself only when Elsa came and asked her what she wanted to wear for dinner. She changed hurriedly and found Carlo was waiting for her in the piazza. One look at his face made her spirits drop. He looked drawn and sad. "I have just received word that my mother has died suddenly of a heart attack. My father wants me to come at once, and of course I must. Will you come with me? We can drive straight to Rome tonight." He looked at her pleadingly. "I need you." How irresistible to be needed by an attractive man on a tragic mission. "You will come, won't you?"

"Of course." Emily looked at her watch. "But I must go back to the *castello* to get some clothes. I could be ready within an hour."

"God bless you," said Carlo, hugging her.

Emily almost ran up to the *castello*. She got the astonished Elsa to pack a suitcase and a bottle bag, telling her she would be back in a few days. Then she told Irma that she had had a call from a sick friend in Rome, but would telephone her and let her know just when she was returning. She looked in on Joe, who was fast asleep. After farewells with Luigia and company, who told her not to worry, they would look after the *signora* and her son, she fled down the path, followed by a gardener with the luggage. She found Carlo looking at his watch and exclaiming with delight, "It took you only forty-five minutes."

They got into his Bugatti and off they went through the night, Carlo silent, Emily filled with compassion. The road was perilous but Carlo handled the car as a sailor handles his boat. They stopped a couple of times for coffee and were on the outskirts of Rome at sunrise. Emily went to the Hassler, where she was known. Carlo would go directly to the palazzo. "I will not be able to see much of you. I must be with my father; but just to know that you are near me will give me courage. It will only be a few days."

It turned into a week. Emily went shopping and sightseeing, and sometimes sat alone in the Borghese garden. She did not want to call up anyone, as it would be difficult to explain her presence there. Carlo telephoned her daily and reported that his father was magnificent—heartbroken, but under control.

By the end of the week, Emily felt that she couldn't leave Irma and Joe at Portofino any longer. She knew that they must be longing to return to New York. But Carlo suggested that she must visit his father first. "I've told him about you," he said. "He wishes to meet you."

Emily was encouraged but still rather shy. What could she say to the old *duca*, and what would he think of her? Carlo had told him that she was not after the family's fortune; that she was not only rich, but extremely rich. The old *duca* was pleased, and when Carlo told him that she would become a Catholic, the old man said, "Bring her to me." So Emily was brought to him, discreetly dressed in black with white collar and cuffs and a black hat which framed her pretty face.

The old *duca* took in everything at a glance, including the huge ruby on her finger and the shining pearls around her neck. They sat down formally in the two-storied library beside a marble mantelpiece proudly held up by dragons bearing the family coat of arms. A tray was before the prince, and he poured out the tea while two menservants with black bands around their arms passed small sandwiches. The *duca* was in a black suit, a black tie, and a black and white striped shirt. His snow-white beard was well clipped. They chatted about the weather and the sights of Rome, but when they had drunk their tea, the *duca* waved his hand and the menservants retired. Emily seized this opportunity to offer her condolences. She was able to speak sincerely, remembering her own feelings when Ben died, saying how sad she was not to have had the privilege of knowing the *duchessa*. The *duca* listened with his head on one side, looking at Emily through half-closed eyes. Was he falling asleep under this avalanche of banalities? Emily wasn't sure; so she turned to Carlo. "I think that I should go, Carlo. I do not want to tire your father."

The *duca* rose to his feet and, taking her hand, kissed it. "Thank you very much for coming," he said in perfect English. "It is very good of you, but you must excuse me. I am not good company these days."

Carlo put his arm around his father's shoulders. "I will take Mrs. Codway to her hotel, then I will come back."

The old man nodded and turned back to the library, as they went into the great front hall. "Your father is a wonderful old gentleman," said Emily. "He was very nice to me. But he doesn't approve of me and I'm afraid I bored him."

"Not at all," Carlo said reassuringly. "I think he liked you a lot. It will take him a long time to recover from Mother's death. Actually, he is a wonderful raconteur and is known all over Rome for his wit."

Emily said nothing. It was worse than she thought. If the *duca* was such a wit, even in his grief there could have been a flicker. Instead of which, he was as bland as an overcooked pudding. Carlo must have felt something too, for he hardly spoke until they reached the Hassler. Then he said, "Father dines very early. If you put off your dinner, why don't you reserve a table on the Hassler roof and I can join you?"

"No, I have to pack and I am tired," said Emily. "I will have something in my sitting room, then you can come and have an espresso. I must get to bed early. I'm leaving tomorrow on the Rome Express for Portofino."

Carlo looked at her sadly. "Father was tired. I could tell that he liked you enormously."

Emily stopped herself from saying, If you think that he acted as though he liked me, I would hate to see how he behaves if he didn't like me. Instead she said, "Well, thank you for taking me there and I will see you later. Unless it is too late."

"It won't be late. I will be here by nine." Carlo saw her through the door and then returned to the car.

The old *duca*, left alone, was preoccupied with thoughts of the future and his relationship with Carlo. He needed Carlo more than ever now. He also wanted Carlo to be happy. He smoked his cigarette until it burned his fingers. By the time Carlo returned from the Hassler, the old *duca* had decided not to risk any coolness between Carlo and himself. He wanted to keep his son. It was in this mood that Carlo found him.

Emily, as she ate her solitary dinner in the sitting room, was far from happy. She wished now that she had not been so old-fashioned in her behavior with Carlo. She wished that she had not talked so much about the difference between her heart and her mind. She wished that she were ten years younger. She wished that she had never come to Rome and never met the old *duca*. She felt like a courtesan, living here at the Hassler, even though she paid the bills and hardly saw Carlo. Still, she was in a stupid position, and the more she thought of this trip to Rome, the angrier she became. She had lost Carlo. He was obviously sitting in the palazzo now, talking her over with his father and losing the battle. At that moment, she wanted Carlo more than she had *ever* wanted anything before. She had been too practical and too unselfish. That was it. And now she had undermined her own interests. Now that Carlo was lost to her, she saw that he was her one chance of future happiness. Perhaps not forever, but who knows what the future holds? Even so, today is what is important and today she had lost Carlo. She felt suffocated, so she went to the window and stepped out onto the balcony. On the Spanish Steps, just below the Hassler, some young people were playing guitars and singing. The smell of the lilies that banked the sides of the steps rose up to her. She stood there and listened, filled with regrets and sadness. Suddenly a pair of arms were clasped around her waist. She let out a cry as she was swung around to face Carlo, quite forgetting that she had left the door unlocked.

"It's me. Carlo," he said joyously. "If I frightened you, darling, I'm sorry."

Emily pushed him away and walked into the room. "You almost scared me to death."

"Well, I couldn't help myself. You looked so small and so dear standing there. Come, sit down beside me. I have news for you."

Emily sat down with a face of stone. "You had a talk with your father."

"Indeed I did, for a long time."

"And . . . ?"

"My father already thinks of you as his daughter. He wants us to spend more time in Rome and wishes to give up the big apartment in the palazzo to us and move into a small one himself. He says that he loved you the moment he saw you." Emily pretended to faint. She threw herself back against the sofa and closed her eyes. "What is the matter?" inquired Carlo anxiously. "Are you ill?"

"No. I am fainting from—I don't know what—joy, surprise, I don't know." Emily jumped up. "Carlo, is it true? You are not making it up?"

Carlo shook his head. "Of course not."

Emily began to sing and dance around the room. Carlo followed her and kissed her. "You are like a little girl tonight," he said.

"I feel like one. I can hardly believe it's true. Your dear, darling, adorable father really likes me?"

"He adores you. He and I are totally in agreement. You are beautiful, charming, intelligent, loving, and the perfect future Principessa Pontevecchio."

Emily put her head on his shoulder and her arms around his waist. "I will make you happy. I will love your child. I will devote myself to your father. And I will be the happiest of all."

# THE PLUM TREE IS DENUDED

IN GENOA, WENDELL PONDEROSA WAS RECUPERATING NICELY. Charlie kept his room filled with flowers. Nuns hung crosses and rosaries on his bed, and the doctors brought him tiny raw asparagus to eat. From the hospital high up on the hill, he could look out over the harbor and was counting the days until the *Conte di Savoia* would glide into port. He was in a mellow mood, and it was then that Charlie came to him and, with trepidation, told him the story of his relationship with Mrs. Shrewsbury. He was straightforward but not explicit about Mrs. Shrewsbury's advances, though he gave Mr. Ponderosa an idea of what he had gone through, and then, in the end, blushing a bit, he admitted his indiscretion with Lady Carter. Mr. Ponderosa, from his bed, watched him closely and restrained himself from laughing, saving that for the time when he could recount the episode (mentioning no names) to his cronies at the Century Club, where being a raconteur counts for a great deal. However, to Charlie he put on a sober face, and when the tale was ended and Charlie said, "I was trying to help the firm, Mr. Ponderosa, and somehow things got out of hand. Perhaps I had better resign,"

Mr. Ponderosa reached out to his bedside table where he had a box of cigars. He opened the lid slowly, selected a cigar, cut the end off with his gold cutter, lit it with his matching briquet. It was only then that he spoke, knowing how he was punishing Charlie, who was watching with anguished eyes.

"Charlie," he said, "you are very lucky." He paused to blow a column of smoke into the air. "Things have changed. When I say that, I mean that young Joe Shrewsbury has changed."

"Changed? In such a short time? But what has that to do with me, sir? How has he changed?"

"He is going to be a chip off the old block," said Mr. Ponderosa. "He has come into some money of his own. I won't go into details, but he got most of it by his own astuteness, which means that he will be a comfort to his mother. *And* . . ." Mr. Ponderosa paused for a long puff on his cigar before continuing, "he has spoken to me. He wants to stay with the firm. He and I will work together, then eventually I will train someone to take my place. There are over one hundred and twenty members of the firm and you, Charlie, will never be seen by the Shrewsburys again."

Charlie drew a deep sigh of relief. "Thank you, sir," he said in an emotion-choked voice.

"We will keep you in the office at 22 Wall from now on," said Mr. Ponderosa, who had thoroughly enjoyed the whole scene. "No more outings for you."

"*No, sir,*" responded Charlie. "I'd like to stick to the office —but not forever. I hope I haven't ruined my future. I don't want to be a mole in the firm."

Again Mr. Ponderosa kept him waiting, taking a long slow puff on his cigar and blowing the smoke up in the air. "Charles," he said slowly, "what you must learn is *finesse.* You should have handled the whole situation differently."

"How, sir?" asked Charlie nervously."

"Well," said Mr. Ponderosa, looking at the ceiling, "the situation should never have gone so far. You should have done research on what Mrs. Shrewsbury's holdings were, what she had been particularly interested in since her husband's death. You should have called Mr. Slocum and Mr. Bumper and Mr. Fox. Did you do that?"

"No, sir," Charlie croaked.

"Well, if you had you could have been your delightful self but have kept the situation in hand. When Mrs. Shrewsbury got a bit moony, you could say such and such a stock had just gone down six points. You could have held your own instead of letting her get the whip hand."

"I don't think I could have done that, Mr. Ponderosa. You have no idea how—"

Wendell Ponderosa cut him off with a wave of his hand.

"My dear Charlie, I was not born yesterday. I have a pretty good idea of what goes on, and you're a novice at this game. But I have enough confidence in you to think that you can learn—and one thing more. Not a word of this to anyone. *In* or *out* of the office. Mrs. Shrewsbury is remaining with us and, as our client, must be protected, *no* jokes. If I hear of such a thing, out you go. Otherwise, I still feel that you have a future with us."

"Thank you, sir," said Charlie humbly. "I certainly appreciate your kindness."

"And now I need a rest," said Mr. Ponderosa. "Come back in a couple of hours, will you?"

"Yes indeed, sir," said Charlie at the door, "and thank you again, sir. I sure am sorry."

Mr. Ponderosa smiled and waved his hand. He had longed to question Charlie about Lady Carter but had thought it an improper thing to do. His curiosity was unsatisfied and he thought perhaps one day in the distant future, after a good dinner at the club, they could talk man to man and he would hear the fine details. He had sent a boy to do a man's work, and the boy had lost his head. Now it was time for a man to take over. Wendell Ponderosa closed his eyes and, when the nun came in to give him a sedative, she found him sound asleep with a smile on his face.

What a saintly face, she thought, crossing herself. He looks as though he were already in Heaven.

When Charlie returned, Mr. Ponderosa was awake and sitting up. "The *Conte di Savoia* will be in any day now." Mr. Ponderosa paused and looked at the travel clock beside his bed. "Actually, Joe and Irma are coming here, almost any moment, so you had better be off. Come back again in a couple of hours."

"O.K., sir," said Charlie, practically rushing out of the door. For the time being he would be Mr. Ponderosa's slave, but one day, perhaps, he'd learn to be his equal.

In less than ten minutes, Joe and Mrs. Shrewsbury were there. Irma settled herself in the chair next to the bed, while Joe drew up a chair at the end. They seemed to be settling in as if for a conference, and Mr. Ponderosa, who was never surprised at anything, waited to see what was on their minds. "Wendell," said Irma, "Emily called me this morning from Rome."

Mr. Ponderosa nodded his head. He knew that Emily had gone to Rome because Irma had called him when she left. "Is she enjoying her visit?" he asked.

"Enjoying!" Irma laughed and so did Joe. "I'll say she is. She went there because of a funeral, and she stayed long enough to announce her engagement."

Mr. Ponderosa raised his eyebrows. "And to whom is she engaged?"

Irma looked at Joe. "I can't remember these foreign names. What is it, Joe?"

"Prince Carlo Pontevecchio. The only child of the Duca di Venturi," volunteered Joe. "I don't know him, but Emily sounded ecstatic. She is coming back to Portofino tomorrow, which is why we wanted to come here today."

"Pontevecchio, the man who was at Reggie's," said Mr. Ponderosa. The name finally took shape in his mind. "Pontevecchio. I know the name well. Our firm once had some dealings with the Duca di Venturi regarding land which the Italian Royal Family owned in California. He came to New York. A fine gentleman, as I remember, and one of the oldest families, close to the Vatican. Emily will have to become a Catholic now."

"Good heavens, I never thought of that. But I can easily imagine Emily changing her religion," said Irma piously, who had no religion herself. "Does she really have to become one?"

"Of course," said Mr. Ponderosa, "and she must have a long instruction period."

"They don't intend to marry for a year," said Joe, "because of the death of the prince's mother."

Irma laughed. "Perhaps in a year Emily will find a king."

Mr. Ponderosa laughed, but Joe remained silent. He felt slightly guilty about Emily and the $1,000. Someday he wanted to talk to her and explain things.

"Well, well," said Mr. Ponderosa. "If you look in that closet, Joe, you will find a bottle of Strega, and some folding cups on the floor. One of the doctors put it there for me. Let's get it out and drink to Emily."

Joe did as he was told, and whether she liked the idea or not, Irma was forced to drink to Emily's health and happiness. The Strega was like fire to her unaccustomed throat, but after a couple of swallows, she turned to Joe and said, "Joe, will you go outside a minute. I would like to speak to Mr. Ponderosa alone."

Joe left, taking his Strega with him, while Wendell Ponderosa braced himself. Irma took another sip of Strega, coughed, and said, "Wendell, there are things that have happened recently that I do not wish to dwell on, but if I am going to stay with your firm, and I want to, I never want to see Charles Hopeland again, nor do I want him to have anything to do with my affairs in any way, not even to get a dog license." (Irma had never had a dog in her life, but at the moment she could not think of anything more trivial.)

"I am sorry if Charles has done something to upset you," said Mr. Ponderosa. "I am sure that it must have been unintentional."

Irma snorted, and Wendell suddenly remembered Lady Carter. "However," he continued, keeping a tight control on himself, "I respect your wishes. Charlie Hopeland will never cross your path in any way as far as the firm is concerned. I only hope, Irma, that you do not hold it against me. After all, I brought him into your life, hoping that he might be of help. I am sorry that he appears not only not to have helped you, but offended you."

Irma started to say something, then checked herself. Wendell, watching her, thought, What next! She suddenly smiled and laid her hand on his counterpane. "Wendell," she said, "in a funny way, Charlie *did* help me. He showed me that I need someone beside me in my life. Now, by a miracle, I have Joe. I never thought he would change, but now there he is like a young James—eager to make money. It is almost unbelievable. He and I are already planning a future, and we both want you in it. Joe has great ideas. Heaven knows what! He thinks we can make lots of money, but I don't want to speculate. What we need is counsel, someone who knows where to go and how to get there. In other words, you. We want you as our partner. Would you like that?"

Would he like it! Mr. Ponderosa almost jumped out of

bed, cast and all; but he restrained himself. "I will be your devoted servant," he murmured serenely, "and I will serve you to the utmost of my ability for as long as you need me, only I cannot leave my firm."

"We thought of that," said Irma, "but we thought that you could be a special partner, we would make it well worth your while, and . . ." She hesitated, tactful for the first time. "Aren't you near retirement, Wendell?"

Mr. Ponderosa winced. "Well, not quite—but Irma, I am sure that we can work something out. I will talk it over with my partners. As I say, I will be your devoted servant, and I do not wish to boast but I know that I will be of help. Whatever happens, you can count on me. In fact, as I think it over," and Mr. Ponderosa put out his cigar, "B.P.&H. have been well served by me. If there is a conflict of interest, you may rest assured that I will stick with you and Joe."

At this moment Joe returned. "Everything settled?" he asked, smiling at Mr. Ponderosa.

"Yes," said Mr. Ponderosa firmly. "I have to speak to my partners, but I am yours."

"Great," said Joe, drawing up a chair near Mr. Ponderosa. "I heard talk before leaving New York that in 1929—that is, next year—the market's heading for trouble. What about leaving the market and going into gold and real estate? We ought to be prepared."

Irma gasped, but Mr. Ponderosa's eyes gleamed. "I think you have got something there, Joe. I've been bearish for a long time." He looked at the window and almost shouted. "There is the *Conte di Savoia* now. Let's all go back with her when she sails. I am fit enough now and we have to talk about your ideas, Joe. Let's get started."

"Fine. Mother and I are ready," said Joe. "Aren't we, Mother?"

Irma smiled. "I am beginning to think 1929 is going to be a great year for us. There is nothing that makes me feel more alive than making money." She looked at her watch. "We have to leave now though, because Emily is coming back, and we might just as well stop at the Italian line and make reservations for the three of us."

So they left, and as they did, Mr. Ponderosa suddenly remembered Charlie Hopeland. He made a note on the pad beside his bed to book him a berth in second class. Then he turned over and fell asleep again. Charlie, slinking in a few minutes later, sat beside his bed and looked at Mr. Ponderosa sleeping so peacefully. He thought to himself how lucky he was to have such a patron as Wendell Ponderosa.